PRAISE FOR VORTEX

"There are two ways to read a Lawrence C. Connolly novel. If *Vortex* is your first encounter with Connolly, just strap on your seat belt and enjoy the ride. He has a knack for writing compulsively readable action that will have you turning pages as fast as you can and will leave you panting for air by the time you're done. But if you've been following this cycle from its beginnings in *Veins* and *Vipers*, you know that there's a deeper side to Connolly, one that comes only from slowing down and taking a leisurely swim in the mastery of his prose. Few writers understand their characters with the same depth, and empathy, that Connolly does. He leaves me in awe. Every time. I am a Connolly fan through and through."
—**Joe McKinney,** Bram Stoker Award-winning author of *Dead City* and *Plague of the Undead*

"With the Veins Cycle, Lawrence C. Connolly creates a world that is eerily familiar to our own, but with hidden surprises around every turn (and page). Writing with power and precision, Connolly evokes sights and sounds that haunt us. *Vortex* is a book you won't be able to put down."
—**Jon Sprunk,** author of *Blood & Iron*

"Delightfully dissonant. Unbridled imagination meets impeccable storytelling. Connolly is amazing that way, like the bull and the matador rolled into one. His work is crazy imaginative and yet absolutely sane in its delivery, reminiscent of other masters of dissonance such as Clifford Simak and Philip K. Dick."
—**John Dixon,** author of *Phoenix Island*

"Connolly delivers a fast-paced mystery with a heavy helping of magical realism that will lose readers in a mystical and frightening world that they won't want to slither out of."
—**Stephanie M. Wytovich,** poetry editor for Raw Dog Screaming Press and author of *Hysteria*

"*Vortex* is the fiction of Wurlitzers and rollercoasters, of fire, of violence and monsters, but it's so much more than that. This is gleeful, intelligent stuff that deserves the widest audience possible. It's a hell of a ride and I, for one, cannot wait to see where Connolly takes us next."
—**Simon Kurt Unsworth,** World-Fantasy-Award-nominated author of *The Devil's Detective*, forthcoming from Doubleday

PRAISE FOR
VIPERS

"[A] breakneck made-for-the-movies celebration of bloody carnage and black scheming . . . fans of summer blockbusters will be happy to crunch popcorn through the car chases, explosions, and brutality."
—*Publishers Weekly*

"[J]aw-dropping, *Vipers* must be read by any serious follower of horror, crime, and dark fantasy."
—**Gary A. Braunbeck,** author of *To Each Their Darkness*

"Connolly shows us once again just how imaginative, intelligent and skillful a writer he is. "
—**Simon Kurt Unsworth,** author of *Lost Places*

"[A] taut novel of horror and suspense that will have you reading chapter after chapter long after you meant to go to sleep."
—**Alice Henderson,** author of *Voracious*

PRAISE FOR
VEINS

"[A] supernatural novel that brings Native American magic to a crime thriller as intense and fast-moving as a Tarantino movie."
—**T.E.D. Klein,** author of *The Ceremonies* and *Dark Gods*

"Some books are good, others are great, but a rare few are tremendous and beg to be read over and again. *Veins* is an unforgettable read."
—**Michael Arnzen,** Bram Stoker Award-winning author of *100 Jolts*

"Connolly writes with clear beauty and a purity of prose."
—**Mary SanGiovanni,** author of *The Hollower*

"*Veins* starts fast, accelerates quickly, and finishes with a flourish."
—**Robert Morrish,** fiction editor of *Cemetery Dance*

"[E]xpert imagery. . . ."
—**Sheila Merritt,** *HellNotes.com*

"[S]ubtly haunting. . . . The plot is fast and intense and the characters are wonderfully real."
—**Laura Lehman,** *BellaOnline.com*

AWARD NOMINATIONS FOR
VEINS

Finalist for the 2009 Eric Hoffer Award.

Appeared on the Preliminary Ballot for the 2009 Bram Stoker Award for Superior Achievement in a First Novel.

Nominated for the 2nd Annual Black Quill Award for Best Small-Press Chill by the editors of *Dark Scribe Magazine*.

PRAISE FOR
VISIONS: SHORT FANTASY AND SF

"*Visions* is . . . the sort of collection that gives genre fiction a good name. . . . The stories display an unusual degree of humanism and a deep regard for nature. Best of all, perhaps, Connolly writes good sentences."
— **Bill O'Driscoll,** *Pittsburgh City Paper*

"Connolly provides plenty of entertaining and satisfying reads."
— *Publishers Weekly*

PRAISE FOR
VOICES: TALES OF HORROR

"'Shrines' hooked me all the way to the last page. I loved it. It must be amongst the best of Connolly's work. The ideas had me guessing and looking into an abyss that seemed infinite."
— **David Slade,** director of *Hard Candy* and *30 Days of Night*

"Lawrence C. Connolly doesn't just get under your skin, he burrows. His style is deceptively unshowy . . . all the better to jolt you."
— **Stephen Volk,** award-winning screenwriter of *The Awakening* and *Ghostwatch*

Nominated for the 2012 Bram Stoker Award for Superior Achievement in a Fiction Collection.

ALSO BY LAWRENCE C. CONNOLLY

The Veins Cycle

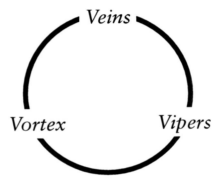

Short Story Collections
Visions: Short Fantasy & SF
Voices: Tales of Horror

From Ash-Tree Press
This Way to Egress

LAWRENCE C. CONNOLLY

VORTEX

ILLUSTRATED BY RHONDA LIBBEY

Lisa —
Best Wishes!
I hope to see you again
real soon — maybe at WHC
in Atlanta. Take care. Larry
Lawrence C. Connolly
1 Nov. 2014

Fantasist Enterprises

WILMINGTON, DELAWARE

Text copyright © 2014 by Lawrence C. Connolly
Illustrations copyright © 2014 by Rhonda Libbey

Designed by W. H. Horner Editorial & Design

Published by
Fantasist Enterprises
PO Box 9381
Wilmington, DE 19809
www.FEBooks.net

VORTEX

Trade Paperback:
ISBN 13: 978-1-934571-05-7
ISBN 10: 1-934571-05-9

ePub:
ISBN 13: 978-1-934571-08-8
ISBN 10: 1-934571-08-3

FIRST EDITION
November 2014

10 9 8 7 6 5 4 3 2 1

For my sibs.

TO THE READER:

The Veins Cycle is not a trilogy, nor is it a series in the traditional sense. As the title states, it is a cycle, and as such the books can be read in any order.

True, the overarching chronology of the 24-hour period that frames the story begins in *Veins*, continues in *Vipers*, and concludes in *Vortex*. But the events are not always sequential. No character lives exclusively in the moment. Like us, they experience the world through a prism of memory, experience, and anticipation—a coexistence of past, present, and future.

A reader beginning the series with *Vortex* will encounter a different set of mysteries than the one who begins with *Veins* or *Vipers*. Nevertheless, in the end, the adventure will be the same. Different onramps, same path.

Now buckle up . . . and enjoy the ride.

Lawrence C. Connolly
Windslow, Pennsylvania
Summer 2013

Space and time are not conditions in which we live; they are simply modes in which we think.

—Albert Einstein

Dark cloud is at the door.
The trail out of it is dark cloud.

—A Prayer of the Night Chant

We are the elements of the earth, and in us resides the spirit of all things, the alchemical power of rock and sky, water and flame.

—Desmond Daystar, PhD

PROLOGUE

Sweating against the elastic that bound her chest, wearing a starched blouse that would draw blood if she turned too quickly, gripping a Bible of tissue-thin pages that glowed with the light of the Word, Samuelle Calder watched the preacher paint pictures in the air.

Sometimes he looked right at her, staring deep with flaming eyes. The heat of his gaze made her soft and wet, like dough before you punched it down. Lately she had been feeling that way about a lot of things. "It's your heart," her mother told her. "*Out of the heart come evil thoughts—adulteries and fornications!*" Her mother's voice always moved to the back of her throat when she quoted scripture, like thunder on the horizon.

The preacher spoke in scripture too, but his voice was different, sharp but muted, a sheathed blade. He was telling the story of the flood, of the days when a vengeful God reclaimed the earth, scoured it clean, started again.

"*And behold!*" The preacher spread his arms, hands wide in the angled light. "*I bring a flood upon the earth!*"

He wore a tailored suit and hand-tooled boots, more like a country singer than a preacher, the kind who sang songs about forbidden things. She wondered if Christ had seemed like this to the people who had heard him preach back in the day. That would explain why the early Christians were so willing to follow him even though it meant defying the law. If this man had a following, if he asked her to be his apostle, she would go with him. She would be his Peter, or maybe his Thomas—though she would never doubt or deny him. And she wouldn't need the light of the Holy Spirit to make her a true believer any more than she would need to be a man to be counted among his closest followers. Yes, those things could happen. Maybe. Someday.

But today she simply listened. And watched.

"*Behold! The waters of justice gather into waves!*" He made a sweeping gesture, painting the air.

"See them now! Mighty waves! They gather above the sinful world! Do you see them?"

The people called out, answering as one: "Yes!"

But Mother held back, cold and reserved. She might speak in tongues at home, but in public she was all ice and stone.

"Do you see it?"

Samuelle tensed, wanted to answer, wanted to leap from her chair and tell him yes, wanted to break the elastic that bound her breasts and scream: "I see it! Everything you've said, I see. Tell me more and let me see that too. Everything you have! Show me!"

But she remained as before, starched and bound in her mother's shadow.

He looked at her, held her gaze, and continued in a voice like cool torrents, carrying her away.

She closed her eyes.

The torrents coiled, fast and hard.

Do you know it, sister? Do you feel the waters?

He spoke inside her now, voice breaking in her private spaces.

And the serpent will cast water over the woman, that he might carry her away!

The water roared.

She gasped.

The chill rushed in.

And she was drowning.

Axle drifted on the edge of a dream, staring at the shadows of curtains on a sunlit window. Patterns shifted, thickened, coalesced—taking shape across the surface of the real.

A wolf-faced apparition appeared, wings extended, hovering above the bed. Axle knew him. It was Kwetis, the nightflyer.

"How bad is it?" Axle said.

"Not hopeless." Kwetis spoke with the light of his eyes, golden heat crackling between veins of black and gray. "Not yet."

"Do you have a plan?"

"A piece of one. But it's risky. It could make things worse."

"Can things get worse?"

"Oh, yes." Kwetis curled his wings, came closer. "A lot worse, but the risk is justified." Sunlight from the window struck his face—part animal, part man, mostly neither. "We'll need to go high and deep, through dream and memory."

"My memory?"

"It was yours . . . long ago . . . before you made yourself forget."

The room turned, passed through a moment beyond time, and arrived at a place where Axle's thoughts were no longer anchored to the bed. He was above himself now, looking down with glowing vision, staring at a sprawled figure on the sweat-soaked sheets: a young man with the earth-toned skin and high cheeks of his ancestors. But his essence was with Kwetis now. He sensed things, truths beyond thought, reasons deeper than logic, the seeds of a plan that might set everything right.

I'll show you! Kwetis said, speaking with the voice of thought, their minds swirling together as man and spirit soared through the open window and upward along a brownstone wall. They cleared the roof and continued on above a landscape of sculpted trees, shooting deep into a cloudless sky that darkened to black as they passed from the sphere of the air.

Stars appeared.

And still they climbed, into empty silence where the earth floated like an island in a blackened stream, clean and pure—no cities or towns, roads or factories. It was the world as it had been long ago . . . as it might be once more if the spirit plan set it right. Axle savored the beauty. And then—together—they angled downward, folded their wings, and fell.

Clouds formed, racing toward them, expanding one moment, swallowing them the next. They fell faster, through a layer of mist . . . into the gray storehouse of rain . . . and finally toward the blue-black depths of a gathering storm. Lightning flashed. They fell deeper, through a region of darkness that gave way to a cloud-dimmed landscape of hills and trees. They leveled off over a blanket of forests and lakes . . . and then out over a winding path that became a road . . . a road that became a highway . . . a highway that wound like a giant snake past fields of grain. They left the road and soared lower still, wings flicking the seedy tops of summer wheat, then rising again to clear a ridge of rolling hills. The storm was behind them now, its wind driving them out over a mining town of placard homes, narrow streets, and a small church whose shadow ran like a blade along the ground.

An updraft caught their wings, lifting them into view of a mountain lake some six miles north, shivering waters held at bay by an earthen dam. In front of it, a deep valley meandered south, cutting through the Pennsylvania forest, then forking as it reached the shoulders of a mountain whose southern face had been cut back to form the highwall of an abandoned mine. Axle knew this place. The locals called it *the crater*.

They flew past it, then over a trailer court of dilapidated single-wides, aluminum homes arranged like fallen dominoes beside a gravel road.

They landed.

It was dark now. Night had come suddenly, arriving without a buffer of dusk or twilight. Rain fell, hard and leaden, striking a gravel yard and a teenage boy who seemed to be clutching something to his chest. He dropped to hands and knees as they crept up behind him. Then he moved forward, crawled beneath one of the trailers.

That's you, Kwetis said, speaking with thought.

But I never did that.

You did.

I don't remember.

That's why we're here.

They followed the boy, gliding across the soft ground. The boy moved by feel, advancing through darkness until he reached a PVC pipe running from the bottom of the home to deep within the ground. There he stopped, started digging.

Axle sensed what was coming. He couldn't name it, but he knew it was terrible . . . unthinkable.

He tried waking up.

Kwetis held him in the dream. *You need to see this. Remember it! Break the cycle.*

But already Axle was pulling away, struggling to return to his sleeping body, trying to wake up before he remembered the terrible secret coiled deep within his past.

Nancy Tully braced against the dash as the news van rocked from Windslow Road Extension and onto the dirt trail that led to the surface mine. The smoke was barely 100 yards away now, rising from a level wasteland of rock and weeds, bordered on one side by a cutaway rock face, on the other by a line of low hills.

Fire trucks surrounded the burning ground, hiding the sinkhole that early reports indicated had been started by an exploding car. Verifying that would be her first order of business, provided she got there in one piece.

"Hey, Bender! I think we can slow down."

Bender was a lean piece of work, tall and good looking in ways that sometimes made her want to scream. He toed the brake, cutting his speed. "Sorry, Nan." He had incredible eyes, blue with hints of red around the pupils, fire and ice. He met her gaze, then turned away, watching what remained of the road.

He had been exceeding the speed limit since leaving Pittsburgh, highballing south on I-79, then west along a series of country roads that led to the mine.

Using her travel time to research the story, Tully had learned that the site and much of the surrounding property had been purchased by a consortium of local businessmen, headed by a strip-club owner named Kirill Vorarov with support from a New York investor known as Ilya Dyadya, sometimes Uncle Ilya. Among the local backers were Arnold Gusky, a venture capitalist currently under investigation for fraud, and Maynard "Bird" Freiberg, trust-fund brat and sole heir to the family-run company that had operated the mine before its closure in the mid-'70s.

The mine was abandoned now, surrounded by deteriorating fences and no-trespassing signs. A tired-eyed cop had stopped them at the perimeter, checked their credentials, then told them to park with the other news van, a safe distance from the rising smoke.

"So what do you say?" Bender asked. "Should we play nice and park with the competition?"

"What do you think?"

"Feel like working some of that Nancy Tully magic?"

"You're reading my mind, Bender. Go in slow. We'll try a little ice breaker."

The burning sinkhole came into view between a pair of emergency vehicles. It was 100-feet wide, smoking like a chimney from hell. A firefighter looked back, saw the van, started toward them.

"Here comes the chief."

He was tall, mid40s, craggy face and nasty limp. She didn't know him, but she recognized sciatica when she saw it.

He moved into their path, held out his arms.

Bender stopped and lowered the window.

"Back there!" The chief pointed 50 feet back, toward the deployed mast of a white ENG van. "With the other crew."

Tully opened her door, stepped out of the air-conditioned cab and into the hot wind from the burning ground.

"That means you too, miss. Over there."

"All right." She kept walking, waving to Bender. "Do as he says. I'll be right with you."

Bender put it in reverse, backed away.

"Sorry about that," she said. "The cop at the gate just waved us through. I'm Nancy Tully." She offered her hand.

He kept his in his pocket. "From Pittsburgh?"

"You've seen me on the news?"

"No. I read it on your van. You're out of your area, aren't you?"

"Yeah. It's my producer. He likes fires." She looked between the trucks, toward the column of rising smoke. "Ever seen anything like this—"

"I need you to get back to your van, Miss Tully—"

"*Nancy.*"

"What?"

"Call me *Nancy.*"

"You need to get back with your van."

"Yes. Sorry." She turned as if to leave, then stopped to give him a look at her profile. It was a hot day. Her on-camera clothes were in the van. At the moment she wasn't wearing much—halter, cutoffs, flip-flops, a killer tan from Beach Tan City. The chief's back might be hurting, but there was nothing wrong with his eyes. "Was it really a car?"

He stared, arms folded. Officially, he was still waiting for her to leave.

"I guess you guys have seen a lot of crazy stuff." She chose those words carefully. *I guess you've seen a lot* would imply that he was old. *You guys* suggested he was part of an experienced team. Consciously, the difference wouldn't register with most people. But this game was all about the hidden persuaders. "But a car? That's crazy, right? How could a car do this?"

The smoke billowed.

"You'd be surprised," he said.

She waited, studied the smoke.

"You've heard of Centralia, right?" he said.

Of course she had. "What's Centralia?"

"A town. Used to be, anyway. It was abandoned in '62. A trash-fire ignited the coal that ran beneath it. It's a ghost now. Fissures running down Main Street, houses teetering on sinkholes. And the ground's still burning."

"Since '62?"

"Centralia, Pennsylvania," he said. "You might want to look it up. That fire started under a pile of burning trash. So to answer your question, it's not crazy. A car fire could do this."

She looked toward him now.

He smiled, or maybe he was just wincing from the pain in his back. Either way, for the moment, he was giving her what she needed . . . and he wasn't telling her to leave.

"We found the chassis burning when we got here. That was before the ground opened up. No getting it out now."

"Too hot?"

"And deep. Bottomless for all we know." He tensed. "That's not for broadcast, Nancy."

"Absolutely. Off the record. Has this mine burned before?"

"No. Not this one. But there was a fire in Ashton three years back. Consol and MSHA were in charge of that one. They drilled boreholes, pumped in a million gallons from a nearby reservoir. That could be done here, I suppose. There's a lake to the north. Lines could be run. It'd be tricky. Water and burning rock?" He tensed, straightened his back. "Too much water and you'll get one hell of an explosion."

"Think you might try that here, running the lines I mean?"

"Not me. Operations like that are above my pay grade."

"Consol and MSHA?"

"Not this time. Not here. This is an *abandoned* mine, Nancy. That complicates things. And there's—"

Fifty feet away, the telescoping antenna on the Pittsburgh 6 van rattled into position, rising like a ship's mast in the mid-day sun. Twenty feet to its left, the rival news team stood amid waves of rising heat. There were two of them, a clean-cut reporter with a wireless mike, a bearded cameraman with a shoulder-mounted Sony.

"You really need to get back with your van, Nancy."

The rival team stared at her, apparently wondering if they should join the conversation.

"Can I contact you later?" she asked.

"Yeah. But not here. This isn't—"

"I'll call the VFD."

"That works."

"Ask for?"

"Chief Gray. *Chris* Gray."

"Thanks, Chris." She offered her hand again. This time he took it.

Something boomed to the north as she returned to her van. The sound rumbled overhead, echoed through the mine.

Thunder?

She stopped, scanned the sky—blue and cloudless above the spreading smoke.

To her left, the rival cameraman looked toward the highwall.

She followed his gaze, scanning the trees at the top of the rise.

Nothing there either.

She continued to the van, opened the cargo door to find Bender sitting at the editing console. His camcorder lay beside him, greeting her with the yellow smiley button that he kept pinned above the lens. He had the communications system fired up, one monitor tuned to Channel Six, the other streaming live from a camera mounted on the 40-foot antenna. At the moment, that camera was shooting east, toward the mine entrance. They'd need to rotate it if they wanted to get some decent B footage.

He slipped a wireless headset from his ears, talked without turning. "Hey, Nan. Marty wants to go live in fifteen."

Tully closed the door, sealing in the cold. God, it felt good! "Fifteen works. I'll be ready."

Bender had set a couple of microphones on the counter: one was an ear mike, the other a handheld wireless with a big NEWS 6 logo affixed to its handle.

"This stuff ready?" she asked.

"Yeah." He met her gaze, held it as if he wanted to ask her something. *Hey, Nan. You doing anything later? Maybe we could get a drink or something?*

She waited.

"Just wondering," Bender said.

"Yes?"

"You get anything from that fire chief?"

Christ, Bender! "A little. Enough for now."

"He'll give you more. They always do."

Not always. She picked up the ear mike. It had a spiral cord, palm-sized transmitter. She put it in her ear, clipped the transmitter to the waistband of her cutoff jeans, and walked to the front of the cargo hold where a dry-cleaning bag hung from a hook behind the passenger seat. "I better get in costume."

"Want me to leave?"

"I trust you."

"Maybe you shouldn't."

Goddamnit, Bender. Cut the crap or cut to the chase.

She tore open the bag, pulled out a skirt and jacket. She slipped the skirt on over her cutoffs and the jacket over her halter. No need to put on shoes. Bender would shoot her from the waist up.

Bender slid the headset over his ears, back to work. "Fire and smoke!" he said, talking to Marty now. "I'll shoot it long, make it look like she's standing right on the. . . . Hold on, Marty." He turned. "Hey, Nan. Is your transmitter on?"

She reached around, hit the switch. "Is now."

"You hear something? Interference? A low hum?"

"I hear it," Marty said, his voice audible in Tully's switched-on ear mike. "It's in your feed."

Bender slid the headset from his ears. "It's ambient." He got up, crossed to the door, pushed it open.

Hot air blew in.

He looked out, the wireless headphones slung around his neck.

Tully came up behind him, looked out. Bender's head and shoulders blocked most of the view. She couldn't see much, only a section of the western wall and a boy sitting way up on the berm of a mountain road. He was a random detail. Just sitting. Hugging his knees. Looking down.

Bender stepped out and looked toward the plateau behind the rising smoke. "Up there," he said. "It's coming from up there."

She stepped down beside him.

Leaves scattered atop the highwall, mist swirled, sparrows took flight, flocked in panic. Whatever was coming, it was moving fast, heading toward the top of the wall.

3

Lying on a gurney in a Green County ambulance, Officer Sharo Jenkins wondered what had become of the morning . . . and what she herself was becoming.

A paramedic leaned over her. He looked young, early twenties, sandy hair, a patch of beard between lip and chin. A plastic badge gave his name.

T. Olson, EMT.

He looked frightened, wobbling as the ambulance accelerated out of the plateau forest above Windslow Mine. "You're going to be fine," he said.

But she knew otherwise. She felt the truth of her condition in the tightness of her uniform, as if her body were expanding, straining at the seams. And her hand? Was that really her hand taking hold of Olson's arm? It looked too large. Not swollen from the snake bites that had nearly killed her, just bigger—as if it belonged to someone twice her size. She pulled him closer. "He changed me!"

"Who?"

"The devil."

A second paramedic tended to a victim beside her. *Zabek?* But the man on the gurney didn't look like Robert Zabek. Only the eyes did. The rest was discolored, misshapen, a monster face with black lips that trembled as they mouthed her name: *Sharo?* It seemed Zabek wasn't sure, as if Sharo's face were as unrecognizable as his. "Sharo? Jesus Christ!"

"The devil," she blurted, knowing how it sounded. But there it was. "The devil changed us." She tried getting up. Couldn't. Straps held her.

Olson put a plastic bag on a hook. Saline? Antibiotics? Sedative?

The ambulance pitched.

"Hold on!" the driver shouted.

Olson lost balance, banged his head on a cabinet, then braced while the ambulance lurched into the uphill lane of Cliff Mine Run, carrying them away from the madness that was still happening above the mine.

Quaking ground. Giant snake. Winged devil.

She couldn't think of those things now. All that mattered was her son. Jordan. Age two and a half. He'd been sick when she left him last night, running a fever so high that she'd almost called off work to stay with him. But duty had prevailed. How long ago had that been? Twenty hours? More? She needed to get back to him.

Olson was still working the IV line.

"Where're you taking us?"

"Hospital." He uncapped a needle.

"Green County?"

"Yeah." He tried pushing the needle into her arm. It wouldn't go. "Your arm." He tried again. "Your skin's—"

"Changed."

"Relax."

"He changed us!"

Olson pushed harder. The needle went in. No pain. Just a sense of something she didn't want.

"I can't go there," she said. "Green County. I can't—"

"Just relax."

"You don't understand. I can't do this!"

The ambulance had two rear windows, each stenciled with an EMT logo: a snake climbing a staff. Snakes had drawn her into this nightmare. Now they were taking her away.

"You need to lie back," Olson said.

Beyond the stenciled snakes, the roadside trees of Cliff Mine Run seemed to race backward toward Windslow.

"I have to get home."

"You need to relax!"

She gathered her strength, then forced up against the straps, popping free with a clatter of snapping buckles and recoiling nylon. She ripped the needle from her arm, shoved Olson away, stood up.

Olson reached for her.

She pushed him back and dove for the doors, threw them open.

Wind rushed in, drowning out the shouts behind her.

The ambulance slowed. One of the doors slammed shut, the other swung wide. She didn't look back, didn't think twice. She leaped from the open door, landed hard, rolled to absorb the shock. Then she was up, running into the woods, over a ridge, down into leafy shadows.

Voices called after her, fading as she continued south, away from Green

County and the doctors who would never be able to reverse the effects of the devil's touch, toward Windslow and the sick child who needed her.

Jordan! Mommy's coming.

Her hands burned, knuckles scraped raw from her tumble on the asphalt. But the pain was minor compared to what she might have suffered if the devil hadn't changed her, brought her back from snake-bite death, made her stronger than any human had a right to be.

The devil!

He had given her the strength to return to Jordan. And right now, getting back was all that mattered.

4

With the bodies from the parking lot chilling in the walk-in fridge and his bloody clothes traded for a tight-fitting pink kimono, jeans, and flip-flops from the dressing room behind the stage, Danny Love locked the doors of the Strip Mine Gentlemen's Club and started drinking.

For company, he watched a television above the bar, flipping channels, pausing when he came to something about the fire out at Windslow Mine. He was starting to calm down when someone knocked on the door.

"Not open!" he yelled. Of course, that should have been obvious. He had closed the gate at the bottom of the drive and changed the message board to read CLOSED TILL FURTHER NOTICE. But whoever was at the door didn't seem to get it.

The knocking came again, harder.

"I said we're closed!"

"Kirill? Is that you, Kirill?"

Danny killed the sound on the TV.

"I'm looking for Kirill."

Danny didn't recognize the voice. "Kirill's not here."

"Pavel?"

What?

"That you, Pavel? Pavel Danilov?"

Nobody in Windslow called him *Pavel Danilov.* Not even Kirill. "Who's there?"

"A friend of Ilya."

"Ilya? Brooklyn Ilya?"

"That's right. Now open up, son. Don't make us talk to you through the door."

Us? Who's us?

"It's important, son."

Danny got up, steadied himself on the bar, crossed to the entrance. But he didn't throw the latch, not right away. He checked the peephole first, looking out at a lean face with gray stubble—not the kind of facial grit you'd find on a derelict, but a smooth salt-and-pepper shadow. "You got a name?"

"Fox."

"I don't know no Fox."

"I'm freelance, son. Ilya sent me. Open up." Danny threw the latch and opened the door.

Fox wore a Stetson, straight-cut suit, open-collar shirt, hand-tooled boots. In all, he looked like no more trouble than an off-duty country singer. Unfortunately, the same could not be said for the men who stood at his side, one a white guy with blond dreads and baggy jeans, the other a jarhead in desert fatigues.

They all stared at Danny.

"So you're Pavel?" Fox said.

"I go by *Danny*."

"Short for *Danilov*?"

"No. Not short for anything. It's my name. *Danny Love*."

"So you changed it."

"Yeah. So?"

"You're the manager?"

"That's right."

"You work for Kirill."

"Yeah, but he isn't—"

Something roared to the east—low and booming, echoing through the hills.

Thunder?

The dreadlock man looked toward it, revealing an ugly scar on the side of his neck.

But Fox and Jarhead kept staring at Danny.

"We'd like to come in, son. Have a look around."

That was the last thing Danny needed. "I told you," he said. "We're—"

"Closed?"

"That's right."

"I don't think he's going to let us in," Jarhead said.

"It certainly looks that way, Mr. Boone."

Danny tried shutting the door.

Boone blocked it with his boot.

Fox stepped back.

Boone grabbed Danny by the kimono.

"Hey!" Danny said.

Boone's jarhead rushed forward, slammed Danny's face.

WHAM!

Danny went down, and the next thing he knew he was sitting in a lap-dance chair, wrists and ankles bound with nylon ties, looking cross-eyed down the barrel of a Colt .45.

5

Looking toward the top of the cutaway hill, Nancy Tully watched a bright-red Firebird accelerate over the highwall and into empty air. It flew above the fire trucks, lost altitude, and crashed a hundred feet behind the van. A fireball rose, too bright and hot to be from gasoline alone.

And Bender? What was he doing? He had retrieved his camcorder from the van, but he was shooting away from the fireball!

"Bender! Jesus Christ, Bender! *The car!*"

He ignored her, training the camcorder on the highwall where something bigger reared against the trees. It was a breaking wave, twenty feet high, uprooting the forest as it thundered toward the brink.

The ground shook.

Tully braced against the van.

The wave spilled across the cliff, fanned into a waterfall, and plunged toward the burning ground.

Too much water . . . one hell of an explosion.

Tully leaped into the van, grabbed the microphone, and raced back outside to find Bender still advancing toward the action. She ran ahead of him, turned, got into position.

Bender panned. The smiley-face button above the lens swung toward her. She raised her microphone.

He gave the signal.

"This is Nancy Tully for News 6 at Windslow Mine, Green County—"

Engines roared. Voices shouted, sounds of panic as water foamed against the fleet of reversing fire trucks. Firefighters scattered. At least one didn't make it, the reflective stripes on his sleeves flashing as the flood dragged him toward the sinkhole.

She gathered her composure, faced the camera.

Bender remained as before, rock steady, recording with a wide angle that erased the distance between her and the torrent. On the screen, she would appear to be standing right on the brink, in the thick of the action. It was career-making stuff. All she had to do was keep it together, do the job, play her part.

"Minutes ago, Blaston Fire Chief Chris Gray spoke of dousing the burning sinkhole with water from a—"

A blast struck her from behind. The world blurred. She dropped the mike, slammed the ground.

. . . one hell of an explosion.

She tried getting up, fell again as the ground moved beneath her. A rift opened to her left, erupting with a roar of shattering rock and ash. She scrambled away. The fissure widened. Something climbed out, a whirlwind of ash that moved as if alive. She found her balance, stood, and ran until something fell in front of her, strewing the ground with plastic, printed circuits, a smiley-face button. . . .

Bender's camera!

A shadow rose behind her.

She turned, and there was Bender, struggling in a living cyclone that had emerged from a rift in the ground, his legs kicking, upper body just visible through the misty shape of a monstrous head.

She stumbled backward, turned, ran for her life. Her flip-flops were gone. Jagged ground cut her feet. She ran faster, looking back to see another living whirlwind giving chase, head crackling with static, eyes glowing with the heat of burning ash. It coalesced as it moved, condensing into solid form, a serpent with gaping jaws.

She ran faster, leaning forward, almost flying until something cut her off. It roared out of nowhere, screamed to a stop. A cargo door opened, a reporter leaned out. "Come on!"

She dove, hit the floor, scrambled in.

The monster stormed toward them, eyes flashing, mouth wide. The reporter slammed the door.

WHAM!

The thing rammed the panel. The van spun, tires grating over stones and slag. Dust blew past the windshield, enveloping the van, so thick that Tully was sure the thing had swallowed them whole. She fell against an editing bay. The reporter grabbed her, pulled her beneath the workstation, and held her tight as the van came out of its spin.

"You OK?" he asked.

She couldn't say anything. Could barely breathe. She'd done something to her ribs. The pain was deep and hot, spreading along her back.

"That thing almost had you." The reporter had a strong chin, prominent cheeks, trustworthy eyes—a face made for TV news. "We've got to get—"

The van rocked, tilting to the side.

"Hey, Jaylen!" The reporter yelled. "Get us out of here!"

"Trying!" Jaylen floored it.

She closed her eyes, holding onto the reporter as the van bounded over heaving ground. It felt good to be moving, getting away, but the ground was still in motion, cracking beneath them as Jaylen hit the brakes.

Tires squealed. The van pitched, bottomed out, stalled. Rock grated against the floor. The van was tilting now, declining toward the cab.

The reporter looked toward the windshield, eyes wide, color draining from his face. "Jaylen!" He pulled himself up on the editing bay. "No! No way! Tell me you didn't—"

"Sit the fuck down, Duane!"

The van rocked. The grating sound came again, rasping beneath the floor.

"Dammit, Duane! Sit the fuck down!"

Duane sat down.

Jaylen restarted the engine, shifted to reverse, gunned it.

The van didn't move.

Tully eased forward, bracing on the island between the forward seats. There was blood on her hands, deep cuts on her palms and forearms. Her knees were worse. Her back spasmed. But something more terrible lay beyond the windshield.

"Get back!" Jaylen said.

Tully couldn't move. She could only stare, looking through the windshield as the van dangled over a bottomless rift.

"Both of you!" Jaylen set the brake. "Move back! All the way back! Now!"

Duane moved first.

Then Tully, past the editing bay, toward the utility closet in the back of the van.

The chassis rocked, settling against the ledge as Jaylen climbed over the island. He was older than Duane, late 30s maybe, though his heavy beard made it difficult to tell. His age was more in the way he moved, the steadiness in his eyes, strength in his hands.

The van stopped rocking, but Tully didn't want to think what would happen if the ground started quaking again . . . or if another one of those monsters rammed them from behind. She crouched on the floor, watching as Duane stepped to a side window, cupped his hands, looked out.

"That thing," Jaylen said. "It still there?"

"Which one?"

Tully peered over Duane's shoulder. Shapes twisted in the distance, crawling among the fire trucks, dragons with glowing wings.

"We should be getting this," Duane said.

"Give me room." Jaylen grabbed his camcorder, pushed it against the glass, hit record.

Duane moved to the editing bay, picked up a headset, started talking. His voice trembled at first, then evened out as he filed his report. Tully envied him the safety of his work. For now, all she could do was watch, crouch in a corner, and clench against the spasms that gripped her ribs.

6

Flying car, roaring waterfall, giant snakes—Benjie had watched it all from the mine's western slope, and now he was totally freaked.

He had stopped by the mine to rest after fleeing the strip-club parking lot where his brother Jason and two friends had been struck dead. And now, fleeing once again, escaping along the upper bends of Cliff Mine Run, he wished he had picked another day to skip his meds.

He hugged himself as he ran, wrapping his arms tight around his shoulders, squeezing hard. He liked the pressure, but the running was making him sweat, forcing him to let go of himself and unbutton his shirt. He pulled it off, exposing a stenciled T-shirt that Jason had given him as a joke, pale blue and printed on the front with yellow letters.

I PEE

IN

THE POOL

He didn't like wearing the shirt by itself, just under things so that no one could see it. But there was no one around now. At least there shouldn't have been.

"Hey, Benjie!"

Benjie kept walking. The voice couldn't be real. The best thing to do was ignore it because if he didn't—

"Is that the shirt I gave you?"

It was Jason. He sat on the guardrail, looking just like he had the last time Benjie had seen him. Well, not exactly the same. This Jason's head wasn't cracked open to the brainpan.

"What the hell, Benjie? You not talking, or what?"

This was the Jason from before things had started happening, healthy and whole and dressed in cutoffs and a baggy shirt that covered his gut.

But it wasn't really him, of course. Even off his meds, Benjie knew the difference.

"Come on, Benjie. Stop and rest."

Benjie tied his shirt around his neck and kept walking. "You're not here!" he said, or tried to. When he was upset, all his words tumbled out in one big lump. *Urnothere!*

"You're blabbering, Benjie."

"Go away! You're dead!" *Goahwayurded!*

"Sheesh, Benjie. You sound like a retard."

"No!"

"No?"

"I'm not."

"What?"

"What you said."

"Retarded?"

"Yeah."

"But you're scared."

Benjie put his head down, watched the pavement, kept walking.

"You're scared, Benjie. And I'm dead! I'm dead . . . Vinny's dead . . . and Ditwitter's dead . . . everyone but you is freaking dead, and you—what did you do when it happened? You left us, that's what! Christ, Benjie! Don't you care about people?"

"Stop it!"

"But you left us!"

"No!"

"What do you mean, *No?* Don't you remember? Forget so soon?" Jason slipped from the guardrail, started after him, running uphill and panting like he was really alive. "Hey, retard! Look at me!"

"No! You're not—" The words collapsed into babble.

"Not what?"

"Now!"

"What?"

"Not here now!"

"What the hell are you talking about, Benjie?"

"Not here now!" He shouted it. "You're dead now!" The words rang against the pavement, and when Benjie turned again, Jason had moved back to the guardrail, scratching his nuts, looking toward a wail of sirens approaching from the north. They sounded close, just around the uphill bend.

"Better move," Jason said.

Benjie leaped aside, ducking behind the guardrail right before a cruiser roared into view. An EMT vehicle followed. Then another cruiser, the cop staring straight ahead as he entered the next bend. Then he was gone, following the other vehicles, nothing left but the dwindling screams of their sirens.

"Good thing they didn't see you, Benjie. They'd probably arrest you or something. Take you in for questioning. Ask you why you ran away when the rest of us were getting killed."

But that couldn't be why those cops were heading south. It had to be the other things happening in the mine. But Jason wouldn't give it up. "Don't deny it, Benjie! The way I see it, those cops have probably been looking for you all day. I mean, that strip-club manager? He saw you with us. Know what I'm saying? He gave them your description, and now you're what they call a *person of interest*. Maybe even a suspect!"

"No."

"Oh yeah!"

"I'm not listening!"

"But you are."

Benjie turned away, ran into the forest. It was safer there. Private. And Jason wouldn't follow. Jason didn't like the woods.

"You can't hide, Benjie! Run but can't hide! Sooner or later, you'll have to come out . . . answer for what you've done!"

Benjie pushed in deeper, continuing until he reached the edge of a terrible river. Then he turned and started walking along it, heading toward home where his meds waited behind a bathroom mirror. Once he got there, he would lock the doors and close the blinds, seal out the world and take his pills. Then he would crawl into a closet and hug himself. And then maybe things would be OK.

Maybe.

The flood raged beside him. All that water. He had seen it draining into the mine. But he had seen it stop too, the waterfall dwindling as the flood changed course, redirecting itself as if it were alive. Going where? Into town? Maybe that would be a good thing. Maybe if it hit the town it would wash over the strip-club parking lot and scour it clean. No more blood then . . . and no more Jason except the one who lived in his mind.

He pushed on, his shirt flapping like a cape about his shoulders, running toward the safety of home.

When he'd gotten up that morning, it had never occurred to Danny Love that by midafternoon he might be shot dead in a pink kimono. Fox sat backward on a wooden chair, leveling his revolver until its barrel became a giant hole. "Talk to me." Fox no longer seemed like an off-duty country singer, more like an aging contract killer, a semi-retired outlaw. "Where's Kirill, Danny?"

Danny raised his hands, covered his face. Nylon zips bound his wrists, cutting his circulation, numbing his fingers.

"Hey, Fox!" Boone the jarhead stepped out of Kirill's upstairs office and onto the catwalk that ran along the side of the main room. He carried a pistol, barrel fitted with a large suppressor. "Check this out!" He held the gun high. "A Stechkin automatic . . . *with a silencer!*"

Fox lowered his revolver, looked back at Boone. "That's a Stechkin, all right."

"And it's been fired!"

"That a fact?"

"There's bullets in the walls."

"Do tell, Mr. Boone."

"This gun was on the desk, but there's others, a whole case of high-end shit. You need to get up here. Take a look."

"All in good time, Mr. Boone."

Boone returned to the office.

"A discharged Stechkin, Danny?" Fox said the words as if tasting them. "I suppose you're going to tell me you don't know about that either."

"It's the truth."

"The *whole* truth?"

"I don't know what goes on up there. It's Mr. Vorarov's office, not mine."

"Your boss discharges an automatic handgun upstairs, and you don't know about it?"

"It must have been before I got here."

"And what time was that, Danny?"

"I don't know." Danny swallowed. Mouth dry. Head aching where Boone had cracked him. He probably had a concussion. "Maybe 7:00."

"This morning?"

"Yeah."

"You always get here that early?"

"No?"

"Does Kirill?"

"No."

"But today you both came in—"

"Not together."

"Kirill got here first?"

"Yeah. I guess. Or maybe he never went home. He was here when I left last night."

"So maybe he pulled an all-nighter?"

"I don't know. Maybe. Or maybe he left and came back."

"That's a lot of *maybes*, son."

"Look, all I know is he was here when I left and here when I came in."

"And what brought you in so early?"

"I heard something."

"Something?"

"An explosion."

"Coming from this club?"

"No. From the old mine. It woke me up. I looked outside and there it was, smoke over the hills. I figured there might be something on the news, so I came here."

"To watch the news?"

"Yeah."

"You don't have a TV at home?"

"Not all the channels."

"Cap his ass!" This came from the white guy with blond dreads. "Do it, yo!" He spoke without looking up, sitting at a table stacked with hardcore smut from the club's porn shop. He was paging through a magazine, pondering each spread as if studying a schematic.

"That's Mr. Prutko," Fox said. "Did I introduce you? Mr. Prutko, this is Danny. Danny, Mr. Prutko."

"Prutko?" Danny said.

"That's right," Fox said.

Danny did a double take: baggy jeans, dreadlocks, nasty scar on the side of his neck. "*Oles* Prutko?"

"That's one of his names."

"Snoop?"

"Sometimes he answers to that," Fox said.

Prutko looked up, flashed a gold grill, then went back to his porn.

Danny put the rest together on his own. Oles Prutko, a.k.a. *Snoop Dogg*! Not that there was much physical resemblance between him and the West-Coast rapper. Dreads and threads notwithstanding, this Dogg looked absolutely Ukrainian, which when you got right down to it was about as Caucasian as you could get.

"He worked for Kirill," Fox said. "Back when Kirill lived in Brooklyn, Brighton Beach. You know the story?"

"I heard he was dead."

"Died protecting your boss? Is that what you heard?"

"Yeah. It was in New York."

"Fox!" Boone reappeared on the catwalk. "You have got to check this out!" He held a giant revolver, one hand on the grip, the other supporting the barrel. "Do you know what this is?"

"No idea." Fox didn't look at it. He just stared at Danny.

"Grenade launcher!"

"Really."

"Multiple shot, handheld. Freaking heavy!"

"Later, Mr. Boone. Let me talk to Danny."

Boone carried the launcher back to the office.

"Your boss has quite a collection."

"He likes guns."

"But I don't need you to tell me that, do I, son? What I need to know is where he is."

"I told you. He said he was going to Harrisburg."

"But he isn't there."

"But that's what he told me."

"Maybe it is, but he's evidently somewhere else."

The TV above the bar was still on, still muted. The image showed a waterfall spewing from the highwall of Windslow Mine. It was all there for an instant, then gone, replaced by people sitting in a studio, lips moving, no sound.

"Tell me what happened this morning, son. About the last time you saw Kirill."

"I already did."

"I mean the rest of it."

"There isn't any more."

"No? I find that hard to believe, son." He looked at Danny's clothes. "Now maybe it's like you say. Maybe you decided to take the day off, put on some stripper clothes, drink vodka and watch TV. And maybe all that has nothing to do with the bullet holes upstairs or your boss going missing. I mean, it might all just be coincidence. But then there's also this small matter of you being so uncooperative, barring the door and acting like you have more to hide than a drinking problem and a fetish for women's clothes."

"I don't have a fetish."

"No?"

"I told you. I was cleaning. My clothes got dirty. I needed to change. This was all there was."

"What were you cleaning, Danny?"

"Stuff."

"Stuff?"

"The bathrooms."

"Really?"

"It's the truth."

Fox considered that, then he leveled his gun, taking aim once again at Danny's head.

Danny covered his face.

"Those hands won't stop a bullet, son. You hold your hands like that, you'll just lose them along with your head."

"I know." His hands trembled.

"So put them down."

The trembling spread, through his arms, into his shoulders. He felt suddenly cold, sick, absolutely certain that he was never going to get out of the kimono alive.

"Come on. Down, son. Little more. That's it. Down."

Danny pressed his hands against his lap, trying to steady them.

"Looks like you got a bad case of the shakes, son."

Danny closed his eyes. The whole room seemed to be trembling, quaking in fear.

"Yo!" Prutko said. "You hear that?"

The room was humming.

Boone stumbled out onto the catwalk. "What the fuck?" He grabbed the banister, holding on as Prutko's tower of porn shifted and toppled to the floor.

Fox tried getting up, lost balance, landed back in the chair.

The building heaved.

"Earthquake!" Boone yelled.

Fox looked around, lips drawn, eyes wide. He glanced at Danny, then looked away as the roar increased from freight-train rumble to jet-plane scream. And then the lights went out.

Someone screamed, a shriek of terror. It was there for a moment. Then gone.

Was it Fox?

New lights came on—harsh, white, and shining from a pair of battery-powered lamps above the bar. They looked like headlights, and Fox was in them, standing now, his shadow stretching onto the stage. He still held the gun, extended for balance while the other hand covered his mouth. He seemed to be biting it, stifling a new scream as he fell back against the bar. Then he vanished, slipping from Danny's view as the lap-dance chair started turning, skidding across the floor like a vibrating phone, round and round until it slammed the stage.

A metal clamp fell from the ceiling, landed with a clang. The place was coming apart, and the club's giant disco ball was right above him, swinging from the rafters as a new sound rose to drown out all the others. It was the pounding concussion of a great avalanche, a deafening crash coming from somewhere just beyond the strip club's walls.

And then, with a blinding flash, the club exploded.

Standing atop the remnants of Silver Lake Dam, Bird watched the last of the flood thunder south through a wave-scarred valley. Waters tumbled and roared, breaking against rocks, erupting into plumes of rainbowed fog. The air smelled of mud and mist, and the whole world trembled with the force of colliding currents.

A road had stretched along the top of the dam, two lanes of double-lined blacktop flanked by low guardrails that had bordered the lake on one side, a 60-degree slope on the other. There were warning signs too.

DO NOT PASS
WATCH FOR CHILDREN

Not that the road had ever seen much traffic.

Most of the homes along the lake's west bank remained unsold.

In any event, the road led nowhere now, its center obliterated by dynamite and water. And the water was still working, eroding the earthen slope beneath the road, leaving blacktop ledges that trembled in the rising mist.

Bird braced against a guardrail post, ragged clothes flapping in the wind, hair whipping about his face. He felt tired, rung-out, and more than a little confused. A few minutes earlier the flood's first wave had chased him and his nitro-charged Firebird over the highwall of Windslow Mine. Now he was here, apparently transported a mile north by the same spirit powers that had kept him alive after the crash. But the presence of such powers did little to calm his fears. Too much had gone wrong.

Axle stood nearby, perched on a section of undermined road. He had wrapped himself in a bed sheet from the guest room of Bird's hilltop home. It draped his shoulders, the ends billowing like wings in the wind. He looked like an Okwe chief—a robe-clad *huyáné* atop an asphalt cliff.

"He's down there," Axle said, referring to the winged creature that lay crushed beneath the broken section of dam. "And this time he won't be climbing out. He'll stay buried. Not fully dead, but close to it." Axle's voice dropped, almost lost beneath the water's roar. "Before this is over, I'm afraid the same might happen to me."

Bird wanted to hold back, give Axle some time to deal with the loss. But the ground wasn't cooperating. Cracks formed, the blacktop threatening to give way.

"Hey, Axle."

Axle remained as before, staring into the mist.

"Axle." Bird reached for him. "Come on. We'd better—" The road heaved. Bird stumbled, his hand closing on empty air as the pavement dropped like a trapdoor. He fell. A section of guardrail dropped with him. He grabbed it, held tight, stopping his fall a few inches above the waves.

And Axle? Where was he? Same as before, standing atop the rise as if nothing had happened. Mist cloaked his body, making it seem as if his head and shoulders were floating on a cloud.

"Axle!" Bird extended a hand. "Help me."

Axle just stared.

"Axle!" The cable groaned, giving way, dropping Bird lower. "Give me a hand, goddamnit!"

"Sorry," Axle said. "Can't."

"What?"

"You're on your own here, Bird." Wind shifted, clearing the mist around Axle's feet. No pavement there. He stood on empty air. "I'm not physically here," Axle said. "I'm back at your mansion, right where you left me."

"Sleeping?"

"Think about it. Where else would I be?"

"You're dreaming this?" Bird considered the realness of the moment: pounding water, rising mist, fingers rubbed raw where they gripped the metal cable. "You're saying this is a dream? We're not really here?"

"Not *we*, Bird. *I'm* dreaming. *You're* here, and you need to get away from that water."

"Christ, Axle!"

"Climb, Bird."

Bird tried, the cable playing out from the top of the rise as more guardrail posts gave way.

"Come on, Bird. Use those skyborn muscles."

The cable slipped again. Bird's feet hit the water. Currents rose, grabbing with a force that seemed almost alive.

"That water will tear you apart if you give it the chance, Bird."

The cable slipped again. Bird fell deeper, currents swirling cold and hard about his waist.

"This is going to get interesting," Axle said.

Waves climbed higher, pulled hard. The cable thrummed. A post angled over the top of the rise, coming loose. Bird tugged, tried climbing. No good. The post broke free, tumbled toward him. The cable went slack. And then he was underwater, somersaulting, slamming into rocks. Water filled his nose, mouth, lungs. The cold shocked him. He heard rumblings, deep and primal—voices in a language that he couldn't comprehend.

But the intent was clear.

Let go. Give up. We've won!

He thrashed, broke the surface, gulped air.

The dam dwindled in the distance. He glimpsed it as the currents spun him. Then it was gone, lost behind the water's green blur as the undertow dragged him down. This time he struck bottom, face-first, cracking his nose so hard that the pain crossed over into colors—blinding whites, piercing blues. The riverbed slid beneath his hands. He tried holding on, but there was nothing there, only flood-scoured rock skidding beneath him until the torrent flung him back toward the surface. He gasped, swallowed a breath that was mostly water.

I'm drowning!

But he remained conscious, his skyborn senses fully engaged as he looked north, back the way he had come. No sight of the dam now. Only mist and rocks.

He called for help.

No answer.

Axle was gone.

Fucking dream master!

Jagged rocks closed in, and Bird was heading for one of them, a wedge of angry shale that cleaved the water like a blade. He tried swimming away, clawing and kicking, redirecting his course. He barely succeeded, moving just enough to miss the rock's cutting edge and slam its flank. He skidded along, past water-slicked rock pitted with fist-sized holes. He tried grabbing on, succeeding only in clawing deep grooves in the shale as the current pulled him under once again.

His breath bubbled out. Should he breathe in, fill his lungs with water, drown and get it over with? Would that even work? He had survived a nitro-and-gasoline fire down in the mine. What were the odds he'd succeed at drowning?

He struggled harder. And then, as fast as it had grabbed him, the undertow set him free. He surfaced, coughed, sucked air. The river had changed.

He was in deep water, turning slowly but picking up speed, heading toward a pass where the flood shattered amid a jumble of broken rocks. He tried swimming away, but the flow was stronger.

. . . tear you apart if you give it the chance . . .

His blood ran cold, but the fight was out of him. He lay back, turned his head to the sky. And that's when he saw that he had more to contend with than falling water.

High atop one of the valley slopes, a dark mass poured toward him. *No! No way!*

It was an avalanche, a mass of dirt and sand coming right at him, matching his course as he accelerated toward the rocks, moving as he moved, taking aim before raining over him in a swirl of stones and clay.

Everything went dark. The water thickened, became a soup of churning muck that closed like a fist. Then he was flying, held aloft by a funnel of airborne dirt that hurled him into an alcove by the shore. He grabbed a ledge, pulled himself out, trailing a skid of mud and clay.

Axle appeared, suspended against the slope, naked but for a shadow of feathers and fur—part man, part nightflyer. "Climb, Bird!"

Bird gagged, coughed up mud, then collapsed.

"Get away from the water. Come on. Climb!"

Bird felt dazed, exhausted, too tired to move.

Axle took hold of his wrist. The touch felt real, guiding Bird up along the bank, away from the flood.

"Axle? How—" It hurt to talk. His throat and mouth were full of sand. "You're—"

"Catch your breath," Axle said.

"You're . . . really here?"

"I've always been here."

"But you said—"

"I'm here in spirit, Bird. Same as always." He backed away, gliding over the wet rock, moving like a projection. "My touch can guide, but it can't carry. Not by itself."

Bird considered the trail of dirt that stretched behind him, a gritty skid mark of grass, roots, twigs, and stones—remnants of the whirlwind that had carried him to the shore. "Your spirit can't carry me?"

"That's what I'm saying."

"But all this dirt?"

"It served its purpose."

"You brought it to life? You used it to—"

"I didn't bring it to life, Bird. It *is* life. Is now . . . always has been."

"So you can animate it?"

"Yes. To some degree. And so can our adversaries, although they're going to be a lot better at it than I am . . . especially now that they're winning."

"Wait a minute! Hold on. If you can do that . . . why couldn't you save the dam?"

"The weight of a man is hardly comparable to the weight of a flood . . . or the force of dynamite. Now come on. You need to get away from here." Axle vanished, then reappeared high atop the slope, hanging over the edge. His coat of fur and feather was thicker now, darker than before.

Bird climbed, pulling himself along the stratified slope, continuing until he reached the high-water line. Here he grabbed the roots of a leaning tree and lifted himself onto a plateau strewn with fallen leaves. He collapsed again.

Sirens wailed in the distance, echoing through the valley.

"Dry off," Axle said, speaking with the light of his nightflyer eyes. "And get out of those wet rags. Even a few drops of that flood might mess with you. It's best to play it safe."

"You want me to—"

"Strip!"

Bird tugged at the fragments of his clothes. The last of the shirt's buttons went flying. The jeans unraveled as he kicked them away. His skin glistened. The beads of water seemed almost alive.

"Dry off."

"How?"

"Channel your inner Okwe, Bird. Use the ground."

Bird settled onto a patch of fallen leaves, rolled until he felt dry. Then he sat, pushed back his mane of tangled hair, and reached for his jeans.

"No," Axle said. "Leave them. You can get dry clothes at home."

"You want me to go home naked?"

"You've done it before."

"Once, thanks to you. And I was driving, not walking!"

"You'll be fine. I doubt anyone's going to be paying much attention to a naked man." Axle turned toward the wail of distant sirens, ears lengthening, flicking toward the sound. "You hear that?"

"Those sirens?"

"Know where they're coming from?"

Bird looked south, out to where a rising cyclone of steam had replaced the smoke above the mine. It looked like something out of a nightmare. But the sirens were coming from the crater. "Windslow?" Bird said. "Those sirens are in Windslow?"

"Yes. The arm of the flood that reached the mine was only enough to douse the fires of our new beginning. The rest skirted the crater, continued south."

"Windslow's flooded?"

"No, Bird. Flooding is what happens when Bottoms Creek overruns its banks." Axle eased down along the slope, stopping when he reached the point where the forest floor ended and bare rock began. "Remember how this valley looked before? Full of trees, vines, undergrowth, loose rocks, soil? You get what I'm saying?"

"So Windslow's—"

"Gone."

Bird felt the chill of it, a town of 5,000 souls crushed beneath a moving mountain of water and debris.

"It's gone, Bird. And we need to stop it."

"Stop it?" Had he understood correctly? "But it's already happened."

"Yes," Axle said. "But there's still time." He stood, growing taller, spreading his wings. He was Kwetis now, speaking with the shimmer of feathers and fur. "Stopping it will be tricky, dangerous—but we need to try."

Bird wasn't sure he was up to something tricky and dangerous. He'd had enough of both for one day.

"You look uncertain, Bird. But you can't back out now. This isn't one of your hobbies. We need to see this through, together."

"You have a plan?"

"I'm not sure."

"What the hell's that mean?"

"I don't have all the answers, Bird. Not yet anyway. Axle needs to do some searching, and you—you need to help buy him time by going home and standing guard."

"Guarding my home?"

"One of the ancient spirits will meet you when you get there. Do as he says . . . and we might be able to try again." He arched his wings, preparing to fly.

"Wait! Hold up." Bird stood, looked east. His home was nearly a mile away. "You really expect me to walk home?"

"Unless you've got a better idea."

"You could transport me?"

"Like I lifted you from the flood? Blow you there in a swirl of dust?"

"No. The other way. Like you did after I crashed my Firebird, when you transported me to the dam."

"I did no such thing, Bird. You hoofed it to the dam on your own."

"Walked?"

"Ran, actually. I don't think I've ever seen a man run so fast. Don't you remember?"

"No. I remember being in the wreckage. Then I was standing on the dam, talking to you."

"You must have blotted it out, denied it, wiped it from your memory.

Horror can do that. Axle could tell you about it. Maybe he will . . . if he gets the chance."

"Horror?"

"I wouldn't worry about it, Bird. You survived. That's what matters. When your mind is ready, you'll remember what happened down there. If not, it makes no difference. The important thing is to head home, play your part . . . save the earth." He spread his wings.

"Save it?"

"That's what this is all about, isn't it?"

"Right. But I've got more questions."

Sirens wailed.

"Who are we saving it for?" Bird asked.

Kwetis's eyes smoldered.

"Come on, Kwetis! I could use a pep talk here."

Kwetis turned away.

"Kwetis?"

He flapped his wings, flew into the air, and vanished like a piece of errant dream.

9

While Duane and Jaylen finished their report, Nancy Tully stood at the van's side window and tried making sense of what she saw.

Fissures radiated from the highwall, arranged like jagged spokes, centered on the sinkhole and a column of slowly turning mist. The flood was gone, the last of its waters trickling from deposits of mud and pulverized trees. And the winged serpents? They had all taken to the air, but other things moved in the middle distance, yellow-clad figures venturing from trailers, trucks, and cars—the firefighters coming out to survey the damage.

Her side spasmed. She tried ignoring it. Injuries didn't matter. What did was that she was standing in another team's editing bay while the biggest story of her career waited just outside.

I have to get back to my van.

She stepped away from the window and crossed to the cargo door. She gripped the latch, tried pulling. Her pain flared. She braced and pulled harder. The van rocked.

"Hey!" Duane said. He was still sitting at the editing bay, still safe within his work. "What're you doing?"

"I'm going out," Tully said.

"Bad idea."

"Maybe not," Jaylen said. He stepped away from Duane, looked out the side window.

"Don't even think about it," Duane said.

"The story's outside."

"Yeah. And so are those dust monsters."

"Looks like they're gone."

"*Looks like* doesn't mean they are."

Jaylen stepped toward the door.

"Don't do it!"

Jaylen grabbed the latch.

"Goddamnit, Jaylen!"

Jaylen pulled. The van shifted, chassis grating against bare rock. But the van stayed put, holding its ground while the door slid open.

Duane steadied himself on the console. "You guys are both—" He turned away, readjusted his headset, listening to a voice in his phones. "Say again! What's that? Windslow's what?"

Tully eased through the door, taking it slowly while Jaylen followed with his camcorder.

"Hey, Jaylen!" Duane yelled. "A flood's hit Windslow! The town's underwater!"

"Flooded?"

"That's what they're saying."

"Windslow?" Tully said. "How far's Windslow?"

"Few miles," Jaylen said.

"We should go."

Jaylen looked toward the dangling wheels. "Not in this van."

"No. In mine." She started walking.

Jaylen called through the door. "Come on, Duane! She's driving to Windslow."

"No way," Duane said. "The roads are out! The town's cut off."

Tully reached the back of the van, stepping into the full force of the wind that blew across the mine. Grit struck her face. She coughed, a simple action that sent pain flaring through her side. She dropped, hugging her ribs.

Jaylen knelt beside her. "You hurt?"

"I think I . . . I might have sprained something." She tried straightening up, couldn't.

"Like a muscle spasm?"

"Yeah." It hurt to breathe. "Oh my god! Hurts!"

"Where?"

"My ribs." She grabbed his hand, squeezed.

"You might have broken them."

"Is that serious?"

"Depends." He helped her up. Both their hands were bloody now, the cuts in her palm leaving skids across his fingers. "You need to—"

"Hey!" Duane stepped down from the van, hurried toward them. "We're supposed to hold up here. They're sending backup."

"But you said the roads were out."

"The ones into Windslow are. Our backup's coming from Blaston."

Tully looked across the mine, through the shifting ash, toward the dirt trail that led to Windslow Road Extension. If the roads from Blaston were open, where were all the other backup teams—the police, EMTs, firefighters?

"What's wrong with this picture?"

Wind gusted. Dust devils rose from the breaks in the ground, miniature versions of the giant funnel at the end of the mine. They formed and dissipated, scattering in the updraft.

Duane looked toward the stalled fire trucks. "Those guys?" He squinted through a squall of dust. "What're those guys doing?"

Fifty feet away, the line of yellow-clad firefighters had gathered before the rising funnel. The mist glowed, flashing from within.

"They're walking toward the sinkhole," Duane said.

He was right. One by one, the figures were stepping into the mist.

"That's fucked up," Duane said, but he wasn't just talking about what was happening at the base of the storm. He looked higher now, up to where the funnel fanned like a wheel against the sky. Shadows circled within the cloud, slender bodies with glowing wings. "Goddamn!" Duane said. "You believe this shit?"

Jaylen shouldered his camcorder, focused, hit record.

The mist flashed again, close to the ground. Silent at first, then rumbling deep and low.

Come to me.

"You hear that?" Tully said.

Jaylen turned his camera toward the base of the funnel. "Thunder?"

"No. I don't think so."

The mist flashed again, speaking first with light . . . then with a delayed rumble.

Come to me.

Tully felt it in her bones, a slow shiver that numbed her pain, put her at ease.

The firefighters kept walking.

Come to me.

The mist swirled.

Don't be afraid.

Jaylen stepped toward it. He didn't have his camcorder. It lay on the ground, abandoned.

Tully called after him. "Hey! What're you—" The question died in her throat. No need to ask. She knew the answer. And evidently Duane knew it too. He walked a few steps behind Jaylen, wireless earphones still clamped to his neck.

Come to me.

She realized she was walking too, effortlessly, without pain or fear, heading toward the rumbling light.

I am your destiny.

nd the serpent will cast water over the woman, that he might carry her away!

A hand gripped Sam Calder's wrist, pulling her from a realm of cold silence and into a place of noise and raging currents. Water broke against her face. She gasped. The hand pulled. "I've got you." The voice seemed to come from everywhere—the water, the wind, her struggling breaths, the hand itself. "I've got you, Samuelle." The hand was rough and cold, more like a mass of clay than something alive, but it held her, squeezing tighter as it pulled her onto a sandstone bank.

She knelt, one hand against the ground, the other gripped by her savior. She tried seeing who it was. Water stung her eyes, blurring her vision. The figure was gray, featureless, indistinct. But his voice was clear. "Breathe, Samuelle."

She opened her mouth.

"It's not like you have a choice."

She knew those words. She had heard them before.

"Breathe or die, Samuelle. Those are your options."

She coughed. Water came out, followed by a rush of pain.

"Slowly, Samuelle. Nice and easy."

She knew that voice. Those exact words. From another time and place . . . another life. She gasped, tried saying his name.

"Don't talk." He gathered her into his arms, held her close. His chest at first felt gritty, smelling of earth and clay, changing as she breathed it in. She remembered now. "Kas—"

"Don't talk."

She gripped his shoulder, the chill of his skin warming beneath her touch.

"Kasdeja."

"Shhhh!"

He picked her up, carried her up the slope to a ledge above the floodline.

A campfire burned there. He set her by the flames.

"Get warm."

The flood had taken most of her clothes. It was a miracle it hadn't ripped her apart.

A miracle!

He took a piece of ragged cloth from the ground beside the fire, shook it out, wrapped it over her shoulders. It felt coarse and damp, a length of unravelling denim. She drew it tight as he crouched beside her. "I need to return to the flood." He touched her face, fingers long and warm. "Just for a moment. Will you be all right?"

"I think so."

He started away, his shape coming into focus as her vision cleared, shifting from the gray outline of a man to something bright, dazzling.

Not a man.

She saw the contours of his body, strong and naked. The nakedness frightened her, but it was an illusion, a trick of the firelight as he passed before the flames. A moment later she saw the robe that draped his shoulders. It had slits in the back, embroidered openings to accommodate a pair of radiant wings, feathers shimmering in the sun. She saw all these things in an instant. Then he was gone, out of sight beneath the ledge.

She pulled the denim tighter about her shoulders. It felt warmer now, softer. Not denim at all, but golden cloth, something an angel might wear.

It was becoming clear now. She remembered the forces that had brought her here—fire, an explosion, rushing waves.

I should be dead.

Kasdeja returned, carrying something wet and struggling. A bone protruded from one end. From the other, a hand opened and closed like a fish mouthing the air. She recognized it by its size, the coarseness of its skin.

"Is that the devil's?" she asked.

Kasdeja didn't answer.

"The devil's arm? Is that his?"

A heavy stick and some coiled vines lay beside the fire. Kasdeja put the severed arm lengthwise atop the stick, then held it in place with a golden foot while he lashed it with the vines.

She coughed, asked him again: "Did that arm come from the devil?"

"What devil?"

"The one back at the dam."

He picked up the stick, swung it over the fire. "The creature that tried stopping you?"

"Yes." She saw the arm more clearly now, its color and texture: dark like clay, ridged like tree bark. "It is, isn't it?"

The flesh smoked. It smelled like beef, but sweeter. "You did well, Samuelle." He turned the stick, cooking the arm. "Your enemies underestimated your faith and vision. But I believed in you. Always did."

"I did what you said."

"That you did."

"I blew up the dam."

"Well, not exactly. You weakened it. The weight of the water did the rest. No matter. The result was the same."

"And I—" She tried remembering. "I was—"

"You were under the dam, inside the culvert where you cornered your winged enemy and placed the dynamite. The blast should have killed you."

She remembered igniting the fire and running for her life, charging for the sunlight. And sometime after that she had found herself lying in a ravine, looking up at . . . up at what?

"Something wrong, Samuelle?"

She shivered.

"Samuelle?"

"I'm fine."

"You're sure?"

"Yeah. Just trying to make sense of it, is all."

The explosion had thrown her from the culvert, leaving her gasping for breath as a tricked-out Firebird pulled beside her, a car with oversize wheels, off-road hydraulics. The driver wore a button-down shirt with rolled sleeves, pants of stone-washed denim. His hair was long and rock-star crazy. She had seen him before. He had been chasing her, trying to stop her. "That man tried helping me," she said. "I called for you, but he came instead."

"He was the servant of the demon master."

"He looked like a man."

"He was once. Not anymore."

"You told me about him before."

"Yes. He calls himself *Bird*."

"*Bird*?" She considered the name. It conjured other memories. "I know that name."

"You know a lot of names, Samuelle."

"My boss . . . Kirill Vorarov . . . he had a partner named Bird. So he was the one? Bird? Bird was chasing me?"

"A transformed version of him, a powerful version. But I knew you could handle him. I've never doubted your strength, Samuelle. Never once."

It was coming back to her now. "He cornered me in a convenience store before I went to the dam. He tried talking to me. There was power in his voice, but I didn't listen."

"You outsmarted him, Samuelle. Outran and outmaneuvered him. You will do the same when you meet his master."

"Bird is the servant?"

"He is now."

"He serves Lucifer?"

"Yes, you may call him that, if you like."

"But you said—"

"Trust your faith, Samuelle. There is power in your beliefs, your convictions. You spent a life denying them, running from them . . . perhaps it's time you run toward them. Embrace them if you can."

"But they're not *my* beliefs."

"They are now."

"They were my mother's."

"She was a wise woman, Samuelle."

"She was crazy."

"Religious people are often dismissed as such."

"But it wasn't religion. She made up her own stories, twisted things so that—"

"You need to accept that part of her, Samuelle. Trust her wisdom. Embrace your birthright."

"*Embrace?*"

"Does that frighten you?"

She thought of Bird, how he had looked as he knelt beside her, his wild hair and high cheeks recalling the look of a particular angel in one of her mother's books. She remembered Bird leaning close, reaching for her. And she remembered recoiling, shouting at him to go away. But that was all. She must have blacked out after that because the next thing she knew the dam had failed and the flood was coming toward her.

"He tried saving me."

"But you didn't need saving, Samuelle. You were already saved."

She peered out along the flood, looking upstream.

"We're about a quarter mile from the dam," Kasdeja said. "Windslow Mine is that way." He pointed south. "Another half mile."

"I should be dead."

"No." He lifted the arm from the fire, touched it, put it back. "Death won't take you that easily. I saw to that. In Colorado. Remember? You'd been snake bit."

"Yeah." That memory was clear enough.

"You changed that night, Samuelle. Not on the outside, but within. And now you're changing in other ways. Take a look. Lift the sash." He pointed to the golden cloth that draped her shoulders, covered her body. "Lift it.

Tell me what you see."

She hesitated.

"Go on. Don't be afraid."

She did as he said, lifting the sash and looking down at what was left of the oversize shirt she had stolen from Kirill's bedroom. She was naked from the midriff down, bare skin slicked with a watery glaze. She opened the sash wider, exposing her skin to the light of the fire. The water shimmered in the heat, not evaporating, but hardening, forming a sheath of interlocking crystals against her skin.

"That's temporary," he said.

She reached to touch it, pausing when she realized her fingers were covered too, gloved in a mesh that tightened as she flexed her hands. She held them to the fire. The coating darkened. It resembled scales.

Lizard skin.

Her arm was covered too. Both arms. Her entire body.

Snakeskin!

She touched her face, then her head: more scales. "My hair?"

"You'll get it back."

She ran her hands along her scalp, scales touching scales.

"Leave it alone for now," Kasdeja said. "Give it time to set."

"But what is it?"

"A chrysalis."

"I don't understand."

"You're changing, Samuelle. It's part of the cycle." He pulled the cooked arm from the fire. "This will help it along."

"That arm?"

"The flood brought it to me."

"And the rest of it?"

"The rest of what?"

"The rest of the devil."

"That winged beast?" Kasdeja gave a half grin, teeth flashing in the firelight. "Under the dam. Buried deep." He poked at the arm, checking to see if it was done. "We don't need the rest of him. This will be enough, for now."

"You made the flood bring that to you?"

"That's right. First it brought you. Then this. It held you both in deep currents, keeping you safe till I came to retrieve you."

"You can do things like that? Wish for things? Make things happen?"

"I wouldn't call it wishing, Samuelle."

"But you can make things happen?"

"At some level I can, when the balance is right. At the moment, it's tipping in our favor." He studied the charred fist at the end of the cooked arm, then lowered it back into the fire.

"We've done this before," she said.

"Tell me about it."

"In Colorado. I was dying. You said you were my guardian."

"No, Samuelle."

"My guardian angel."

"That's not what I said."

"It's what I remember."

"Does that make it true?"

"Yes. I think it does. At least . . . I believe it does."

He held her gaze, firelight glinting in his eyes. Then he turned away and lifted the arm from the fire. She sensed he was playing with her, testing her, suggesting things and then denying them so she would think the revelations were her own.

"What else do you remember?" he said.

"You said your name was Kasdeja."

"Did I?"

"Yes. I'm sure of that."

"What else?"

"You fed me snake meat."

He pinched the cooked arm, peeled the skin like oily paper.

"You said it would cure me."

He stripped off a strand of meat. It struggled between his fingers. "Maybe you're not remembering at all. Maybe that time is this time. Maybe this is the only time there is." He passed her the twitching meat. "Eat while it's moving, while it's still strong."

The meat recoiled as she brought it to her lips.

"Hold it tight, Samuelle. Eat it fast."

She pushed it into her mouth, biting hard, chewing it into submission. It was richer than snake meat—sweeter, denser, dryer. It fought her as she chewed.

Kasdeja seemed amused. "A little gamey?"

She pressed her hands to her mouth, holding the meat in as it tried slipping free.

"I'd offer you water, but I think you've had enough of that for a while. Some things work faster when taken straight."

She swallowed. The meat came back up. She clamped her jaw and swallowed again. This time it stayed down. But an aftertaste lingered, ripe and strong.

"Not much I can do about the flavor, Samuelle. Think of it as medicine . . . antivenin."

He said that before . . . the last time . . . in Colorado.

He handed her another piece. "And there's something else I need to tell you." He watched her wrestle the second bite between her lips. "You'll need to keep eating to sustain your powers."

"More devil flesh?"

"No. This meal is simply to get you started. From here on, ordinary food will do."

She swallowed, winced. The meat was still moving, wiggling in her belly.

"I'm not much for eating," she said.

"Some people live to eat, you eat to live. Is that it?"

"Something like that."

"You're not big on the joys of flavor and appetite or savoring the pleasures of life. No matter. That might change as your senses expand. You'll soon find that food tastes richer than you ever imagined. And your other senses will open as well—colors, sounds, textures. It would be a shame not to indulge just a little . . . if there's time, if the others make it possible."

"What others?"

"Your helpers."

"I don't have any helpers."

"Not yet. But you will. They'll share your expanded sense of taste. It's a survival trait, after all. But their other senses will remain more or less as before. Full dilation is for leaders, not followers."

"Followers? My followers?"

"Soldiers for the soldier, Samuelle." He put the arm back into the fire. "I think your first follower's already here, carried upstream by the same forces that delivered this arm . . . the same forces that delivered you." He looked toward the river.

She followed his gaze, peering through the smoke and down the hill to where something lay close to the water's edge. It looked like a man, facedown, lifeless. Or maybe it was only a smear of shadow, a stain on wet rock. But then, slowly, it began to move.

Danny opened his eyes.
Still alive!
The strip club hadn't exploded. The deafening crash and shower of sparks had come from the giant disco ball breaking loose and smashing behind him. All that mirrored glass, each shard reflecting the glare of the lamps above the bar, engulfing him in false fire. Still alive, still sitting in the club, still tied up and at the mercy of three goons who claimed to be working for Ilya.

"Earthquake," Boone said, standing on the catwalk, backlit by the open door of Kirill's office. There were windows in there, the only ones in the entire building. Each looked directly out onto the face of a cutaway hill, good for letting in a little light and the wail of emergency sirens, but nothing more. "That had to be an earthquake."

Fox straightened up and holstered his gun. He stepped away from the bar, glass crunching beneath his boots. He retrieved his hat from the floor, put it on, glanced at Danny, then looked away.

Prutko emerged from a jumble of furniture by the stage. He shook his dreads. Bits of glass fell like crystal dandruff.

Fox picked up his fallen chair, set it on its legs. "Boone!"

"Yeah?"

"Go start the Humvee."

"We leaving?" Boone descended the stairs. "What about him?" He pointed to Danny.

"He's coming too."

Boone headed for the door.

"Prutko. Go with Boone."

Boone opened the door. Light spilled in, spreading in a wedge across the floor as he stepped into the glare.

Prutko followed, leaving Danny alone with Fox.

"You get many earthquakes around here, son?"

"No."

"I didn't think so." Fox pulled two nylon zip ties from his pocket. His hand trembled. Not much, but Danny noticed. The man was still shaken.

"Listen, Mr. Fox—"

"Hold still, son. This'll only take a moment." He fastened one tie around Danny's neck, leaving it slack while he threaded the second through it. Then he pulled the first one tight: *zzzzzZZZZt!* "That too snug, son? Can you breathe?"

Danny's pulse beat against the noose.

"Answer me, son? Can you breathe?"

"What're you doing?"

"Keeping you close." Fox sat beside him. "Making sure you don't bolt or try something stupid." Fox set a hand on Danny's shoulder, looped the second zip around his own wrist, pulled it taut. He and Danny were tied together now, Fox's hand resting on Danny's shoulder as if they were best buds, maybe father and son posing for a portrait. "You saw I was scared, didn't you, son?"

"No."

"You heard me cry out."

"I didn't."

"Don't lie, son. I see it in your eyes, but don't take my scream as weakness, son. It's more complex than that. You listening?"

"Yes."

"You know what I'm saying?"

"I think so."

"A man is many things in the course of his life. I used to be a man of the book, a preacher. I travelled the country, telling stories, saving souls— though I think I did better with the telling than the saving. It just seemed to come natural. You following this, son?"

"I think so."

"The point is . . . the thing I need you to understand is . . . those stories have a way of staying with a man. That's all I'm saying. I need you to know that."

"I didn't think you looked scared, Mr. Fox."

"And something else. Something else you need to know." Their faces were close, almost touching. "I have a short fuse when it comes to liars."

"I'm not lying. I swear to God."

"Careful, son. Careful who you call as your witness. And don't doubt me. If you remember that, you might just come out of this with your skin intact. OK?"

"OK."

"Good boy. Now let's take care of something else." With his free hand, Fox produced something that looked like the handle of a knife. No blade. Just a handle.

Switchblade!

Fox thumbed a button.

Click!

The blade appeared.

"One of the tools of my current trade." Fox tightened his grip on Danny's shoulder. "Bend with me, son." Fox bent down, pulling Danny with him as he pushed the blade against the zip that bound Danny's ankles. He flicked his wrist.

Snap!

"There you go, son." He straightened up. "Now you can walk." He pressed the blade against the chair, folding it back into the handle. "We'll leave your wrists as they are." He pocketed the knife. Then they crossed the lounge toward the open door.

The parking lot looked much as it had the last time Danny had seen it: level, bare, more-or-less free of the blood that he had hosed away after hauling the bodies to the cooler.

Above the lot's eastern end, traffic had stopped on the interstate overpass. People were out of their cars, leaning on the concrete barrier, looking north. Some had their cell phones out, snapping pictures. A few looked as if they were placing calls, or trying to.

There were only two vehicles in the parking lot, Danny's blue Nissan and Fox's black Humvee. The white truck that had brought the college boys was gone, hauled away by a friend who had owed Kirill a favor.

The black Humvee wasn't running, and Boone and Prutko weren't in it. They stood twenty paces away, stone still at the side of the building, looking out to where the level lot ended and a wide valley began. Sirens blared, ringing louder now, closer.

Prutko looked back, brow raised above the rims of his shades, lips drawn as if he were about to take a humongous crap in his baggy jeans. He didn't say anything, just looked at Fox, then turned again to face the sirens.

Fox led Danny on, around the club's northeast corner and into view of what should have been a low expanse of placard homes and false-front stores. But none of those things were there. Windslow was now a mass of muddy water, floating debris, tar-roof islands. To the west, the tower of the municipal building rose like a brick spindle. Atop it, sirens blared—rising, falling, rising, falling. . . .

"You believe this, yo?"

Miraculously, the strip club, positioned on a bluff above the town, remained untouched.

"We're cut off, yo! Jesus Christ! It's a goddamn—"

"Prutko!"

Prutko lowered his shades, looked at Fox. "What?"

"It might be wise to temper your tongue."

"What's over there?" Boone pointed past the Hummer, out to where the bluff's eastern edge declined beneath the overpass. "Is that an exit?"

"Danny?" Fox said. "Answer the man."

Danny swallowed, found his voice. "It's . . . it's just a slope."

"Can we drive it?"

"I don't know. I don't go over there much."

"There's one way to find out." Boone took out his keys, headed for the Humvee. "Let's have a look."

Prutko followed.

Fox held back, looking toward the mine now—out to the northern horizon where the rising smoke had become a funnel of steam, its top a spreading wheel, widening against the otherwise clear blue sky. "*Behold the storm of the Lord,*" Fox said, his voice rising from someplace deep in his throat. He pulled Danny closer, spoke into his ear. "Ever see a cloud like that, son?"

"No. Never."

Fox seemed about to say something else, but then he just tightened his grip on Danny's shoulder, turned, and led him toward the Humvee's open doors.

12

Soaring on the spirit wind, Kwetis flew to a part of the dream where Windslow Mine was once again silent and abandoned, a scar that had never healed, a place of memory and regret.

He banked along the highwall, descending toward a ledge that held a pressboard shack and fenced-in generator. His winged shadow rippled beneath him, expanding against the stratified rock, merging with his taloned feet as he touched down. He folded his wings, straightened up, and crossed to the drop that overhung the floor of the mine. At first his winged shadow moved with him. But then it shifted, pulled away and rose to stand on its own. It was a separate entity now. And Axle? The dreamer? He was himself again. A man, no more, no less, standing alone before the shape of Kwetis.

Kwetis stared, eyes like embers, then he turned and walked toward the edge of the cliff. He had his own shadow now, one that moved independently of the light, swinging over the brink as he dropped to a crouch. "Sit with me, Axle." He swung his head around, cocking his neck until one eye glowed across the arch of a wing. "Don't be afraid of the drop. We need to talk, spirit to man."

The ledge was much as Axle remembered from the first time he had seen it, weathered rock overhanging the crater floor.

"Remember the first time we came here?" Kwetis said. "We visited your great-grandmother's dream."

"I remember."

"Remember what she said when she saw us?"

"She asked if we'd come to thank her." Axle remembered other things too, how the visitation had taken place nearly a year before his own birth, a time when his father had still been alive.

"Time travel," Kwetis said, as if reading Axle's thoughts. "Easy enough to do in the spirit realm, not so easy in the living world." He peered into the mine, leaning until Axle feared he was going to fall. But he stayed rooted to the rock, looking down at something far below. When he spoke again, it was with a voice pitched just above the whistle of the wind. "Your great-grandmother might have embellished things, but she had a remarkable spirit, Axle—a fine sense of destiny." Kwetis looked toward Windslow Road Extension, two lanes of weathered blacktop visible beyond the limits of the mine. "She knew about paths too, about how one always leads to another—forking, diverging, doubling back. It's why she called our plan the *oohaate*—the path that must be followed."

"But it's not really called that?"

"No. She gave it that word in her dreams, carried it with her when she woke—all in an effort to understand things she could never really know."

"And what about you?"

"Me?"

"She called you *Kwetis*."

"She did. That was her pronunciation. The ancient Okwe would have said it like this: *Kwë'tís*." He gave the word a more measured sound, adding a pause between the syllables. "Do you hear the difference?"

"I think so."

"It means *nighthawk*. Do I look the part?"

"Like a nighthawk?"

"Do I?"

"You have wings."

"Anything else?"

Axle considered: long legs and torso, black fur, wolfish face. "Not really."

"And I'm not really what you see when you look at me either. This form is merely a collection of approximations: hawk wings for swiftness, bright eyes for intellect, long arms for a reach that exceeds a man's. But I am not really any of those things. In truth, I am no thing."

"Nothing?"

"No thing."

Again, Axle heard a break between the syllables, like the pause in *Kwë'tís*.

"I am no thing, Axle. Yet I am. I was ancient when the Okwe sensed my presence in their sacred mountain, older still when your great-grandmother dreamed me, heard my name in the winds of memory. And now I'm even older, as old as the oldest rocks, ancient yet appearing to you much as I did to the Okwe—as a collection of approximations."

"Am I supposed to understand that?"

"I think you do. But there's something else you need to know . . . a bit of wisdom for the eyes." He gestured along the rock wall, leaning more severely than before—so far beyond his center of gravity that Axle felt dizzy just watching. "Come on, Axle. Look with me."

"I can look from here."

"Right. But can you *see?*" Kwetis reached back, grabbed Axle's shoulders. "Bend with me." The words had a strange resonance, as if coming from somewhere else—another life beyond the dream. The impression was there one moment, then gone as Kwetis pulled Axle forward, turning his face to the void below. "Relax. You won't fall. Not this time."

The sun blazed gold against the vertical wall beneath the ledge, setting fire to the strata: yellow sandstone, green shale, ruddy clay. And there were coal veins too—black voids between the colored bands.

"I've seen rocks before," Axle said.

"But this is not about the rocks. Not *just* the rocks." He gestured, casting a long shadow over the wall. "Each layer is an era, a band of time—millions of years, epochs beneath the surface of *now.*"

"OK." Axle tried sitting back, but Kwetis held him tight. "And the point is?"

"Imagine a truth deposited beneath a thousand such layers, a concept buried under ten-million years of myth and legend—each successive layer farther removed from the truth than the one below it. That's what I am, Axle. The buried truth."

"You're losing me."

"You're a mechanic, not a philosopher. Is that what you're saying? These concepts are beyond you?"

"Something like that." Axle shifted, pushing back against Kwetis's hand. It was like shouldering an outcrop of rock, hard and unyielding.

"You sell yourself short, Axle. These concepts aren't beyond you. They *are* you. You've been pondering them all your life. Now look there." He pointed toward a mineral deposit filling a diagonal crack in the strata. "See that? That angled line? It's a vein, newly formed rock crosscutting down through ancient layers, crosscutting time."

"And you're telling me this because?"

"Because crosscutting time may be our only chance to salvage the plan."

"Didn't we already try that?" Axle said.

"You mean following that boy beneath the trailer?"

"That didn't work so well, did it?"

"Because I was there," Kwetis said. "I think you need to try again, on your own."

"Follow the boy?"

"Yes."

"When?"

"As soon as you can find your way back to him."

"And how do I do that?"

"Any way you like, Axle. It's your dream. And finding him on your own might be the only way of finding the truth that sets everything right."

"The truth?"

"A forgotten truth."

"Can you be more specific?"

"Something buried deep."

"Beneath ten-million years of rock?"

"Or a decade of denial. Look inside yourself, Axle. Find it there, in the rock of memory."

"Go back ten years?"

"Easy enough to do in dreams. Any man can do it."

"But it's risky?"

"Dreaming always is."

"And what about you?" Axle asked. "What will you do?"

"Meet with Bird. Work with him to hedge our bets. Then I'll hover close. If necessary, I'll meet you when you wake, join you once again."

"Mind and spirit?"

"More tangible than that . . . but we'll worry about that when the need arises." The glowing eyes shimmered, speaking with heat. "Right now, you have work to do." Then, without another word, Kwetis slipped from the ledge and dropped until his wings caught the spirit wind. A moment later, he was heading east, toward Windslow Road and the hilltop estate that still held Axle's sleeping body.

Axle wondered what would happen if he woke up now. He thought of Bird's question, the one Kwetis had kept him from answering when they had been standing together above the flood, the question about the fate of the earth.

Who are we saving it for?

Axle sat back, shivered. And then, from behind him, a voice called out from long ago: "Come to thank me?"

13

Dalton Davies climbed out of the flood and collapsed onto a stone ledge. He was naked, cold, and still too close to the water. He needed to keep climbing, and he would . . . in a moment . . . but right now he pressed his head to the stone and let the tension bleed from his body. He was beginning to drift when he realized he wasn't alone.

He rolled to his side, gathered into a crouch, and looked up the slope toward a thread of rising smoke.

People!

There were two of them—a man hunched before a fire, a woman sitting beside him, shoulders wrapped in what looked like a pair of shredded jeans. Her hands moved beneath the folds, scratching as she glanced at Dalton. She was bald. Her skin shimmered.

Waterborn!

The word rose unbidden. Dalton had no idea what it meant or where it had come from. He did not think he had ever heard it before, but it felt familiar. More importantly, it felt true.

She's waterborn! And so am I.

He looked at his hands, turned them in the sunlight. They shimmered like the woman's skin, slicked with water, hardening into scales.

Real scales! Not painted!

For months Dalton had painted his body, covering every place he could reach with snakeskin patterns. Now he was covered for real: bands on his arms, ridges along his belly, feathery quills sprouting from his groin. And what was under those quills? He didn't want to look. Better to leave that for later, especially since the man by the fire was staring at him, gesturing with a long-fingered hand, beckoning.

Closer, the gesture said. *Come closer.*

Dalton climbed, away from the water, toward the ledge, stopping when he was close enough to smell the smoke. The man was cooking something.

A snake?

The smoke blew toward him, stinging his eyes. Dalton blinked, looked again.

Not a snake. An arm!

And the man wasn't a man.

Shaped like a man, but not a man.

Dalton backed away.

"No," the man said. "Too late for that. I made this for you." He lifted the arm from the fire. "Come and eat."

The arm shifted, struggling in its lashings even though some of the flesh had been cooked and stripped from the bone. And then, as if it all weren't strange enough, somewhere to the south, the sky screamed.

"Here they come," the man said. He looked at the woman. "You're going to like this, right out of one of your mother's visions. Or almost, anyway."

She looked toward the sound.

Dalton did the same, tracking the scream as it passed overhead, glimpsing something as it cut across the disk of the sun. The glare blinded him, the sun momentarily black in the core of his vision. He shielded his eyes, tracked the sound north, and finally saw its source: a chevron of flying snakes—seven of them in V formation.

"Like a seven-headed dragon!" the man said. His voice was rough, like grinding stones. "There're certainly more of them still circling down at the mine, though fewer than there would have been if you hadn't flooded their nest."

"I did that?" the woman said.

"Oh, yes. That and more. Score one for our side."

The woman looked toward the sky, shielding her eyes with a scaled hand as the snakes continued northward. "What are they doing?"

"Riding the winds. But they won't get far. Not in their current condition. They're weak . . . weaker than they would have been if your flood hadn't forced them into the sky. They'll need to come down and eat if they're going to survive the day." He turned the arm in the fire. "In some ways, they're like you, Samuelle. Just like you . . . and just like—" He looked toward Dalton. "Just like our guest."

Dalton blinked, the sun's ghost appearing as a blackened halo around the man's head. But he wasn't really a man. Just the rough likeness of one, like a figure molded from dirt.

"What are you?" Dalton said.

"What do I look like?"

Again, the smoke stung Dalton's eyes. He blinked, rubbed, looked again.

The man had long arms, broad shoulders, and the coarse semblance of wings folded tight against his back.

Angel wings?

Dalton remembered the last thing his dead girlfriend Polly had said after painting their living-room carpet with blood from her slashed ankles and wrists.

I see angels. What do you see?

But this thing wasn't an angel, just an animated mass of dead matter— clay, stones, roots, leaves. . . .

"You were an artist, weren't you, Dalton?"

"You know my name?"

"I know what you know. You lived in an old farm house a quarter mile downstream. You used to make statues out of trash, junk-art devils with plastic wings."

Dalton considered running. Maybe that would be the best thing. Down the slope and back into the flood. He'd take his chances with the currents. What was the worst that could happen if he did that? Drown? Get smashed against the rocks. At least those things made sense.

"Ever wonder about that compulsion to sculpt winged men, Dalton? Ever considered why you did that?"

"It was . . . just a thing. Something I wanted to do."

"Like painting yourself with scales?"

"You know about that too?"

"Maybe those things were rooted in premonition, a way of getting you ready for dealing with me."

"You a devil?"

"I can be. That's up to you. Samuelle calls me *Kasdeja*." He gestured to the woman. She didn't seem to be listening, too busy scratching. "She's got things pretty much sorted out, but then her baggage is a bit richer than yours."

"Kasdeja?"

"If you like. It's an angel name."

"You're an angel?"

"I can be."

"But are—"

"We can answer that later." He pulled the cooked arm from the flames. "Right now, it's time to eat."

"You want me to eat that?"

"Not all of it. Just enough to help things along."

Dalton noted the length of the arm, the size of the fist.

"Something on your mind, Dalton?"

"That's *his* arm."

"Whose?"

"My guardian's."

"Is that what you called him?"

"He was my friend."

"Oh? Well then, I suppose you'll be needing a new one of those."

"You killed him?"

"No, Dalton. Not me. Samuelle did that. She killed him, blew him to pieces, buried him in a culvert. Most of him, anyway. All except for this arm."

The woman was scratching her head now, dragging her fingers roughly over the scales.

"Samuelle blew your friend to smithereens, Dalton. The dam came down and this arm went flying." Kasdeja picked at the cooked skin. "The rest of him . . . what did you call him? Your *guardian*? The rest of your guardian is buried under the dam." He peeled off a piece of flesh, watched it twist in his earthen grip. To Samuelle, he said: "This meat's calmed down a bit since you had yours."

Samuelle looked at Kasdeja as if she had forgotten he was there. Then she went back to scratching, dragging her fingers over her head, raising a dander of scales.

"Guess she's got her hands full," Kasdeja said, turning back to Dalton. "And you . . . you need to eat this. Seriously. Things could go badly if you don't."

"They're already bad."

"No. Not at all. I know bad. Believe me, this isn't it."

"You want me to eat my friend?"

"Just some of his arm."

Dalton backed away.

"Come on, Dalton. We need you to be strong. Right, Samuelle?"

"I don't need anything from him."

"You need to work with him, Samuelle."

"I work alone."

"You mean like you did on that hill behind the interstate, shooting those three guys in the strip-club lot, picking them off from a distance? No one helping? Just you and your gun?"

"I don't want to talk about that."

"No? Then what about that kid, the one who lived by the lake . . . back when there was a lake. He helped you with the dynamite. What was his name? *Paxton*?"

"Him neither." She stopped scratching, inspected her fingers. "I don't want to talk about any of that."

"Right. But you worked with him."

Dalton figured this might be a good time to make a run for it. But his body seemed to have other plans. Against his will, he stepped forward—onto the ledge, toward the fire. Then he sat.

"There you go, Dalton. Much better."

Up close, Kasdeja looked even less defined than before. His head bore only the faint suggestion of a face—black stones for eyes, a root for the nose, dark gash for a mouth. And there were other things too. Worms and sow bugs and millipedes and ants—all mingled in among the molded dirt.

"You're hungry, Dalton." It wasn't a question. "You want this. *Need* this." Kasdeja offered the piece of twitching flesh.

Dalton took it.

"Ata boy! Now hold it tight. Pinch hard. That's it."

It felt like a greasy slug, curling across Dalton's fingers, trying to escape. Bits of dirt peppered its surface, residue from Kasdeja's hand.

"Go on, Dalton. Eat before it gets away."

Dalton pushed the meat into his mouth.

"Chew!"

Dalton worked his jaws. The meat dodged the first chomp, succumbed to the second.

"Now swallow."

Dalton forced it down. No good. It came back up, over his tongue, against his teeth.

"Come on, Dalton. Big swallow! You can do it."

The meat wiggled out through his lips, twitching like a half-chewed tongue.

"It's getting away, Dalton!"

Dalton sucked it back, chomped it with his molars, swallowed hard.

Kasdeja passed him the rest of the arm. "Go on. Take it."

Dalton just stared.

"Don't think of it as the flesh of a friend. Think of it as something he'd want you to have."

Dalton took the end of the spit, grasping it in his right hand, his good hand.

"There you go! Now eat up! Good for you."

Dalton probed the meat with his left hand, the one where tissue damage from an old snakebite had left his thumb withered and useless. Now that thumb looked like a lump beneath a snakeskin glove, almost as if the scales were acting like a bandage, nursing the old wound, helping it heal.

He brought the arm to his mouth and peeled off a hunk of wriggling flesh with his teeth.

"Burns!" Samuelle said.

Kasdeja looked at her. "Those scales starting to get hot?"

"No."

"No?"

"Not starting." She scratched with both hands, clawing at the top of her head. "Been burning for a while. Itching and burning."

"It's all that scratching you're doing."

"But I can't stop."

"I didn't say you should. Actually, scratching is good. Keep it up and—"

Her scalp split, a finger-size tear opening near the top of her head.

Dalton stopped eating.

The break in her scalp opened wider. A swirl of red spilled across the scales, into her eyes.

Blood!

The tear widened. The red became a torrent, covering her face. But it wasn't blood. Wasn't fluid at all. It was hair, bright red and shimmering in the sun.

"Want some help?" Kasdeja asked.

"No!" She tugged at the break in the scales, pulling it wider.

"That's right." Kasdeja turned toward Dalton, clay lips twisting into something that might have been a grin. "She likes to work alone."

The scales crackled, peeling back to reveal an inner face, smooth and radiant.

"Fire and water," Kasdeja said. "Tempered flesh. Very rare. You'll be a reckoning force, Samuelle!"

She threw the ragged jeans from her shoulders, tossing them to the ground. She was nearly naked underneath. Nothing but scales and the remnants of a scorched shirt. She grabbed the shirt's collar, pulled it off, flung it away. She was naked now: slim, muscular, covered with scales from the neck down.

"You go, girl!"

She threw herself backward on the ground, knees in the air, rubbing her shoulders in the dirt.

"Work it, Samuelle! Shed that skin. You can do it!"

She rolled to her side, saw Dalton looking. "Hey!" She grabbed her shirt, pulled it over her breasts. Not that there was much to see, just twin mounds covered with iridescent scales. "Don't look, you shit!"

"It's all right," Kasdeja said. "Nothing to be ashamed of, Samuelle."

She went back to pulling at her scales.

"You really ought to let Dalton help you."

She gave up trying to cover herself with the shirt, sat up, and peeled herself to the waist. Her upper body was all skin now, iridescent flesh, naked as a flame.

"Some things really shouldn't be done alone, you know?"

She turned her back to them, stood and shoved the scales past her butt.

It was all coming off in one piece, curling inside-out as it reached her ankles. Then she was on her back again, kicking hard. The scaled skin broke free, landed in a heap beside the fire. She gathered it up, wrapped it around her waist, tied it tight.

"Not bad," Kasdeja said. "Like a miniskirt. Turn around."

She did.

The snakeskin face hung behind her like a tail.

"You'll be staring them down coming and going, Samuelle."

"Meaning what, exactly?"

Dalton looked away, pulled off another hunk of meat, and busied himself with chewing. He wasn't going to risk pissing her off by telling her she had a snakeskin face on her butt. Let Kasdeja tell her. Safer that way.

"Meaning," Kasdeja said, "that you'll want to find some proper clothes first chance you get."

She tugged the scales, straightened the skirt. Then she put the ragged shirt back on, tied it like a halter. It was an interesting look: ragged blouse, bare midriff, iridescent skirt, bare feet.

"Guess you won't be needing this anymore." Kasdeja picked up the scrap of ragged denim, draped it over his shoulders like a sash. Then he turned toward Dalton. "And now for you."

Dalton swallowed. "Me?"

"Time to change."

There wasn't much left of the cooked arm. Kasdeja took it, set it across his knee.

"Time for *me* to change?" Dalton asked.

"That's right."

"But I'm not itching."

"Didn't expect you would be." Kasdeja extended a finger, long and slender, tipped with a shale blade. He ran it along the scorched lashings that held the arm to the spit. The lashings popped and slid free. The arm followed, coming apart as it fell, bones and gristle plopping to the ground. "Things are going to be a little different for you, Dalton." He took one of the blackened bones, ran his hand along it to brush away the remaining meat and gristle. Then he raised the bone, held it like a club. "Things are about to get interesting." He swung the bone, caught it in his palm.

Thwack!

"Whenever you're ready, Dalton."

"For what?"

"As I said, Dalton." *Thwack!* "Whenever you're ready."

14

Exhausted from his battle with the flood and fearful of what awaited him at home, Bird walked naked through the forest that lay between Silver Lake and the Frieburg Estate. Hilly and overgrown, the ground assaulted him with stones, thorns, and an endless barrage of colors and smells—some familiar but newly alive to his skyborn senses, others overwhelmingly strange and disorienting.

He passed through a stretch of tangled woods that quivered with the fuzzy scent of sumac and hogweed, then emerged into a shale valley where a narrow creek glowed with oily rainbows. He eyed the water cautiously as he stepped over, then hurried up the next rise, climbing toward a clamor of racing engines on Windslow Road. The route seldom got much traffic, but now a line of vehicles forced him to hide in the undergrowth. Most were from Blaston, all highballing south as if getting to Windslow faster would make any difference, as if all weren't already lost. He waited till the roar of the engines faded, blending with the distant peal of emergency sirens. Then he pushed on.

His property lay over the next rise, a sprawling estate that employed an army of seasonal workers in the spring and fall. Summer was relatively quiet. Currently, the full-time staff consisted of two live-in servants, neither of whom were in sight as he reached his mile-long driveway. The pavement burned his feet, forcing him onto the 40-acre lawn where he stopped to rest beside a padlocked shed used for storing tools and fertilizer. The eaves tossed a thin shadow over the grass.

The shade whispered.

Rest.

At the top of the hill, his mansion's towers rose above the curve of the lawn, conical roofs flashing in the sun. So far away.

Rest.

He stepped into the shade. The coolness soothed him.

Lie down.

He resisted. Axle needed him. That was part of the reason he had to keep moving. The other part was the prospect of being found naked and asleep on the front lawn. The servants already thought he was odd. He didn't need to give them more to wonder about.

But it was over half a mile to the top of the rise.

And the shade was cool, intoxicating, insistent.

Rest.

He hunkered down and closed his eyes, taking a moment to rest his legs. Then he rose and walked on, stepping out into what should have been a glare of sunlight.

Instead, the world dimmed, wind rose, dust covered the sun.

Aw, hell. I didn't!

He looked back toward the shed, and there he was, sprawled on the grass, naked as a worm, dreaming.

And I'm the dream.

The sky darkened.

Should he try waking up? Or was this dream important, Kwetis's way of showing things that couldn't be explained? If so, he would need to ride it out, pay attention.

Light flashed to the south, spreading like a sunrise, but brighter, hotter . . . and closer. The light wasn't coming from *beyond* the trees. It *was* the trees. They were burning, and the fire was coming toward him, fanned by serpentine shapes that emerged from the rising smoke, flying serpents with glowing wings.

U'këë Ushaista!

The realization came matter-of-factly, the way such things do in dreams. He knew these creatures, partly from having read about them in books and online journals of Okwe lore, but also because he had dreamed about them before. The dream memory was fresh, incredibly vivid.

But that wasn't a dream!

It came back to him now. He had seen these things in the mine, had run from them as the ground ruptured and dust gathered into slithering shapes. And now he was running again. But this time he didn't get away. The serpents overtook him, driving over him in a wave of searing heat. He screamed. The grass ignited. Trees exploded.

Then silence, darkness, a void that ended with him awaking within the dream to find himself face down on a blasted wasteland.

Soot swirled above him, a dark haze broken only by a ghostly smear of noonday sun.

He stood.

The sky brightened, sunlight diffracting through rising heat. Images appeared in the shimmering air, mirages of dead forests, molten cities, charred mountains.

"Kwetis." He whispered it, then shouted aloud. "Hey, Kwetis! What's this mean?"

Something popped behind him. The sound came again. Then again. But it wasn't until a drop struck his head that he realized what it was. The dust had gathered into clouds, and now rain was falling, clearing the air, cooling the ground. Streams formed. The ground shimmered, bristling with shoots of grass. In a blink the earth came alive again—grasses, weeds, small trees. But the ground beneath his feet remained bare, a narrow swatch of hard-packed clay stretching away in both directions.

A path that must be followed.

Up ahead, smoke rose behind a crumbling wall.

A camp? Village?

The path led through a gate of broken stone, into an enclosure of some 5,000 square feet. A mix of dwellings stood near the center, some fashioned from woven branches, others of animal hide, and a few of materials that seemed to have come from another time and place. Among these were two cone-shaped huts that might have resembled teepees if they hadn't been made of hammered tin. And beyond them, in the center of the village, a kind of long, triangular hall had been fashioned from iron panels, tilted together in A-frame fashion. What was it? A meeting house? Storage shed? The interior seemed empty, ignored by all except a statue of metal and plastic that towered over it. The shape was crude but recognizable: broad wings, long face, pointed ears—Kwetis.

Villagers gathered beyond the edge of the statue's long shadow. They were nearly naked. He might have fit right in, but no one noticed as he stepped into the winged shadow. He was a *tsiskë*, a visitor from another place, another time.

He crouched beside a man who sat facing the others. A leader? Storyteller? The man was a head shorter than Bird. He wore a loin cloth, hemp moccasins, and piercings of colored plastic and glass fastened with pins and wire. He seemed to be telling a story, gesturing with painted arms. Bird tried listening. The words sounded like English, but garbled, strangely accented.

"Who are you?" Bird asked.

The man kept on talking.

"Why am I here? Do you have something to show me?"

Some of the men laughed. Not at Bird, but at the storyteller. So he was telling a funny story. That was good. At least comedy wasn't dead.

Bird turned back to the statue of Kwetis. An array of junk lay at its feet:

washers, screws, rivets, a flywheel, an oblong of heavy iron. There was also something that looked like a candleholder, broken where it had once been part of a candelabrum. And there was another item, one that looked older than the others. It was an Okwe artifact, made from stone, carved to resemble an elongated bird. The Okwe had called such objects *birdstones.* Some scholars believed they had been used as spear throwers, others suggested they had been merely ornamental, but one writer—the philosopher Desmond Daystar—claimed that the Okwe had valued birdstones as legacy gifts. A young man who received one from a dying elder was said to be trusted with the memory of the giver, thus ensuring that the giver's spirit would live on in the words and deeds of the receiver. Bird had always fancied Daystar's theory, but at the moment, the intriguing thing about this birdstone was not what it represented.

Bird leaned closer, studying the intricate patterns in the variegated shale, making sure.

It's mine!

He had purchased this birdstone from an online dealer. He recognized the markings, the slight imperfections, the patterns in the shale. This was that same stone!

But what's it doing here?

He considered the other artifacts—the oblong of iron that might have been the engine block from one of his sports cars, the broken candleholder from his mother's heirloom candelabrum. . . .

It's all mine!

And it didn't end there.

He stood, looking around. Those teepee structures of conical tin were the roofs of his mansion's towers. And the iron slabs beside the statue, they were the heavy shutters that his father had installed on the mansion's windows and doors in order to secure the home during winter. And the stone walls surrounding the village? They had been part of the mansion itself, its outer wall, eroded and broken by fire and time.

This was my home!

A shadow moved over him. It was the statue of Kwetis, walking on metal legs, speaking with the reflected light of its glass eyes. "Now you've seen it, Bird. Now you know."

"Know what?"

"The answer to the question you asked when Axle and I pulled you from the flood. What you're fighting for. The prize at the end of the struggle. This is it."

"What? This settlement?"

"Not just this one. There are others. A few thousand scattered across the earth, all inhabited by the survivors of the great cleansing."

"That firestorm?"

"Yes. You and Axle were supposed to make that happen. You were to have become the caretakers of the smoldering mine, guarding it while the great heart's fires strengthened underground. When the time was right, the fire would have risen and spread, engulfed the earth, scoured it clean."

"That was the objective?"

"Yes. Part of it."

"I thought we were trying to fix things!"

"You were. You will. That was always the plan."

"You call that *fixing*? Decimating the human race . . . cutting it down to—what? Neolithic numbers? A few thousand scattered tribes?"

"Fewer perhaps."

"And what about the rest?"

"The rest?"

"The eight billion or more who will die in your firestorm! What about them?"

"They'll be fine, Bird."

"They'll be dead."

"No. Not entirely. Their collective essence will simply return to a truer state, at one with the earth, the destiny of all living things."

"I didn't sign on for this."

"Trust me, Bird. It's for the best." Kwetis gestured toward the villagers. "A hundred years after the cleansing, these remnants of the human race will leave their burrows and assume their proper place upon the healing land."

"Proper place?"

"Caretakers, not masters."

"I don't think I'd like that kind of world."

"I understand. You'd rather employ caretakers than be one. That's why we played along with your Okwe stories as long as we could, but those tales were never more than fantasies, spun by people who lived so close to the heart of the world that they couldn't help sensing the shadow of the shadow of the truth."

"The shadow of the shadow?"

"Occasionally they saw more."

"You're saying the Okwe legends foretold these things? But there's nothing Okwe about enveloping the earth in fire, burning it in order to—"

"What about *U'këë Ushaista*?"

"No. Not the way the Okwe depicted them. The *U'këë Ushaista* cleared forests, not civilization."

"Civilization *is* a forest, Bird. Tangled and overgrown."

"You're twisting things, talking bullshit."

"Really?"

"The *U'këë Ushaista* were a rejuvenating force, a symbol of rebirth—"

"And what comes before rebirth, Bird?"

"But the entire earth? How many *U'këë Ushaista* will it take to torch the globe?"

"They are the tinder. The spark. The works of man will do the rest. Bombs, chemicals, warheads—once the chain reaction begins, it will all be set free. A terrible burning, Bird. But the spirit of the earth is still strong enough to recover."

"No. No way. Count me out!"

"We knew you'd react that way. It's why we never shared it with you before."

"So why tell me now?"

Kwetis's eyes shimmered, flickering like ashes in a draft. Something about the color suggested laughter. Was the nightflyer amused?

"What?" Bird said. "Am I missing something?"

"I'm telling you now, Bird, because I want you to stop it from happening."

Bird stared at the glowing eyes. Had he understood correctly? "Stop the rebirth?"

"For now."

The sky screamed.

The village vanished.

The maintenance shed returned. Beyond it, winged shapes swirled within the spreading cloud above Windslow Mine.

"The vectors of change have been released too soon," Kwetis said. "A crucial stage of their cycle has been compromised by rival forces who want to see the world poisoned beyond its ability to heal. They're the ones we're fighting now, and the only way to beat them is to reset the plan, cycle back to a time before our adversaries claimed the higher ground."

"Keep the earth as it is?"

"As it was," Kwetis said. "As it was yesterday . . . before the plan was compromised."

"And the human race—"

"It will continue a little farther down its path."

"And you want that to happen?"

"Yes. It's the only way."

"What's the catch?"

"There isn't one. Not for you. You'll just go back to what you were."

"Dead?"

"What you were before that."

"Alive?"

"For a while."

"Skyborn?"

"No. Just highborn . . . the privileged Maynard Frieburg living off the fat of the land in his hilltop castle, looking out at his manicured lawns and doing as he pleases."

"You're playing me."

"Perhaps . . . but that doesn't change the truth of what I'm saying. You'll have your old life back, the world as it was."

"And how does that serve your plan?"

"That's for me to work out . . . provided I can make it happen, and that means keeping Axle safe and undisturbed while he searches his dreams for a piece of forgotten truth. He's the center, Bird. His memories are the key. If he believes the right things, we can try again."

"But wait a minute. Hold on! You're saying . . . if your adversaries succeed, your plans for a scorched earth get canceled? In that case, maybe I should just wake up Axle myself. That way I stay skyborn, everything continues as it is. Am I right?"

"An oversimplification—"

"But I'm right, aren't I? That's what you said. The world continues as it is—"

"Yes. As it is. Windslow destroyed, thousands dead, and an incomplete burning of the earth already underway."

"But civilization will survive."

"Yes, for a while, but soon—in fifty years, maybe less—the planet will be poisoned beyond the point of healing. When that happens, there will be no place for the human race, no place for any living thing—and that includes skyborn spiritmen."

"And these adversaries. Who are they?"

"Spirits. Masters of the flood who are now challenging our dominion of land and sky. And they are succeeding."

"But why would they want to destroy the world? What's in it for them?"

"Everything," Kwetis said. "They're not of this earth, and when this world is gone, theirs will be all that's left."

"So my choices—"

"Retreat or eradication."

"And if I choose retreat, things go back to where they were yesterday?"

"Yes. Almost where they were. A few changes. None that you'd notice."

"For how long?"

"We'll find that out together, but first you have to play your part, get ready."

"Go home?"

"Stand guard. Your adversaries will arrive tonight at the height of a terrible storm. At that point, it will be up to you to hold them off, and that won't be easy. Not in your current condition."

"I feel fine."

"Your body's spent, Bird. When was the last time you ate?"

Bird tried remembering. It had been a while ago, sitting in his study, sharing a late dinner with Kirill Vorarov's attorney. "Yesterday," he said. "But I'm not hungry."

"No. And you won't be. You're beyond hunger. The spirit assumes dominance as the body weakens. But you need to leave such things to Axle. While his hunger devours his body and feeds the dream, you need to eat, stay strong, and prepare for the coming danger."

"Eat and stand guard?"

"Yes. And you'll want to secure the house, seal the windows and doors. Close the shutters your father had installed. They were designed to keep out six months of winter. Perhaps they'll be strong enough to survive this night. And get your servants someplace where they'll be out of your way."

"Such as?"

"The servant's quarters should do."

"The bungalow? Will they be safe there?"

"Their safety isn't our concern, Bird. But the truth is they will be considerably safer alone in their bungalow than with you in your stone mansion. Our adversaries aren't interested in them. Just be sure to get them out of your way before the siege begins."

"What kind of siege are we talking about?"

"Hard to predict exactly. For now, focus on preparations. Eat, seal the house, and hope that when Axle wakes, he has the key that will let us try again."

"Fine. But just so you know. Next time? I'll be on to you both—you and your rival spirits. Decimation and oblivion can't be the only choices. I'm for finding a third option. Screw the both of you."

"There is no third option, Bird. But if there were, the path to it would be the same. Stand guard. Give Axle time to finish his search."

Bird turned away, toward the shed where his dreaming body lay sprawled like da Vinci's Vitruvian Man.

"All right, Bird?"

Bird looked south, back to where the spiral storm rose from the mine, gathering strength above the distant trees.

"All right?" Kwetis's voice seemed to come from somewhere close but far away.

Mr. Frieburg?

The dream dimmed.

Mr. Frieburg? Are you all right? Mr. Frieburg?

15

Benjie continued north along the sudden river, the waters falling by the time he reached Silver Lake Dam. He climbed an intact section of slope, pausing to catch his breath when he came to a patch of shattered road. A drainage basin of rocks and mud stretched before him, shimmering in the sun, pulsing with the shadows of darting clouds.

But they're not clouds.

There was something strange about the way those shadows moved, turning and twisting, banking against the wind.

Not clouds.

He looked up, and there they were. Flying snakes. Seven of them. Big as trucks and circling the basin.

He couldn't look away.

But they're not snakes . . . can't be snakes.

It wasn't just their wings or size that told him that. It was the way their scales shimmered like charged dust, glowing and flashing as they moved. And it was other things too, things that Benjie sensed but couldn't define.

Not snakes . . . monsters!

One of them was having trouble, its wings crumbling, coming apart as it broke formation. The others ignored it at first, closing ranks, circling tighter until the lone monster dropped from the sky.

Benjie wrapped his arms around his shoulders, hugging tight as the thing fell headfirst, wings breaking apart, body whipping in the air. . . .

FhhhooooMMMMMMM!

It struck the lakebed a hundred feet out, mud rising as the long body fragmented in a shower of grit and ash.

The other monsters broke formation. They arched their necks, beat the air, and landed like serpentine swans to gather around the shattered body. The mud sizzled beneath them. Their scales darkened. They moved in close, heads low, inspecting the remains of the fallen monster.

Are you OK! their movements said. *Come on! Get up!*

They seemed concerned, as if they wanted to help but didn't know how. Maybe they weren't terrible monsters after all. Maybe in a way they were like him, frightened and confused.

Maybe.

Benjie had no desire to stick around and test his theory. He turned and ran, following the road toward a neighborhood of peaked roofs, high gables, and cantilevered decks that bordered the drained lake. They were giant homes, cottages for people with too much money. But there were no people there. The place was silent, empty. And yet, at the end of the street, a figure stood in the beaming sun. She was a hundred feet away, wearing a see-through robe, waving and calling: "Hey! Hey!" She leaned over a porch rail, looking right at him. "Hey, Paxton!"

Benjie stumbled.

"Paxton!"

He needed to get away, but instead he stopped as the woman started toward him, robe fanning like the train of a ghost, crazy eyes getting bigger and stranger with each step. He didn't know this person, had no idea who she was, and yet she kept coming.

"Paxton!"

What did that mean? Was it someone's name?

She reached him, grabbed his arm. "Where were you?" Her face was suddenly the biggest thing in the world. "Been looking all over!" She was so close now that her two eyes seemed to be one eye—a big, crazy eye going wider as she studied his face. "Hey!" Her breath smelled like booze, a dry lemony stink.

He pulled away.

She noticed his shirt.

He covered the printing with his arms, hugging himself.

She glared. "You're not!"

Not what?

"You're not Paxton!" She said it like it was his fault, like he'd planned it to piss her off. "Who are you?"

He didn't want to look at her. But he did. Not at her eyes or her face, but at her see-through robe. At her body. She had droopy titties, hanging low like puppies that knew they'd been bad.

Bad, titties. Bad! Bad!

"What're you looking at?"

He stepped away.

"Hey! I'm talking to you!"

Houses lined the street, close together, narrow yards in between—just enough room for a snake monster to crawl through.

"What're you looking at now?"

A shadow moved against a brick wall, first the shape of a head, then a long curving neck.

He tried telling her about it. *A monster's coming! Between those houses!* But the words got stuck in his mouth, came out jumbled.

"What?" she said. "I can't understand you."

A triangular head slid into view, then stopped beneath a high gable. Its scales no longer shimmered. It looked heavier than before, more like a creature of flesh and blood than shifting dust.

But the woman didn't see it. She was too busy staring at Benjie, scrunching her face, looking disgusted. "What're you—" She turned to see what he was looking at. Her eyes went wide, but she didn't scream. She just recoiled, her face going like "holy shit!"

The monster eased forward. Its throat pulsed once. Its jaws opened as if trying to dislodge something. Deep in its mouth, a static glow flickered and died. Then the monster froze again. No other movement. Just looking, staring at Benjie.

"Shit!" This time she said it out loud. "Aw shit!" Then she turned and ran, slipping on the grass as she tried getting back to her porch. A tree stood in the way. She stumbled around it, tripped on a root, and suddenly her butt was in the air, mooning the sun. It might have been funny if it hadn't been real. And it was. It had to be. He could never imagine anything as crazy as this.

The monster started for her, gliding over the street, picking up speed.

This was Benjie's chance. He could run, be someplace safe before the monster finished with the woman. He wanted to do that . . . needed to do it . . . but an inner voice stopped him.

Christ, Benjie! Don't you care about people?

It wasn't Jason this time. It was his own mind, almost shouting.

Don't you care?

The woman got up, arms flailing as she stumbled away.

Don't you?

The monster moved in for the kill, head swinging low, mouth opening. . . .

The voice in Benjie's head screamed louder.

Run!

He did as it said. He ran. Not to safety, but toward the monster, right beneath the shadow of its jaws where he grabbed the woman and pulled her into a flat-out dash toward the porch.

The monster followed.

Benjie and the woman climbed the stairs. The door was ajar. He threw it open, pulled her inside. She slipped, landing hard as he slammed the door. Then he threw the bolt and backed away, hugging himself as he waited to see if the monster would smash through.

But nothing happened.

The woman sat by a flight of stairs, knees drawn to her chest. "Is it me?" she said.

Benjie held his breath.

The door thumped, strained against its hinges, then settled back.

"Is it?" she said. "Is it me?"

The door shifted in its frame. No thump this time. Only a soft twitching. The movement repeated, the door easing slightly inward, the monster nudging it, testing it.

"It isn't, is it? Tell me it isn't."

What was she talking about?

"Tell me it's not me." She got up, bare feet tracking dirt from her run across the lawn. She took his arm. "That thing, that snake—"

Not a snake!

"I'm not making it up, am I? It's real."

Benjie swallowed. He didn't like being touched, especially by strangers.

"It's not my imagination, right? You saw it too."

The booze on her breath was hot and sour. He couldn't breathe with that smell in his face.

"It's real, right?"

He tried pulling away.

"Hey!" She gripped him tighter. "I'm talking to you!"

They were in a foyer with a winding staircase, chandelier, and second-floor rooms visible behind the balustrade of an open hallway. Nice place, but dark and stuffy. No lights or AC.

Power's out.

"Hey! Are you listening to me?"

He worked his mouth, but there was nothing there. His voice was somewhere in his chest, tangled up with his pounding heart.

"Can you talk?"

He shook his head.

She released his arm and crossed to the stairs, sat down with a plop. She had gritty scrapes on her cheek and hands from where she had fallen. One arm bled in a slow, steady smear. "Are you some kind of mute?"

The first floor extended beneath the staircase to a pair of French doors and a sun-washed patio. At the moment, only a sliding screen stood between the hall and the world outside.

"Come on. Just nod if I'm right. I need to know you're not some kind of pervert."

A shadow moved along the patio. A head appeared beyond the screen.

The woman didn't see it. She was on the stairs, looking the other way, toward the front door and the monster that was no longer there.

"Is it a physical or mental condition?" the woman said, taking her time on the last word. *Con-dish-hun.*

The monster peered through the screen, looking at Benjie.

"I mean, are you some kind of retard?" She said it without meanness. *Just asking.*

The monster pushed against the screen, testing it.

Benjie wanted to tell her they should go upstairs, find a closet, climb inside, hide until all the snake monsters went away.

"Hey?" Her tone changed, as if she'd suddenly realized he was looking at the French doors. "Is there something back there?" She pulled herself up, saw the monster. "No." She dropped back down. "No! I can't do this!"

The monster pushed harder. The track groaned. The screen popped free, toppled, landed with a bang. The giant head jerked back, froze. A forked tongue appeared, tasting the air. Then the monster eased forward, entered the hall.

Benjie leaped over the banister, grabbed the woman.

"Hey!"

He dragged her, pulling her toward the second floor as the monster slid alongside the stairs. Then it was in the foyer, scales grating against the wall as it made the turn.

They reached the landing.

The woman stumbled, pulled him off balance. They both fell. He was on top of her now, eyes closed, waiting for the monster to grab them.

But it didn't.

When he looked again, it was backing away, recoiling down the stairs and into the foyer where it struck an S-pose beneath the chandelier.

The woman pressed against him. He didn't like that. He wanted to move away, but he didn't. When they had been outside, the monster had chased the woman when she ran, ignored him when he stood still. Maybe, like ordinary snakes, it was attracted to motion. In any event, they weren't moving now . . . and neither was the monster. It just sat there, neck curved, eyes wide. Its throat pulsed, jaw twitched.

Patches of char covered its flanks. In some places the skin looked ragged, peeled away. Not like normal snakeskin, which came away in one piece. This stuff was falling away in ugly patches, like crumbling dirt or burnt rags.

It's sick.

And its wings were gone, the last bits of them having scraped away on the stairway wall. Black smears covered the wainscoting, with bigger pieces strewn like burnt coal across the foyer floor.

Like ant wings! Good for one flight only!

But ant wings didn't turn to ash.

"Why are we sitting here?" the woman said.

A master bedroom lay to their right. Unmade bed, night stand, vodka bottle. Benjie didn't like the looks of it. But there was another room at the far end of the hall, a smaller room with a computer beside a window, movie posters, closet in the corner. That was where they needed to go, make a run for it, lock themselves away until the house was safe.

"What're we doing?" she said. "Why're we sitting here?" She pulled away, got up, stumbled toward the master bedroom. That was all it took. The monster's head shot forward, past the chandelier and over the balustrade. The woman didn't have time to scream. The thing grabbed her by the head. Her slippers flew off, one of them catching on the chandelier, the other sailing into the master bedroom.

The monster reared back.

The woman's feet kicked, back and forth like she was running upside down. Then, with a jerk, she was gone—nothing left but a lady-shaped bump in the monster's throat, still kicking.

Run! Run! Run!

He leaped back from the balustrade and dashed into the other bedroom.

He closed the door and opened the closet. He liked closets. They were safe. Dark and quiet. But he couldn't hide in this one. No room. It was crammed with stuff. Toys, clothes, magazines, computer equipment—all jumbled together and piled in tight.

What now?

He crossed to the window, threw it open, looked out. No screen. It was fifteen feet to the ground. He'd break a leg, maybe his neck. But a rope dangled along the wall, ending at a stain of grit and moss, as if someone had been hanging wet things out to dry.

The rope was anchored to a desk.

Would it hold?

Something moved behind him.

Tap.

The door shifted.

Snick!

He'd closed the door . . . but it hadn't latched.

Now! Go now!

The monster entered the room.

Benjie gripped the rope and dropped over the sill. The desk shifted, and suddenly it was skidding across the floor, dropping him fast until it slammed the wall.

WHAM!

The rope burned through his hands. He let go, fell the last seven feet, landed hard. The monster was at the window now, the tip of its mouth peeking out, grit flaking away from its jaws as it tried pushing through. But that monster didn't matter. What did was the sound of something else advancing from the other side of the house, a second monster coming up behind him, gliding in for the kill.

Benjie ran, leaping for the low fence at the edge of the lawn. He didn't make it. The monster grabbed him. He would have screamed if he could, but a terrible pressure gripped his throat. It was his shirt sleeves, the ones he had tied around his neck. The monster had grabbed the back of his dangling shirt, not him. The sleeves squeezed tighter, and then, with his feet kicking against the sky, the knot let go, dropping him into a long somersault toward the ground. He landed hard, ran, jumped the fence. . . .

This time he made it, but there was something wrong with one of his ankles, a burning pain that grew with each step. But he kept going, eventually coming to a dirt path, then to a two-lane road.

Cliff Mine Run?

It didn't matter. Wherever he was, he had to stop.

A leaning pine grew near the road. He collapsed beneath it, pulled off his left shoe, peeled off his sock. The ankle looked swollen. He stripped the other foot and put both side by side. The left was noticeably larger. And the pain was getting worse.

What now?

He was stranded, lost and alone . . . or nearly alone.

Deep in the forest, something stirred.

He tensed, listened.

More sounds. A snapping branch, shifting leaves. Louder. Closer. A figure lumbered into view, took a few crouching steps, then stopped to peer from the shadows. A mane of tangled hair framed its face. It wore a ragged uniform, dark blue, shiny buttons. It looked sort of like a person, but in the way that the monsters had looked sort of like snakes.

Like a person but not a person.

The wind shifted, pushing the clouds, stirring the trees. The forest darkened. The creature vanished, swallowed by the dimness.

Silence.

Was it really there?

A twig snapped.

Leaves rustled.

The creature emerged, stepping into the light, walking straight toward him.

16

Thwack!

Dalton watched as Kasdeja swung the bone with one hand, caught it in the other.

Thwack!

The sound was flat and dry, like rock striking dirt.

Thwack!

Dust spilled from the back of Kasdeja's earthen hand.

Thwack!

"Hear that, Dalton?"

Thwack!

"That's no ordinary bone." He pushed the bone back into the fire, working it like a poker, stirring the coals. "Now watch." He gripped it with both hands, raised it high, then slammed it hard against one of the rocks that lined the pit.

THWACK!

The rock shattered.

"See that?"

The bone was still in one piece. The rock was gravel.

"Earthborn bone," Kasdeja said. "Fire cured, flood washed, air cooled." He held it high, turning it in the light. "Earth, water, fire, and air. Know about those, Dalton?"

"Classic elements?"

"Good answer. You're a college boy, aren't you?"

"Was."

"Then maybe you'll understand what we're doing here." He extended the bone as if he wanted Dalton to take it.

Across the fire, the woman sat in her snake-skin skirt and ragged halter, stone-still, watching.

Kasdeja shook the bone. "Come on, Dalton."

"Come on, what?"

"What do you think?"

Dalton reached for the bone.

Kasdeja swung it back, out of reach.

"Hey!"

"Hey what, Dalton?"

"I thought you wanted me to take—"

Kasdeja swung the bone straight out, swinging hard, clubbing the end against Dalton's shoulder.

Thwack.

"Ow!"

"What?"

"I said 'Ow!' That hurt!"

Kasdeja swung again, still sitting, but putting his weight into it this time, striking Dalton's calf.

Thwack!

Dalton recoiled. "Goddamnit!"

"Hurt?"

The club blurred and came again, hitting Dalton's other leg.

THWACK!

Something broke.

Dalton screamed.

The woman leaped to her feet. "Hey!"

Dalton tried getting up.

Kasdeja remained sitting, swung again, striking Dalton's head.

THOONK!

The world grayed out. When it returned, Kasdeja was standing, towering like an outcrop of rock, ready to put the full force of his earthy weight into the next swing.

The woman drew closer, right behind the raised bone. "Why're you hitting him?"

"Keep out of this, Samuelle."

THWACK!

Dalton tried crawling away.

Kasdeja followed. "Crawling, Dalton? Working on that snake routine?"

THWACK!

Dalton's face hit the ground, breath rushing out in a silent scream, hot and metallic. "Hurt, Dalton?"

THWACK! THWACK!

"Does it itch?"

Dalton rolled onto his back, curled into a ball. He couldn't breathe.

Kasdeja raised the bone, ready to swing again.

"You're killing him!"

"Yes, Samuelle. It certainly looks that way."

Dalton covered his face.

"What's it look like to you, Dalton? Am I killing you?"

Dalton coughed, tasted blood.

"No answer?"

The blood was thick and hot, coming from someplace deep inside, filling his throat, mouth, and nose.

No more! I can't let him hit me again!

Kasdeja swung.

Dalton summoned his strength, grabbed the bone. Held on.

"Nice catch, Dalton!" Kasdeja yanked the bone free, gave it a twirl, then knocked it against the ground—*thump! thump!*—like a batter getting ready.

Samuelle pushed closer.

"Get back, Samuelle. Let me finish."

Dalton tried covering his face, but the fight was out of him, pain crossing over into numbness, deafening silence. No point struggling. Nothing to do but look up as the clay man reared back—arms raised, bone poised high above his head.

"Please," Dalton said.

The bone came down.

17

Back in the lap-dance chair with fresh zips around his ankles, Danny watched Fox search for something behind the bar.

"Where're the drinks, Danny?"

"You mean alcohol?"

Fox opened a cabinet, looked inside. "This is a bar, isn't it?" He slammed the cabinet and kept looking.

Their drive to the far end of the lot had brought them into sight of the interstate's exit ramp, cut off by an arm of the flood that flowed around the cutaway hill. A dry stretch of Windslow Road lay beyond the water, but for now—at least until the runoff drained—Fox and his buddies weren't going anywhere.

Boone and Prutko had remained outside, scanning the news on the Hummer's radio.

And Danny was alone in the club with Fox.

"Here we go." Fox found the VIP cabinet near the register. He reached in, took out three bottles, set them on the bar. "But this can't be all you got."

There were cases of the stuff in the back, but the bodies from the parking lot were there too, bagged and wedged inside the walk-in cooler. There was no way Danny wanted Fox snooping around back there.

"Can I ask you a question?" Danny said.

Fox found a plastic cup, filled it halfway with whiskey, leaned on the bar.

"If you're working for Ilya," Danny said, "how come you don't know how this place works?"

"How it works?"

"It's a BYO club," Danny said.

"That a fact?"

"So how come you don't know that?"

"Like I said, son. I'm freelance. My specialty is asking questions, getting answers—kicking ass and taking names. People know my skill set. When

I'm needed, they call. Today it was Ilya, told me to contact Boone and Prutko, said they had a job for me."

"So you don't really know Kirill."

"I work on a need-to-know basis, son. And right now the main thing we need to know—"

The front door opened. Boone walked in. "We're screwed!" He crossed the room. "People on the overpass are making calls, but we can't get a signal for shit."

"Could be the elevation," Fox said. "Where's Prutko?"

"Playing the radio." Boone stepped to the bar, cracked the seal on a bottle of vodka. "Stinks in here."

"It's the drains," Fox said. "Backed up from the flood."

"Smells like shit."

"I suppose it is. You might want to open the door." Fox rounded the bar, carrying his drink, heading toward Danny. "None of this changes anything, son. You know that, don't you?" He seemed eager to get back to business, resume the routine as if nothing much had happened.

Danny had seen this sort of thing before, back in Yekatarinburg on the night his mother got the call that the police had found his father's body, shot dead in a field. She had hung up the phone and went back to baking bread, denying death by escaping into the routine of life.

Fox sat beside Danny. "Ilya is paying me to get answers. Pretty soon, I'm going to find a way to get in touch with him. When I do, I'd like to have something."

"But I told you all—"

"You've told me shit, son. Pardon my French, but that's the way it is."

Boone opened the door to the parking lot, propped it with a chair, then returned to the bar.

Fox sipped his drink, then set the cup on the floor. "Maybe you're think-ing there's no point in pursuing any of this, and maybe if we all weren't stranded here . . . well, me and my associates, we might cut our losses and leave. But the fact is, we are stranded. And the other fact is, I think you know a lot more than—"

"Some fool blew up a dam!" Prutko came through the door, dreadlocks bouncing, cuffs bagging around his snow-white sneakers. "Just said so on the news. A dam!" He kicked a chair, sending it clattering across the room. "*Koorvah!*" His voice shrilled from the rafters. "*Koorvah layno!*"

"*Corvette lame-o?*" Boone said. "What is that? Rapper talk?"

Prutko saw the remaining bottle on the bar, made a beeline to it, picked it up. "Not rapper talk!" He opened the bottle, drank.

"The hell is it then?"

"Ukrainian?" Fox said.

"Ukrainian!" Boone looked at Prutko. "That's right. You're Ukrainian. I keep forgetting."

"*Ya sru na tvayu mat!*" Prutko said.

"What?" Boone said.

Prutko took another drink.

Boone glared at Danny. "What's so funny, kimono boy?"

Ya sru na tvayu mat!

Scared as Danny was, there was something impossibly funny about Prutko threatening to take a crap all over Boone's mother.

"You laughing, kimono boy?"

"No," Danny said.

"Like hell! What is it? What'd he say?"

"That's enough!" Fox said.

Boone took a bag of chips from a bar display, ripped it open, started eating.

"Those chips good?" Prutko said.

"*Corvette lame-o.*"

"I could go for some real food, yo."

"Yeah." Boone swallowed. "Hear that. Hey, kimono boy! This place have a kitchen?"

Danny tensed.

"Something wrong, son?"

Danny considered his options. If he said there wasn't a kitchen, Boone would probably just go snooping around and find it anyway. If he said there was, Boone would go straight to it and find the bodies in the cooler.

"Son? Boone's talking to you."

Danny had jammed those three trash-bagged bodies right inside the door. Once Boone found them, it'd be all over. There was only one thing to do. "You want me to make you something?" Danny said. "Sandwiches?"

"Fish sandwiches?" Prutko said.

"Yeah. I could do that."

"Really?" Fox said. "With zip-tied hands?"

"You could untie me."

"I don't think so, son."

"But it's not like I'll get away! Like you said, we're trapped."

"You sound anxious, son."

"I'm just trying to help."

"Doesn't sound that way to me. I'd say there's more to it. You're up to something."

"So there's a kitchen?" Boone said. "Where?" He looked toward the swinging door behind the bar. "Back there, right?"

Danny felt all clenched inside, throat closing, gut twisting into double knots as Boone rounded the bar, pushed through the doors and into the glare of an emergency lamp that burned above the sink. It was the only other battery-powered light in the club. The cooler, if Boone found it, would be completely dark. Maybe that would help, but Danny didn't think so. Maybe he should just hurry up and tell Fox what was back there, tell him all the things he hadn't told him before. Maybe full disclosure was the only option left. "Mr. Fox, listen—"

"No, son. You don't negotiate. You're tied, and you're staying tied."

"I'm not negotiating. You can keep me tied—"

"I intend to."

"I just want to—"

Something banged in the kitchen.

"Boone?" Fox said.

"Goddamn bucket! Looks like someone was mopping up."

"Mr. Fox," Danny said. "I have to—"

"Found a cooler!" Boone said. A clicking sound followed, a latch disengaging . . . then the soft *snick* of an insulated door swinging open.

"I don't doubt you know your way around back there, son. And if I were to let you go, you might just seek the advantage of familiar territory. Hide in the darkness, slip through a back door—"

"There isn't a back door. Not in the kitchen."

"So you say. But how can I—"

"Hey, Fox!" Boone's voice sounded farther away now, muffled. "Holy shit!" A new sound followed, something heavy dragging across the floor.

Danny couldn't speak, couldn't move. He wanted to close his eyes, crawl inside himself, implode.

"Damn!" Boone said. "Fox! Damn, Fox!"

"Boone?"

The kitchen doors banged open. Boone stepped out, eyes wide. "You're not going to believe this!"

"Try me, Mr. Boone."

"There's dead guys in the cooler!"

"Dead?"

"Three of them."

Fox looked at Danny.

"One of them's real big," Boone said. "Could be our guy."

"Kirill?"

"He was a big man, right? This guy's 300, easy."

"Three bodies, Mr. Boone?"

"Yeah. Trash bagged!"

"Can you bring them out?"

"Could use some help."

Prutko was already on the move.

"Well, son. It just gets thicker, doesn't it?" Fox set his chin in his hand, scratched the country-singer stubble on his cheeks. "Talk to me, son." He seemed both pissed and amused. "What in the world have you been up to?"

18

Sam's life had been a study of violence. She had not cultivated it that way. It had simply grown organically, rooted in her mother's sense of biblical justice and her own uncanny grasp of distance and trajectory. Fear had also played a part, particularly a fear of people, of getting close, of the devils that lurked within men . . . and men within devils.

When Kirill Vorarov had offered to support her need for isolation by putting her shooting skills on retainer, she had signed on without regret, and although most of the jobs had involved threats and warning shots, she had never shied away from killing when killing was ordered. But such violence had always served a purpose. It had never been random, and except for those times when she had found herself on its receiving end, it had almost never been up close and personal. In short, it was nothing like the violence she was witnessing now.

Kasdeja hefted the bone and swung it hard. He didn't stand up. He didn't need to. His arm was that strong, as if he were made of stone and not angel flesh.

THWACK!

He struck Dalton across the leg, right below the knee.

Dalton shrieked. "Goddamnit!" He seemed confused, and so was she. Was Kasdeja just kidding, horsing around, making a point? But then Kasdeja hit him even harder, on the thigh this time, and suddenly Sam was reliving the ordeal behind the strip club, the fat kid swinging a crowbar, knocking her down, pinning her. . . .

THWACK!

Dalton screamed, his voice ringing back from the rocks and trees, echoing inside her. She leaped to her feet. "Hey!"

Dalton tried getting up.

Kasdeja swung again, striking Dalton's head, knocking him down.

"Why're you hitting him?"

"Keep out of this, Samuelle." Kasdeja stood up, flexed his radiant shoulders, got ready for the next swing.

Sam tried holding back, staying out of it. But suddenly the thing in Kasdeja's hand was no longer a bone. It was a crowbar. And Kasdeja was a kid in untucked flannel. What was his name?

Jason!

She shivered, remembering. . . .

She had been behind Kirill's club changing a tire on her Jeep, exhausted and off her game, not paying attention to anything but the tire. She had not realized Jason was behind her until she turned to see him coming on fast, swinging the crowbar.

THWACK!

The sound was just like that.

Dalton rolled onto his belly, the scales on his bald head shimmering as he tried getting away along the ground.

"Crawling, Dalton? Working on that snake routine?"

THWACK!

"Hurt, Dalton?"

THWACK! THWACK!

"Does it itch?"

Kasdeja leaned into each swing, his body a series of levers, each flexing to deliver maximum force.

There had to be a point to this. Kasdeja—the angel who had saved her from death in Colorado and given her a second life on this ledge above the flood—couldn't be doing this simply to torment Dalton. It had to be about her . . . some kind of test.

What was she supposed to do?

Kasdeja's wings were partially extended now, feathers glowing in the light, moving with the effort of his arms and shoulders. And now he was lifting the bone again, getting ready for another swing.

"You're killing him!"

Kasdeja looked back at her, the delicate curves of his nose and mouth obscured by the downy arc of a wing, but his eyes were visible. Icy blue. No malice. The eyes might have been carved from polished stone. "Yes, Samuelle. It certainly looks that way." Then he turned back to face his target. "What's it look like to you, Dalton? Am I killing you?"

Dalton gasped, bleeding from nose and mouth, struggling for breath as he rolled onto his back.

"No answer?" Kasdeja pivoted, blocking Sam's view.

This is it. He's going to kill him.

The bone blurred, struck hard. But the sound was different this time, strangely muted.

Sam stepped forward, coming around the arch of a wing to see that Dalton had caught the bone, gripping it in a trembling hand, forcing it back from his face.

Kasdeja seemed unimpressed. "Nice catch, Dalton!" He tugged, muscles working like steel cables beneath his skin as he pulled the bone free.

It's a test. It has to be a test! But who is he testing? Me or Dalton?

She took another step. She was in range now. He could strike her if he wanted. But he wouldn't do that. He was her guardian angel. She could trust him. Couldn't she?

He extended his arms, slapped the bone on the ground, getting ready. "Get back, Samuelle. Let me finish." Kasdeja shifted his feet. They were broad and long, glowing beneath his robe—*like bronze from a furnace!*

Sam stepped back, moving behind Kasdeja's wings until she could no longer see the blood bubbling from Dalton's nose and mouth, sign of a ruptured lung, maybe something worse.

Kasdeja reared back, raised the bone.

Dalton coughed. "Please." His voice was wet, choking.

Kasdeja swung.

THWACK!

He reared back, ready to swing again.

"Stop it!" Sam grabbed the bone by its end. It seared her hand, still hot from the fire. But she held on. "Stop hitting him!"

But it was too late. Dalton wasn't moving. His head lay broken, bleeding out on the ground.

Kasdeja turned. "No, Samuelle!" He pulled her closer, their faces almost touching. "You've grabbed the wrong end." He was so close that she could see her reflection in his eyes. "Let go."

She did.

The bone had left a gash in her palm, a deep V-shaped wound the color of boiled liver. And the pain! It felt like something burrowing through her skin.

"Try it this way!" He flipped the bone, offering the small end. "Take it." Her hand was swelling now.

"Hurry, Samuelle." He grabbed her hand, set it on the bone.

The pain vanished.

"Now the other. Hold the other end with your left. Complete the arc!" He grabbed her left hand, slammed it hard against the broad end. "Hold tight!"

She did, one hand on each end while he gripped the shaft in the center.

"Feel the power, Samuelle? Like a devil's touch, it has the power to heal, resurrect, transform . . . and kill. I'm transferring those powers to you now. One power for the left hand, another for the right."

"Devil powers?" She couldn't release the bone. Her hands felt locked. "What if I don't want them?"

"What makes you think that matters?"

Fire and ice coursed through her, up one arm, down the other. She tried tugging free.

"Easy, Samuelle! Hold tight."

She had no choice. Her hands were fused to the bone.

"Water is less than earth," Kasdeja said. "Earth is less than air. But you've been tempered in fire! That makes you a worthy vessel for the powers of earthborn touch."

"What are you talking about?"

"Hold tight."

Her hands spasmed, clenching until she feared they'd break.

"Tighter."

The bone crumbled, became dust, sifted through her fingers until her hands gripped empty air.

"Don't let go!"

But there's nothing there!

"Hold it tight, Samuelle!"

Things changed inside her—shifted, realigned, and exploded in waves so intense that her legs gave way. She fell forward, ready to embrace him. But he stopped her, grabbing her wrists. "Careful now."

She regained her strength.

He released her and stepped back, out of reach. "From now on, you'll need to be careful what you touch."

Her hands tingled, the ghost of the bone pressing against them. She opened the right. The palm was smooth, more like stone than flesh, and imprinted along it were seven marks, faintly star-shaped, arranged in a V.

"Something wrong, Samuelle?"

She closed the hand.

"If that palm frightens you, what will you make of this one?" He stepped forward, took her left wrist, raised her fist high. "Open it. Look at it."

She did as he said, unclenching the hand to find the flesh split wide with a terrible wound, but there was no pain—only the lingering weight of the bone. "What is it?"

"Death," he said. "Don't fear it." He rolled the fingers closed, squeezed them tight. "This hand's power is balanced by the other. With them, you need never fear anything ever again." He let go of her wrist and turned toward Dalton's body. "Test the powers, Samuelle."

"What?"

"Touch him."

"With my—"

"Use the right hand if you want to restore him. And you should. He's no good to you dead."

"So this *is* a test?"

"Partly. Violence for a purpose, Samuelle. You know all about that."

She knelt beside the body.

"Go on."

"Where do I touch—"

"Wherever you like."

She opened her hand. Pale light rose from the palm. She held it over Dalton's face, illuminating the wound.

"Lay on the hand, Samuelle."

She brought the palm down, cupped the wound.

Dalton remained as before.

"Nothing's happening."

"The healing takes time," he said. "The left hand works a little faster, but evil is like that." He gripped her wrist, pulled the hand from Dalton's head. "That's enough for now." He helped her to her feet, then held her close, wrapping her first in his arms, then in his wings. His scent enveloped her, rich and earthy. "Relax." His wings closed tighter. She was in darkness now, buried tight, alone with his voice. "Empty your mind, Samuelle. Make room. Let me in."

She pushed her face to his chest.

The darkness deepened. She drifted, thoughts dissipating the way they did when edging toward sleep. And then. . . .

He opened his wings and stepped away.

She stared, amazed.

He was more radiant than before, glowing from within, smiling like the sun as he folded his wings against his shoulders. "Walk with me. I have more to show you."

She glanced at Dalton's body, unchanged, still dead.

"He will join you when he's ready, Samuelle." He turned toward the forest that rose behind the ledge. "Come. I have visions to share."

She followed, and as they walked, he told her about the end of the world.

19

Mr. Frieburg? Are you all right?

Bird stirred, rising from the dream.

"Mr. Frieburg."

He opened his eyes.

"Are you all right?"

Bird focused on the weathered face of Jim Dooley, the estate's grounds-keeper. The bastard seemed to be suppressing a laugh.

"Mr. Frieburg."

Bird sat up, the toolshed's wall rasping against his shoulders. A moment ago, he'd been talking to Kwetis. Now the dream spirit was gone. The world had returned. Back to normal, or nearly so.

"I brought this for you, Mr. Frieburg." Jim unfolded a robe, set it across Bird's shoulders. The fibers felt coarse, itchy on his skyborn skin. No matter. He slipped it on.

"What happened to your clothes, Mr. Frieburg?"

"It's a long story, Jim."

Trees stirred along the mile-long driveway, leaves turning belly up, casting shadows in the rising wind.

"Should get you inside," Jim said. "Rain's coming."

Not rain, Jim. Something worse.

"You want me to help you up?"

"No. I'm fine."

"Pardon me saying, Mr. Frieburg. You don't look fine."

"I had . . . had an accident at the mine."

"The Company?" Jim always called Windslow Mine *the Company*, short for *the Company Land*. He'd been doing that since the days when Bird's father had run the place from an office in the mansion's east wing. "You were down there?" Jim looked concerned. "Then you've seen them?"

"Them?"

"The fire and flood," Jim said. "A reporter on the news said that's what happened. First a fire, then—"

Bird stood, bracing against the shack. He remembered what Kwetis had told him about fueling his body. "I need to eat."

"Let's get you to Bridget, then."

Bird put his hand over Jim's shoulder. A moment later they were riding in the golf cart that Jim used for zipping around the grounds, accelerating toward the stone towers of the coal-baron castle on the hill.

The house was dim. No electricity. A battery-powered radio crackled in the kitchen, mingling with smells of meat and vegetables. Jim's wife Bridget appeared in the archway, a slender woman with thistledown hair, wearing the same white apron she'd worn when Bird was a child. She took one look at him. "Oh my!" And that was it. From that moment, she was all business.

For years Bridget had adhered to a daily schedule established by the elder Mr. Frieburg, serving breakfast at 8:00, lunch at noon, dinner at 4:00, supper at 9:00. Those meals were still ready on time, eaten if Bird wanted them, stored if he didn't. "There's a chop in the fridge, Mr. Frieburg."

"He'll take it," Jim said. "And whatever else. The lad's hungry."

She hurried away.

Bird settled into the captain's chair at the head of the table.

"Anything I can do, Mr. Frieburg?"

"Yeah. Close the windows. Seal the shutters."

Jim considered the dining-room windows, casements open to the clouding light, curtains shifting in the breeze. "Worried about the rain? Think it'll be bad?"

Oh, Jim! You have no idea.

"It'll get dark, Mr. Frieburg. With the shutters closed and the power out—"

"Close them anyway. And the doors too, outer and inner. Close and bolt them. Upstairs, too. But stay out of the guest room above the patio. I'll do that one."

Bridget entered with a glass of ice, pitcher of tea, saucer of lemons—all balanced evenly on a silver tray.

"And sugar," Bird said.

"But you don't take sugar, Mr. Frieburg."

"I'm taking it today."

She set the tray on the table, then returned to the kitchen while Jim started on the shutters. No doubt they both had questions, and Bridget, who had a sixth sense about everything under the Frieburg roof, was certainly curious about the stranger in the bedroom above the patio. But she and Jim obeyed without comment, leaving him alone with the brightest lemon slices he had ever seen.

He pulled the saucer close, picked up one of the wedges. The rind felt tart in his skyborn hand. He popped it into his mouth, the zest exploding as he bit down. *Oh my god!* He took another. Then more. By the time Bridget returned with the sugar, the slices were all in his mouth, juice dribbling over his chin.

"Those slices were for the tea, Mr. Frieburg."

He wiped his mouth and kept chewing. God, he had never known such lemons. Kwetis had been right. He needed to eat.

"I have proper fruit if you'd like," Bridget said. "Apples and oranges."

He swallowed and reached for the sugar. "Bring it on." He raised a spoonful, shoved it into his mouth.

Oh . . . my . . . god!

Jim finished closing the shutters. The room was dark now, but Bird's skyborn vision had already adjusted.

"I'll get some candles too," Bridget said, returning to the kitchen.

Jim followed her.

Bird kept eating, nearly finishing the sugar by the time Jim appeared with an heirloom candelabrum retrieved from deep in the pantry. It held six candles, each lit and cradled in a wrought-iron arm.

"Not too close." Bird pointed to the middle of the table. "Over there is fine."

Jim moved it. One of the candleholders jiggled as if loose. Bird felt a sense of déjà vu, a vague impression that faded as new smells wafted from the kitchen, meat and vegetables warming in the oven.

"She's getting that chop for you now, Mr. Frieburg."

"Right." Bird poured a glass of tea, dumped in the last of the sugar. The granules sparked in the candlelight. "Hey, Bridget. That chop. Just bring it cold, OK?"

Jim backed away. "I'll get the upstairs windows."

Bird drank his tea, thrilling at the taste. No lemon. Just tea and a trace of sugar—almost overwhelming in its undertones.

Bridget reappeared, plate in hand. "Chops shouldn't be eaten cold, Mr. Frieburg. You'll get a bilious."

"I don't think so. Not today."

She set down the plate: meat, potatoes, and peas. He picked up the chop, gripping the bone like a skillet handle while she positioned his silverware.

"Are you well, Mr. Frieburg?"

"I'm fine, Bridget. Never better. Just need to eat." He bit into the chop, snapped the bone, ground it between skyborn molars. The taste was remarkable—sweet, gritty, and salty with char. He talked around it. "You got any more?"

"Bones, Mr. Frieburg?" Her tone was flat, Irish deadpan.

He grabbed a baked potato and pushed back from the table. He stood, feeling stronger. "I'm going to help Jim with the windows."

"I'm sure he can manage."

"Still, I'd like to get it done. And—" He waved the potato at the table. "Bring more food. Whatever you got. You said there's fruit?"

"Yes. There's that."

"Put it out too." He walked away, eating as he headed for the stairs, feeling her gaze burning into his back, following him as he climbed toward the second-floor hall.

He passed beneath a stained-glass skylight, an addition that he'd commissioned after inheriting the house. His father never would have approved, but Bird had been interested in the skylight's designer, dating her just long enough to make the purchase. The thing leaked when ice froze and thawed around its frame, but today it would provide some much-needed light once the shutters were all closed.

The door to Axle's room waited at the end of the hall. The last time Bird had opened it, he had found himself standing beneath the hovering form of Kwetis, wings spread against the ceiling while Axle lay dreaming on the bed.

What would he find this time?

He set his hand against the door. It shifted in its frame, pushed and pulled by the wind from the room's open window . . . or maybe it was the wind of a dream.

"You need some help, Mr. Frieburg?" Jim had finished with the shutters in the master bedroom and had returned to the hall.

Bird waved Jim away. *Keep working.* He pushed the rest of the baked potato into his mouth, chewing as he wiped his hand on his robe. He felt stronger than before, more alert. He turned the knob to Axle's room, opened the door, stepped inside.

A wing-like shape moved across the bed, but it was only the shadow of a curtain billowing from an open window.

Axle lay in the center of the mattress, knees bent, hands fisted to his chin. He looked more like a fetal man than a skyborn master, locked in a lucid dream.

20

Come to thank me?"

The voice came from the direction of the pressboard shack in the center of the ledge, but the ledge was gone now, replaced by a gravel lot of singlewide homes. One stood a little apart from the others. Vinyl siding, screen door, wooden porch—the trailer where he had come of age under the half-blind gaze of the great-grandmother he had called *Yeyestani.*

Trees surrounded the lot. Sun angled through them, painting everything with the light of dream and memory. But there were shadows here too, deep ones that darkened as he drew nearer.

"Yeyestani?"

She answered by limping into view, pushing the screen door open on its rusty spring and stepping onto the porch. She looked older than he remembered, frail as a twig, brow knitted with worry . . . or was it pain?

The door clapped shut behind her.

"Have things gone well, Akeo?"

Akeo. It wasn't a proper name. Just an Okwe word meaning "left behind." The last time she had called him that had been on the night of her death, the same night she had taken him to Windslow Mine and forced him to find his way home alone.

"Are you here because you've succeeded, Akeo? Or has everything gone *yakôtyes?*"

She had always talked that way, peppering her speech with terms passed down from her elders.

"That isn't it, is it, Akeo?" She squinted. Her eyes were as he remembered, one dark, the other stone white. "You've failed. That's why you're here. You've come to tell me your father died for nothing."

"Don't say that."

"All right. So maybe it's you. You died for nothing."

"That neither."

"Are you going to fix what's wrong?"

"If I can."

"And if you can't?"

Something rumbled in the distance, a low earth-shaking sound like the roar of a train. But there were no tracks anywhere near Coals Hollow. No active ones, anyway. They had all been shut down along with the mine. But this sound was too loud to be a train anyway. Loud and getting louder.

He grabbed the porch, holding on as a wall of roaring darkness barreled past the edge of the lot. It looked like a churning mountain, a pulsing wave of trees and rocks, a section of landscape racing along both lanes of Cliff Mine Run. The pavement shattered beneath it, asphalt vaporizing to smoke.

The whole court shook with its passing, homes rattling, threatening to come apart. But the tremors subsided as Yeyestani called to him, her voice close yet far away, loud but dimmed by distance. "That doesn't concern you, Akeo. Not yet. Not here." She opened the door, walked back inside.

Time seemed to pass.

It was darker now. Nighttime. A fluorescent light flicked on, blue-white through the screen, illuminating the porch.

He climbed the stairs.

She stood inside, working at a small table. She had her back to him, shoulders moving, hands rising and falling to the sound of a grating rhythm. She seemed to be filing something, raising a small cloud of grit that drifted in the light.

"Yeyestani?"

She kept working.

He stepped closer, pressed his face to the screen. It felt real, too real to be merely the artifact of a dream.

"Yeyestani?"

A moth fluttered beside him, struck the screen, bounced off to try again.

"You need to invite me in, Yeyestani."

"No." The file rasped with the rhythm of her words. "I don't have to. This isn't *that* dream. And you're not Kwetis anymore." She filed faster, harder. "New dream, new choices." She stiffened, stopped working, studied her hand as if she had cut herself.

"Yeyestani? You all right?"

She turned to face him. "You need to be careful, Akeo." She fixed him with her white eye, the one that saw the future. "Understand?"

"I'm trying."

"No. Not really. Not even close." She cradled her hand to her chest as she stepped nearer. "You're not the nightflyer, Akeo. Not in this part of the dream." She pushed the door open, stepped into the doorway.

The moth fluttered in, chasing the light.

"Here you're barely a man, Akeo." She raised her cupped hand, opened it to touch his temple. "Flesh and blood." She drew the hand back, showed him the blood on her fingers. "You've been shot."

"That was before."

She frowned. "Before doesn't matter here, not in dreams. There's a bullet in your brain. Your friend Bird put it there."

"He wasn't my friend when he did that."

"He is what he is. Then and now."

He felt something wet trickling from his temple. He touched it. It was blood. Not his though. The head wound was part of another life. The blood had come from her hand, smeared there when she had touched him.

"It's you," he said. "You're the one who's bleeding."

"No." Blood fell from her fingers, forming a puddle on the porch. "It's not what you think. Nothing is."

The air grew still. No sound now but the hum of the fluorescent bar in the kitchen ceiling, the clicking of the moth banging against it.

"This all means something, doesn't it?" he said.

She didn't answer.

"Yeyestani?"

She was gone now. Only her blood remained, staining the threshold between porch and kitchen.

He stepped inside, into the fluorescent glow. The trailer's other rooms lay to his left, cloaked in darkness.

A hand file sat on the table in the center of the kitchen, resting beside a piece of partially carved slate, seven inches from end to end. He picked up the carving, turned it over in his hand. The shape was vague, unfinished, but with features that suggested it was on its way to becoming a knife.

He touched the blade, lightly at first, then harder. It didn't cut. Yet Yeyestani had been bleeding.

He put it down and backed away.

He wanted to wake up, but even now the dream was becoming richer, more detailed as the trailer's other rooms brightened to his left. It wasn't as if the lights were coming on. Instead, it seemed the rooms were condensing out of the darkness, gathering form and substance as he looked at them. They were all exactly as he remembered from life. Snacks on the coffee table, television tuned to MTV. The sound was cranked up a little too loud, drowning out music from Yeyestani's bedroom. Not quite a song, but a piece of one, a word chanted over and over.

He entered the living room, flicked off the television.

The chanting grew louder.

It tugged at him.
He walked toward it.

21

The figure stopped, crouched, stared at Benjie.

He didn't return its gaze. Animals didn't like being stared at. And the figure looked like it might be part bear. He studied it from the corner of his eye. Broad shoulders, big head, a mane of tangled fur . . . or was it hair?

It made no sound, not even when it started moving again, keeping a safe distance as it climbed toward the shoulder of Cliff Mine Run. At least for now, it was respecting his space. It moved silently along the gravel, hunkering down when it reached the guardrail.

He could look right at it now, sizing it up as it peered cautiously toward the uphill bend in the road. It wore a tattered uniform, ripped across the shoulders, shredded and torn along the arms. The wild mane on its head and shoulders was definitely hair.

It's a person.

It turned, met his gaze.

It's a woman.

He looked away.

"You all right?" she asked. Her voice was low, almost a whisper. She moved toward him.

He froze, closed his eyes. He heard movement, shifting gravel, a snapping twig.

"Hey?" The voice came from in front of him now. "That ankle. It looks like it hurts."

He held his breath.

"OK if I have a look?"

Since she had said *it looks like it hurts*, he knew she was having a look already. But that wasn't what she meant. What she meant was she wanted to examine it.

"You a doctor?" he asked.

"No. But I know some first aid." There was something in her voice that made him want to trust her. He opened one eye, peered through his eye-lashes to find her staring at the words on his shirt.

"I don't," he said.

"Don't?"

"Don't pee in the pool."

She made a half smile, one side of her face going up, the other weighted down by a heavy scar. "I didn't think you did," she said. "If you did, it wouldn't be funny."

"You think it's funny?"

"Sort of. That's why you wear it, right?"

"Sort of."

"Can I look at your ankle?"

He nodded, looked away. "OK."

She moved closer. She had some BO. Not the bad kind that came when you wore the same clothes all week and didn't shower. Just the kind that came from working out, getting sweaty. It was an OK smell, more proof that she was human, or at least more human than something else.

He tensed as she lifted his foot, cupped it in her palm. "Can you move your toes?"

He did.

"Does it hurt to do that?"

"Yeah."

"How about this?" She turned the foot to the left.

"Yeah."

She moved it the other way.

"*Ahhhhhhhhh!*"

She set the foot down, gently. "I don't think it's broken."

"Hurts."

"Sprains generally do. You'll need to keep off it for a while."

"But I need to go home."

"Where's home?"

He looked toward the uphill bend in the road.

"That way?" she asked.

"I think so."

"Far?"

"I don't know. I'm lost."

"Yeah. Easy to do in these woods."

"You ever get lost?"

"Sure. Lots of times. Just don't tell my chief."

"Your chief?

"That's right. I'm police. My name's Sharo."

"OK."

"And you?"

"I'm not police."

"But you have a name, right?"

"Uh-huh."

"And it is?"

"Benjie."

"Pleased to meet you, Benjie."

"Yeah."

She tensed, looked toward the road. She had a nice face, almost normal when he saw it only from the side that wasn't scarred. "Something's coming."

An engine raced, getting louder as a cruiser rounded the uphill bend.

She hunkered down.

The car raced past, lights flashing.

"That your chief?" he said.

"No. That's a Blaston car. I'm Windslow."

"So you hide from Blaston?"

"From everyone, Benjie. At least until I get back home."

"Where's that?"

"Windslow."

"You going to walk?"

"Yeah. Unless I get a better idea. But let's see what we can do for your foot." She took one of his socks from the ground, stretched it taut. "This will do."

"For what?"

"Support." She lifted his foot, wrapped the sock around it, starting at the heel, working up along the ankle. The pressure felt good. "I'll have to pin this."

"OK."

"Can you hold it for me?"

He set his fingers beside hers, pressing down as she removed a name tag from her shirt. She pinned it to the top of the sock. A few adjustments, and then she was done.

He turned his foot to see the tag.

S. JENKINS

"Now let's get the other sock over it, to hold it in place." She rolled the other sock up along his foot, pulling it snug.

The ankle didn't hurt so much now. It just throbbed, chugging like an uphill train.

She picked up his shoes, handed one to him. "Put this on your good foot. I'll be right back." She returned to the woods, reappearing a few minutes later with a long branch. It was shaped like a hockey stick, or maybe a leg with a foot on it. She wedged the foot-shaped end into his other shoe, pressing it against the ground until it was good and snug.

"Wooden leg?" he said.

"Sort of." She laced the shoe up tight and turned the stick so that the shoe was upside down. "But the shoe's not for walking on. It's more like a cushion. Goes under your arm."

"Like a crutch?"

"Exactly." She helped him up. "There's a roadblock." She pointed up the road. "I passed it a half mile back. They're stopping everything heading south. You get that far, someone will take you home."

He leaned on his crutch, his bad foot cocked behind him.

"Go on. Try walking with it."

He hobbled toward the road. The crutch worked OK, but the stick felt rough against his palm, digging in.

"That roadblock's just around the bend," she said. "Below the intersection with Highland and Old River Trail."

"What about—" The words wouldn't come. He swallowed, tried again. "What about you?"

"I have my own home to get to."

He pictured the route she would take, the shortest path to Windslow—through the mine.

Don't let her!

"Good luck, Benjie." She started away, back into the forest.

Christ, Benjie! Don't you care about people?

He tried calling after her, but he was suddenly scared again, the words catching in his throat as she vanished into the shadows of the windblown trees.

22

Leaving Dalton's body by their dying campfire, Sam and Kasdeja climbed a slope of tangled undergrowth and entered a stretch of forest that shimmered with mist. The ground had buckled here, shaken into fissures and ridges. Some of the rifts were narrow enough to step across, others were yards wide, sheer and bottomless. Kasdeja carried her over these, holding her tight as he took to the air. Sometimes she looked down, into glowing darkness where coal veins smoldered like burning serpents. Each time she clung to him, one fist pressing his shoulder, the other balled against his chest. She had no idea what would happen if she touched him with either of those hands, and she had no intention of finding out. For now, she'd had enough surprises.

As they walked, he talked to her of choices, of how the human race stood at a crossroads, one path leading to fire, the other to paradise. And in time they came to a ridge that was different from the others, a heap of dust and clay that shimmered like scales in the changing light.

"We won't climb this one." Kasdeja cut in front of her, crossed to her right, took her fisted hand in his. "Stay close. We'll walk around it."

It was the remains of a giant serpent, heaped beneath a ring of splintered branches.

"It fell from the sky?" she said.

"Yes. As they all will." He led her to the monster's head, a mound of smoldering ash. "You did this, Samuelle."

"Me?"

"Your flood forced them to the air before their time." He eased closer, bent toward her, spoke into her ear. *"I put enmity between them and you, and you put an end to them."*

She tensed, stepped away.

"Something wrong?"

"Don't do that."

"What?"

He knew. He had to know. He knew everything.

He's testing me!

"Talk to me, Samuelle."

But she didn't want to. Better to change the subject. "I thought you were going to tell me about the end of the world."

"The end to the world as you know it," he said. "Which can either be a curse or a blessing." He drew her away from the serpent. "Walk with me. We're almost there."

The ground angled upward, toward a break in the trees and a dark cloud that spread against the sky—a gathering storm . . . or something *like* a storm.

"Where are we going?"

"To the mine."

"Why?"

"It's the center."

"Of?"

"Everything."

Thunder rumbled.

Wind rose. First in the high branches, then whipping low as Kasdeja led her onto a table of hard-packed earth. Straight ahead, the ground fell away, ending at the machined cliff that marked the crater's edge.

"*Let darkness and the shadow of death stain the face of the deep,*" Kasdeja said. "*Let a cloud dwell upon the abyss.*"

She pulled away again.

"Something wrong?" he asked.

"I think you know."

"Do I?"

"You said you know everything."

"I know what you know."

"Then you know who you sound like when you talk scripture."

"Was that scripture?"

"Almost. Not exactly. But that's what she did. She changed things, got things wrong, twisted words to suit her—"

"Who are we talking about, Samuelle?"

The cloud flashed, twisting atop its stem, a dark weed spreading against the sky.

"Samuelle?"

"My mother," she said. "When you talk scripture, you sound like my mother."

"Really?"

"Don't play me, Kasdeja. You know what I know . . . so you know about her . . . all about her."

"She was a prophet, Samuelle."

"I don't think so." She put an edge in her voice, making it clear the topic was closed. Then she peered over the sandstone precipice, straining to see the base of the storm.

"You're too far back," he said. "Come closer. You needn't fear falling. Your body is strong . . . if you break it, it will heal."

"What do you mean?"

"Exactly what I say. I'm not speaking parables, Samuelle. Not this time."

She drew toward him, stopping a few inches from the brink. There was no barrier to mark the edge, no raised rim or ridge of rock, certainly no rail. The ground just ended, fell away. She didn't dare lean forward, but she did look down, one foot behind the other as she lowered her gaze to take in the entire length of the spinning funnel, a tapering cord plunging into a mist-covered hole 60 feet down.

"See?" he said. "Not so bad when you face it straight on. It's often that way. Now steady yourself. Our journey doesn't end here."

The ground quivered, flexing as if alive, groaning as the ridge extended beyond her feet. A bridge formed, a stone arch curving through the air, piercing the stem beneath the spreading wheel.

"Trust your balance," he said. "Stay on the path." He stepped onto the bridge, robe billowing as he walked along the upward curve of the arch.

She held back. The path was barely a yard wide, tapering as it approached the funnel—so narrow at that point that it would be impossible to place two feet side by side.

"Don't think about it, Samuelle. Follow me . . . trust the way."

Wind rose as she stepped forward, blowing the frayed ends of her knotted shirt as she stepped from the wide ledge and onto the rising arch. The stone pulsed as it took her weight, hard but yielding, somehow alive. She didn't look down, but trusted her feet to stay the course as she focused on Kasdeja's folded wings. His nearness reassured her, keeping her balanced until he reached the storm's spinning stem. The mist broke against him. Then he was gone, swallowed in a whorl of displaced mist. She was alone now, moving along the ever-narrowing span.

Trust your balance. Stay on the path.

The spinning funnel was right in front of her, banded like a serrated blade, defying her to take the final step.

Trust the way.

She extended her fists, pushed them into the crosscutting winds, kept walking as the currents took hold, steadied her, drew her in. Something passed through her, a jolt of static that moved along her arms, into her body. The path darkened. Wind buffeted her. She took another step . . . then another . . . and then the darkness parted. Light greeted her, beaming down through the eye of the storm. She seemed to be standing in a deep well, surrounded by walls of banded rock. But the bands were fluid, shifting, turning clockwise as they rose toward a circle of cloudless sky.

Kasdeja stood a dozen steps ahead of her, balancing at the highest point of the arch, the place where the bridge should have begun its downward curve to the other side of the abyss. But there was no downward curve. The bridge ended in midair, not a bridge at all . . . but a needle of stone projecting out into the hollow core of the storm.

Wind howled around him, lifting his hair like a pillar of flame. "Keep coming, Samuelle." He removed his sash and flung it to the wind. It unfurled, rose, vanished into the light. "Won't be needing that," he said. "Or this." He lifted his arms. His robe billowed, sliding from his body. An instant later it hovered above him, sleeves extended, hem rippling. It turned, dancing in the air, then followed the sash into the circle of sky.

She averted her eyes, afraid of his nakedness.

"The robe and sash were baggage, Samuelle. They'd only weigh us down." He spread his wings, then turned to offer her the anvil of his back. "Come on." He bent low, into the wind, feathers splayed and trembling. "Don't be afraid."

His flanks were like polished stone, sculpted yet undefined, more mannequin than man.

An irrational urge moved through her. She wanted to strip off her shredded halter and snakeskin skirt, toss them away, ride him skin-on-skin as he took to the air. But she couldn't. Not yet. She approached him, put her arms around his neck.

"Hold tight," he said.

She drew her legs over his hips, flattened one fist against his chest, the other across his shoulder.

"Move with me." He kicked off.

A jolt shook her as he grabbed the air, a jarring transition from standing to flying, but after that it was all rhythm and flow. His wings pushed and pulled, reaching up and angling back, like oars in the wind.

She hugged him tighter, eased forward, pressed her face to his. Below her were more stone projections, layers and layers of incomplete paths jutting out into the eye of the storm. The image was there for an instant, then gone as Kasdeja reentered the spinning mist, passed through, and emerged over the mine.

The crater floor lay far below, more like a topographical map than real-world terrain. Yet she didn't feel afraid. Not yet. Not until he folded his wings and dove.

She gasped, held on.

Don't be afraid.

She held her breath. Closed her eyes.

You needn't fear falling.

Straight down. Faster and faster.

She opened her eyes, and there was the ground, so close she saw the falling shadow of Kasdeja's wings spreading dark against the water-carved clay. Closer and closer. She opened her mouth to scream, but then he caught the wind, broke their fall.

"*Ahhhhhhhhh!*" The scream became a purging breath, a long exhalation as gravity and momentum pressed her hard against his back.

"Now watch," he said. "Look down."

They flew over a jumble of fire trucks and vans, some mired in muddy drifts, one tilting precariously over a break in the ground. The vehicles were visible for a moment, then gone as green shoots engulfed them, growing from the crater floor. Leaves unfurled, meshing into a canopy of interlocking branches.

"What is this?" she asked.

"A vision." He turned, circling. "This is the Windslow Mine that would have been if your adversaries had taken control of the land, sealed the perimeter, and given their plan time to run its course."

Leaves sparked in the sunlight, a sea of yellow-green pulsing in the wind.

"It's beautiful," she said.

"It is. But evil hides in beauty. And this forest is only a cover . . . a mask for terrible forces gathering strength beneath the ground."

He banked toward the setting sun, orange against the western hills. And in that glow, the trees began to move.

"Behold, Samuelle. The day of fire!"

The branches swayed, rippling as something rose beneath them.

Kasdeja circled.

She watched.

The forest heaved, swelled upward, then dropped back as the ground gave way. Trunks snapped, trees fell, spilling toward the center of the crater where a pit opened like the pupil of a giant eye. And the pupil was burning, filling first with smoke, then with exploding light.

The forest ignited.

Fire spread, radiating outward. Flames broke against the highwall, a blazing surf capped with blackened ash. And rising out of those breakers, appearing first as whirlwinds of smoke, flashing with static as they condensed in the rising heat, a swarm of serpents screamed and took to the air. They flew close. She felt the heat of their scales, the rage of their eyes. There were hundreds of them, then thousands, each more terrible than the one she had seen dead in the forest. That had been an infant, a stunted dwarf set free before its time. These creatures flew on wings of burning ether. Spikes lined their backs, trailing lightning, igniting the sky as they scattered to the wind.

Kasdeja flew higher, above the heat and smoke, into the realm of crystal air where thread-like clouds scattered in his wake. He leveled off. The earth lay far below them now, curved like an inverted bowl, dotted with the fires of burning cities and towns.

"The vectors of a scorched earth, Samuelle. If your adversaries had gotten their way, these creatures would have gathered their strength underground and then hatched to breathe fire over the land. And after them more would have followed, enough to overwhelm all the works of man. Watch now. I'll show you." He folded his wings, descending back into the heated air, back to the site of Windslow Mine where something massive rose from the burning crater. A wedge appeared, jagged and serrated, a blacked peak riddled with glowing veins.

"*A stone cut without hands!*" Kasdeja's voice thundered in her ears. It might have been a memory of her mother's voice. But it no longer frightened her. Such fears paled in comparison to the mountain taking shape beneath them. "But this isn't the rock of Daniel, Samuelle. This is not a stone to *replace* the world. This is the rock of burning fruit . . . the rock of *decimation.*"

Meteors flashed, slicing the air with streaking light. And atop the mountain, a glowing tree unfurled leafless branches that spread like veins against the sky. And from those branches, a terrible fruit sprouted and began to scream.

"*But the fruit of this tree you shall not eat!*"

It grew in clusters, tangled masses of serpentine seedpods, sprouting wings, ready to fly.

"But it won't happen," she said, gripping him tighter. "It's only a vision! I stopped it, right?"

The seedpods broke free, took wing, scattered. And now, in the distance, new trees sprouted, terrible clouds with glowing trunks and mushroom crowns.

"Yes, Samuelle. You stopped it . . . for now."

The vision vanished.

The world went dark.

When it brightened again, she was standing beside him on the edge of

Windslow Mine, shivering in the chill of the still-gathering storm.

"A parable?" she asked.

"Some of it was." He embraced her, first in his arms, then with his wings. "Sometimes that's the only way to know the unthinkable."

She felt safe in his embrace, shielded, locked up tight. She pressed her head to his chest, heard what she thought was his heart, then realized it was her own.

"But the reality would be just as terrible, Samuelle. And it could still happen. Right now, the demon master lies within a stone fortress, searching through his dreams for a way to undo the good you have done. You need to stop him. Wake him and kill him."

"How?"

He gripped her wrist, lifted her fisted hand. "Use your power."

"My hand?"

"A terrible weapon, Samuelle."

"But I'll have to get close—"

"Yes."

"Real close."

"No more long-distance killing, Samuelle. You're a death angel now."

"And you'll help me?"

"I already have."

"Will you take me to it, the stone fortress?"

"No."

"Then how can I—"

"You know how this works, Samuelle. All I can give is what you already know."

"No. That's not true. What about the vision you just showed me?"

"From your mother's stories, amended to suit a greater truth."

"And what about the stone fortress? That's not something I know about."

"Perhaps in a way it is. Sound the depths, Samuelle. Look deep."

"I don't have time for that! You need to tell me what to do."

"No. You need to realize who you are, what you've become." He gripped her wrists. "Think, Samuelle. Say the words. They're inside you. Find them. Speak them."

"I don't know what you're talking about!" But she did. Even as she denied them, the words were there, wrapped in the memory of her mother's voice.

"Speak the words, Samuelle. Know them and make them real." He held the wrists higher, showing her the marks on her hands. "Speak the words."

"I—" Her voice caught. She swallowed, tried again. "*I am one who lives. . . .*"

"Keep going!"

She closed her eyes, feeling a chill as she realized how perfectly the words described her. Written two thousand years before her birth, often quoted by a mother she had learned to despise, the words were all about the thing she had become. A prophecy! She braced herself, drew another breath, tried again.

"*I am one who lives, and was dead, and behold, I am. . . .*"

"Say it!"

"*I am alive forevermore!*"

"All of it, Samuelle. Keep going!"

"*I am alive forevermore . . . and . . . and I have—*" She looked at her right hand, emblazoned with pulsing stars. "*And I have—*" She looked at the other hand, winced at the dark thing in its center, clenched it tight. "*I have the keys of Hell and Death.*"

"And of life."

"It's from Revelation."

"You remember!"

"I don't want to."

"But you do."

"And the vision—"

"Your mother told you of such things, images from her own prophetic dreams, symbols she tried explaining through the only religion she knew. Her life was one of searching, looking for answers. Remember how she took you with her, long trips to hear preachers on the fringe of Christianity, speakers and healers who performed for donations. Most were charlatans, but she was a searcher, Samuelle. A true pilgrim. An apostle in search of a message. And she's part of you . . . always has been . . . still is."

She was crying now.

He released her wrists.

She went to clasp her hands, press them together as if in prayer.

He stopped her. "No." He grabbed her wrists. "No folded hands for you." He held them apart. "Good and evil can't mix." He let go.

She crossed her arms, hugging herself with balled fists.

"You have the power, Samuelle. With your right hand, you will raise an army of seven. With your left, you will silence the dreams of your enemies, both the demon master and the servant who guards him."

"But I still don't know where they are . . . who they are."

"You met the servant before the flood carried you off. He knelt beside you in the valley. We talked about him earlier. He calls himself *Bird*."

"Kirill Vorarov's partner?"

"That's who he was, not what he is. Like you, he's changed."

"But where's the fortress? Where do I find him?"

"That's for you to answer. You'll get no more from me."

"Never?"

He grinned without humor. "Never is longer and deeper than you think, Samuelle. Let's just say *for now*."

She wanted to argue, but she held it in, swallowed it back, let it smolder. "So I'm to find a stone fortress I've never seen, confront a demon master I do not know, stop a dream that isn't mine?" It sounded like one of her mother's stories. "And I'm to do it with an army of seven, raised by my own hand."

"And your first recruit is close. He'll come to you soon, though not exactly in the form you remember." Kasdeja opened his wings, releasing her into the light of day.

They were back on the ledge, the same one where she had eaten devil flesh. She stepped to the brink. Water flowed below the overhang, but more slowly than before. The flood was falling. Overhead, clouds spread, wheeling above the trees.

"Wait for him here," Kasdeja said, speaking behind her. "Enlist him. He'll serve you well." Wind gusted from the valley. Kasdeja's voice changed, dropping in pitch, becoming one with the churning air. Dust whirled. When she looked back, he was gone.

She looked toward the side of the ledge, the place where she had once pressed her life-giving hand to Dalton's cleaved skull. But all that remained was Dalton's skin, limp and shimmering on the blood-smeared ground.

23

The emergency lamps faded, not much brighter now than the darkening day beyond the strip club's open door. Dim light spilled in, pooling against the bodies that Boone and Prutko had placed beside the bar.

Danny wiped his eyes with zip-tied hands. He needed to pee but wasn't sure he should say anything about that. Not yet. Not until he got a sense of what Fox thought about the story he was telling—a stammering, dry-mouth spew about four college kids who had shown up that morning before the club opened.

"One of them—the big one—was really mad," Danny said. "He told me he'd been roughed up by a girl he picked up hitchhiking, said the girl was one of Kirill's dancers and wanted me to set things right. You know, like compensate him."

"So you shot him?"

"No. That wasn't me. That was the girl."

"The dancer shot him?"

"Except she wasn't a dancer. He just assumed that because she worked for Kirill."

"So she shot him for Kirill?"

"No. It was personal. She messed with his truck, screwed it up so it wouldn't start. When the guys tried leaving, she shot them."

"You said there were *four* guys."

"Yeah. The big guy's brother got away."

"And the three that didn't? You helped the girl put them in the cooler?"

"No. The girl was gone by then."

"But you said she messed with their truck."

"Yeah, and then she hid out, probably on the hill beyond the overpass. Shot them from there."

Fox looked impressed. "That's some fancy shooting."

"She's like that," Danny said.

"And the truck? Where is it now?"

"Towed away. I called a guy who does things for Kirill. Favors."

Fox glanced toward the bar. "How'd you explain those bodies to him?"

"He didn't see them. I moved them first, got them out of sight."

"By yourself?"

"That's right."

"Cleaned the lot?"

"Yeah," Danny said. "Hosed it down."

"That's a lot of work, son."

"It's my job. I'm the manager. I need to keep everything in order."

"So you dragged the bodies inside. Then when the tow guy left, you lock the club, bagged the bodies, hauled them into the cooler. That's dirty work."

"Yeah."

"You must've got some blood on you."

"I was covered."

"So you put on some off-duty stripper clothes?"

"It was all there was . . . all I could find."

"It's an interesting story, Danny. I'm not saying I believe it, but it's interesting."

"It's the truth."

"In any event, it's not exactly the truth I came here for, is it? Where's Kirill?"

Danny wondered if he should just make something up. It wasn't as if Fox was in a position to disprove anything he said.

"Something on your mind, son?"

Danny shifted, trying to take some weight off his bladder.

"Nervous son?"

"No . . . I mean, yeah. But the thing is." He lowered his voice. "Mr. Fox. I really have to go."

"Go?"

"Piss."

"Really?"

"I was drinking before you got here."

"Trying to relax?"

"Yeah. It was a stressful morning."

"Now you got to pee?"

"Yeah. Real bad."

Fox patted his shoulders. "Understandable, son. Completely understandable."

"So . . . can I?"

"Can you what?"

"Take a piss."

Fox folded his arms across the back of the chair. He looked toward the hall that led to the restroom, then back at Danny. "It's like the truth, isn't it?"

"What?"

"Piss," he said. "It's like the truth. A lot like it, when you really think about it. I mean, the way it builds up, gets heavy, makes a man squirm. It doesn't like being kept in, either. And after a while, if you don't let it out? Well, it just comes a gushing on its own. Embarrassing when that happens, but there it is. Know what I'm saying?"

"I really have to go, Mr. Fox."

"And you will, son. One way or the other."

Have to tell him something . . . anything!

"The way I see it," Fox said. "You can relieve yourself of two burdens just by telling me what I need to hear."

"But, Mr. Fox—"

"Kirill, Danny. Where is he?"

"Morgantown."

Fox looked surprised.

"He's in Morgantown," Danny said.

"You just remember that?"

"No. But he made me swear not to tell."

"I see. And you're a man of your word?"

"Yeah."

"But now you're breaking it?"

"Do I have a choice?"

"No, Danny. I don't suppose you do. But Morgantown's a big place. Can you be more specific?"

Danny gave him the name of a hotel.

Fox considered it, then stood up.

"So I can go?" Danny said.

"Take a piss?"

"Yeah. Can I?"

Fox turned to the bar. "Boone! Prutko! Got a job for you."

What was he going to have them do? Carry him in? Help him aim? Danny didn't care. Whatever it took.

"What?" Prutko said. "What's the job?"

"Keep an eye on Danny."

"Keep an eye on him?"

Fox started away, heading toward the stairs to the catwalk.

Danny called after him. "Mr. Fox! You said—"

"Tell it to Prutko, son. He'll handle it."

"Where you going?" Boone said.

"Need to make a call."

"Lines are down, yo!"

"Land lines are. But Boone said it looked like people on the overpass were making calls. Could have been the elevation. Might as well give it a try."

"You going to the overpass?"

"I'm thinking the roof will do." Fox started up the stairs.

"What was he saying?" Prutko looked at Danny. "You want me to handle something?"

24

The singing grew louder. A single word, over and over: "Bird." It came from Yeyestani's bedroom, crackling with static as if playing on her old AM radio. "It's my beacon," she used to tell him. "A homing signal, for when I get lost in dreams."

Now it was guiding Axle . . . drawing him into the trailer's narrow hall. The bathroom was on his right. After it, his bedroom, also on the right. Yeyestani's room was straight ahead, but in this dream there was a fourth door as well. It was bigger than the others, carved from solid wood. The knob was brass. It stood closed on the right side of the hall. No space for a room there. It had to lead outside. He passed it by, kept moving, drawn by the singing.

He'd heard the song before, though never coming from Yeyestani's bedroom. She preferred talk radio over oldies stations. And this was definitely an oldie, a novelty hit from the mid-sixties, something about *Bird* being the word.

He set his hand on the door, the inane lyrics playing a counterpoint to his fear, terrible memories of finding Yeyestani dead and covered with blood.

The singing grew louder as the door swung inward, but the room he found waiting for him was not Yeyestani's.

A man sat with his back to the door. A sawbuck table stood beside him. On the table, an open briefcase. All these things were familiar. Axle knew the room . . . and the man. They didn't belong in Yeyestani's trailer, but Axle knew them, remembered them.

Part of him wanted to run, but the same compulsion that had drawn him down the hall was now pulling him closer.

The man in the chair wore a leather jacket, jeans, work boots. A stained T-shirt covered part of his head, tied in the back to staunch bleeding from a bullet wound. His face was swollen, one eye rolled back, the other staring right at Axle.

"You're me," Axle said.

The music came from the sawbuck table, from the briefcase that wasn't a briefcase at all. It was a portable record player, lid raised, disk spinning beneath a skipping needle.

"You're me, aren't you?"

The man sat back, lifted the needle.

The room fell silent.

"You are, aren't you? You're me."

The man gave a left-sided smile. There was blood on his teeth, caking his lips like chewed tobacco. "It's *all* you." He gestured to the room. It had two doors, one open to the hall of Yeyestani's trailer, the other sealed with plywood and heavy beams. Taped to one of the beams, a hand-lettered warning:

DANGER
NO EXIT

"It's *all* you," the man said. "Me. My wound. The bullet in my brain. You and me. It's all you because . . . think about it! This dream is all happening inside you, living in your mind."

"You've lost me."

"No. You've lost yourself. A piece of it anyway. And you need to get it back because she's coming." He turned his good eye toward the door that led back to Yeyestani's trailer. It was closed now.

From outside, the sound of footsteps. Running. Coming on fast.

"She's you too, you know? A bad part, like the bullet in my brain, *our* brain. She'll kill everything if you give her the chance. And this time there'll be no resurrected father to save you. Your earthborn guardian is gone. She's taken his power, and she'll use it against you if you give her the chance."

The running was louder now, closer.

"You can stop her," the man said. "You can do it, provided you brought it with you."

"Brought what?"

"You didn't ditch it again, did you?"

"What are we talking about?"

"Another piece of you. A part of your past. Something denied and buried deep."

"But you can't tell me—"

"I can only tell you what you know . . . what you're prepared to accept. Otherwise—"

The running stopped.

"Please tell me you brought it."

Something slammed the door, shaking it in its frame. The latch groaned, but it held . . . for now.

"Tell me," Axle said, his voice seeming to come from far away, somewhere beyond the veil of sleep. "Tell me what to do."

25

Tell me what to do."

Bird almost answered Axle, almost shook him awake to ask what he needed. But Kwetis's instructions had been clear. Axle was to remain asleep. Bird was to leave him undisturbed. Whatever was happening in the dream realm, it was Axle's to deal with on his own.

The steel shutters rattled, shaking in the rising wind as Bird got up and steadied himself beside the bed. He felt dizzy, suddenly confused—as if his thoughts were not entirely his own.

He looked down at Axle. The guy was stone still now, hardly breathing.

I need to get out of here.

He headed toward the door, pausing again when he saw his reflection in a mirror above a bureau. The reflection surprised him, as if he had expected to see someone else.

Just me.

He left the room and returned to the darkened hall, feeling more like himself again as he emerged into the overcast glow of the skylight.

He went to his bedroom, removed the robe and left it on the floor by his walk-in closet. Then he entered the adjacent bath and tried taking a shower. No good. The jetting water felt like needles on his skyborn skin. Within a minute, sensory overload drove him back into the bedroom where he hunted his closet for some loose-fitting clothes. He found them, and something else too, a stone amulet hanging from a leather strap. It was his birdstone—the one from the dream.

He turned it over in his hand, examining the elongated body, blade-like tail—exactly as he had dreamed it.

A sign? An omen? It couldn't have been a coincidence. He slipped it around his neck and returned to the dining room.

Bridget had set out a bowl of fruit and platter of cold beef. But for now, the food could wait. He went into the kitchen. Bridget was there, staring at her crackling radio, listening.

". . . atop PPG tower. I can see part of it now, hanging over the side. It seems to be . . . wait a second! It's coming around, turning . . . it's—" Static.

Bridget reached for the dial, tried getting the station.

"Bridget?"

She jumped, looked around, eyes red.

The radio crackled.

Bird stepped closer, reached around her, tuned the station back in.

". . . can see what looks like a head, big as a truck, peering down from atop . . . hold on. Police are moving us back, away from the building. We're moving back. This is Tracy Glick, Pittsburgh News 6 at PPG—"

The feed cut out.

"Bridget? What's going on?"

She stared, eyes wide, unfocused.

"Bridget?"

She turned away, crossed to the fridge. "I forgot the sauce." She opened the door. "For the meat."

A new voice came on the radio, talking about additional sightings, unconfirmed reports from Waynesburg, Canonsburg, East Liberty. . . .

"Bridget! What's going on?"

She closed the fridge, leaned against it. "It's snakes, Mr. Frieburg. Flying ones."

Now it was his turn to steady himself, lean back against the sink. It was happening. "I need to get you and Jim out of here."

"Out of here?"

"Someplace safe."

"And where would that be, Mr. Frieburg? The other station says the Silver Lake Dam's let go. They say there's roads washed away, bridges out. They say—"

Bird left the kitchen, entered the hall, shouted up the stairs. "Jim! Hey, Jim! Finish up and—" He stopped, afraid of waking Axle. So many concerns . . . too much to worry about.

Jim appeared along the top rail. "Just finishing up."

Bird waved him down.

Bridget entered the hall. "But aren't we safe here?"

"No."

"Where then?"

"Your place," Bird said.

"The bungalow?" She turned to Jim as he descended the stairs. "Mr. Frieburg wants us in the bungalow!"

"It's safer than here," Bird said. "Trust me."

"Nasty storm brewing," Jim said. "Sky looks black from the north tower. It's—"

"Come on." Bird took Bridget's arm, waved for Jim to follow. "I need both of you out of here now." He walked toward the back door that led to their home, a wood-frame house on a patio foundation, no basement. They didn't argue. He was their employer, after all. Even without the power of his spirit voice, they had little choice but to trust him. But then, as he opened the door to a howling wind, Bridget stepped back, pulled free of his grip.

"My radio!" She returned to where it stood by the sink, picked it up, then followed him out beneath the threatening sky.

26

Dalton's skin tumbled across the ledge, turning somersaults in the wind, stopping when it snagged the rocks of the burnt-out campfire. It flopped onto the coals, then lay flat and still—like the shadow of a man who wasn't there.

Sam stood beside it, alone with the sound of flowing water and hissing leaves. Overhead, the disk-shaped cloud wheeled, dark and angry. And descending from its center, just visible above the trees, the funnel flashed like an arcing cable. The world seemed strangely alive, imbued with an intensity of colors that she had never noticed before. It would distract her if she let it. Better to tune it out, stay focused.

She walked to the end of the sandstone ledge, looking past the high-water line of exposed roots and leaning trees, deep into the valley to where the flood had fallen back to a shallow stream. Between the high-water line and the trickling water, the valley was naked rock, the bones of the earth laid bare by the torrent that had come and gone. And amid that expanse of gray, a man in a fire suit appeared in the distance, coming around a bend in the valley. No shoes, just a bright yellow jacket and pants standing out in stark relief against the rock.

Dalton?

He looked smaller than before—more compact, and seeing that made her wonder how much she herself had changed.

She waved.

He shielded his eyes, his yellow sleeve flashing in the uneven light. Were her heightened senses playing tricks with her eyes, or were his clothes uncommonly bright?

He called to her, voice echoing in the tight valley: "Is he still up there?"

"What?"

"That clay man."

"Who?"

"Your freaking friend."

"Kasdeja?"

"He up there?"

"No, but he's around."

Dalton stopped.

"You scared of him?" she said.

"Wouldn't you be?"

"You mean because he hit you?"

"That what you call it? *Hitting?*"

"He had to do it. It was *for* you, not *against* you."

Dalton rubbed his head as if remembering the beating.

"That a fire suit?" she asked.

He raised an arm, looked at the reflective stripe on the sleeve as if reminding himself that he had it on. "Yeah." He fingered a shoulder patch. "Blaston VFD."

"Where'd you get it?"

He pointed south.

"The crater?"

"There's some trucks down there," he said. "No people. Just—"

"What were you doing in the crater?"

"Getting away."

"But you came back?"

"Yeah." He was walking again. "It's like I'm supposed to be here. Like something's . . . pulling me back." He stumbled, kept walking, advancing until he was barely twenty yards downstream.

"Stay there," she said. "I'm coming down." She turned, stepped from the ledge and descended the slope. She climbed like a gecko, hands and feet flying across the smooth rock until she stood beside him.

"Do you have something for me?" she asked.

"What?"

"Kasdeja said you'd help me if I brought you back."

"Brought me back? I walked back."

"Before that. Back to life."

"I was dead?"

"You don't remember?"

"I remember him beating me. That's what I remember! After that I was just sitting there, up on that ledge, itching like a bastard. I did just what you did, scratched right out of that skin. Then I left, figured I'd get away before he came back to beat me with another bone or some damn thing."

"He crushed your head, Dalton."

He rubbed his scalp, bone smooth. No bumps or scars, nothing but his memory to verify what she was telling him.

"He crushed it, Dalton. Beat you dead . . . then I brought you back, healed you with this." She showed him the hand, the marks on her right palm.

"Those stars?"

"Something like stars."

"What do they do?"

"Give life. Kasdeja didn't beat you to be mean. It was to help you transform."

"He didn't beat you."

"No. But we're different. I needed to bring you back to finishing making you what you are."

"Yeah?" He studied his hands, the skin almost luminescent. "So what am I?"

"My helper. That's what drew you back here. Part of you wanted to get away, but another part knew you needed to be with me."

"What kind of helper?" he asked.

"I don't know. Maybe the kind that tells me where to find a stone fortress."

"A what?"

"Bird's house."

"A birdhouse?"

"All right. Guess information isn't your area."

"What's a stone fortress got to do with a birdhouse?"

She pushed past him, walking downstream, heading toward the one place where she was pretty sure she could find some answers.

27

The pounding from the hall grew louder as Axle turned to the boarded door. It was boarded for a reason. There was nothing beyond it, just empty air and a long fall to the floor of the mine. He couldn't get out that way, not unless he sprouted wings and flew.

"But this isn't that shack, not entirely," the man said. "It isn't only the place you remember. It's also the place where your body lies dreaming this dream . . . the place you'll be when that killer at the door comes for you in the waking world."

"All those places?"

"Past and future," the man said. "They're all the same in dreams."

The door to the hall shook more violently, trembling in its frame, but still holding . . . for the moment.

"You haven't answered my question," the man said. "Did you bring it?"

"What?"

"You'll never break the cycle if you keep leaving it behind."

Axle turned to the boarded door, grabbed one of the nailed beams, yanked hard. The hand-lettered sign came loose and drifted to the floor. The beam followed, its end striking the sawbuck table.

"Not that way," the man said. "Don't you remember?"

"But it's part of me." Axle gripped another board, pulled it free. "If I want it to be an exit—"

"Really? You think it's that easy to change who you are?"

Axle pried the final beam free. Only the plywood sheet remained, nailed to the frame.

"This isn't about fantasies," the man said. "It's about working with truths, facing things as they are."

Axle gripped the edge of the plywood, ripped it free. Wind grabbed it, sucked it through the opening. He grabbed the empty doorframe, struggling in the racing air that threatened to pull him from the room.

"Some things are too terrible to be denied," the man said. "You can cover them up, but that doesn't change them."

Outside, the plywood sheet dwindled, tumbling on the wind.

"You'll never find the answer by running away," the man said. "Face your fear. See where it takes you."

The door to the hall exploded, splintering to dust as a giant fist lunged into the room. It knocked the man aside, sent him crashing into the saw-buck table. The record player fell with him, but it was a briefcase now, spilling papers that scattered in the churning wind.

The fist reared back, struck a cobra pose, turned toward Axle. Then it opened to reveal a palm split with a dark and terrible wound.

The man dragged himself to a corner, drew himself into a hunch, hugged his legs. "There are things worse than death," he said, shouting over the wind. "You'll find that out if she touches you."

She?

The hand lunged.

Axle leaped away.

The hand turned, followed.

"Don't run from it, Axle! Don't let it take hold of you . . . but don't run. You've been running too long. Time to take a stand, get atop your fears."

The hand lunged again, the wound dilating to reveal a deep throat, ribbed and pulsing.

Axle ducked beneath it, crawled behind the toppled table.

The hand knocked the table aside, reached for him.

He scuttled back, cowering against the frame that opened onto the abyss. He considered jumping.

Don't run from it!

The hand opened wide, fingers splayed, wound dilating, throat glowing.

Axle leaped. Not into the abyss, but upward against the wind, between the fingers, over the knuckles, and onto the back of the hand.

The arm reared back, slammed him against a wall. He leaped free, through the door to land in Yeyestani's trailer. He was in the hall once again, the long arm writhing beside him, stretching toward the living room, vanishing into darkness.

He got up, tried running.

The arm flexed, blocking his way. He couldn't return to the pressboard room, couldn't flee into the darkness of Yeyestani's home. The only option lay right beside him, the hallway's fourth door, the one that had never existed in the real-world trailer. It had to lead outside. He threw himself against it. It opened onto darkness. He stepped through, slammed the door behind him.

Silence.

He wasn't outside, but in a darkened room with paneled walls, high ceiling. And the thing that had chased him? It had already punched down one door to get at him, but now it seemed to have given up. The carved door remained intact, shifting slightly in its frame, pushed and pulled by a draft at Axle's back. It was a mere breeze compared to the one that had nearly sucked him into the abyss. It smelled of dust and pending rain.

He turned, his eyes adjusting to reveal a sight that was, in its own way, even more disturbing than what he had found waiting for him in the pressboard room.

28

Sam and Dalton came to a fork in the valley, one way branching toward Cliff Mine Run, the other down a narrow ravine where the flattened remains of a wood-frame home lay packed beneath a bridge.

"My house," Dalton said. "What's left of it."

"You lived under that bridge?"

"No. The house used to be upstream. I was inside when the flood hit, carried everything here."

"Must have been one hell of a ride."

"Yeah. Wouldn't want to do it again."

The flattened house wasn't the only thing compacted beneath the bridge. Wattled amid the bricks and beams were masses of rock, mud, and trees. Atop it all, wedged in but strangely intact, a section of roof lay tight against the bridge deck.

"You have to climb over it," Dalton said. "At least, that's what I did."

She started climbing.

Much of the debris was surprisingly dry, wrung out by the forces that had packed it into place. She imagined the flood racing under the bridge until the flotsam formed a temporary dam, diverting the surge toward Cliff Mine Run. It was amazing that the bridge had held up under so much pressure. "They don't make them like they used to," she said.

"It was a good house."

"I mean the bridge." She reached the top, climbing from the roof to what remained of the span. The bridge deck was gone, nothing left but the steel support. She balanced on a beam, holding on as wind hammered her back. The funnel looked bigger and meaner than it had when she and Kasdeja had stood before it on the edge of the mine. Lightning flashed within the cloud. Thunder pulsed like a beating heart. And there was another sound, a thumping *whooomp-whooomp-whooomp* of spinning blades.

"Helicopter," Dalton said, climbing up beside her. "I saw two of them when I was in the mine. One came in real low, like it wanted to land. But it couldn't. The wind is crazy down there. Worse than here. Lots worse." The sound faded, moving south.

She and Dalton were now some 30 feet above the valley floor, barely 100 feet from the highwall's brink.

Dalton gripped a bridge beam. "Like I said, the climb down is harder. I almost fell a couple times."

It wasn't really that high, barely twice that of the upstream ledge. *I can do this.* She felt Kasdeja's gaze bearing down, watching as she began her descent.

Your body is strong, resilient . . . if it breaks, it will heal.

Dalton followed, climbing more slowly, finally catching up with her as she reached the end of a mud-clogged spillway that ran to the highwall.

Way out toward the center of the mine, a helicopter came in low, struggling in a shearing wind.

"That's not one of the choppers I saw before," Dalton said.

Sam noted the markings. "It's not police. Not EMT."

"Who do you think?"

"Could be anything. Freelance news. Disaster tourists." She considered the vehicles that lay strewn across the crater, one of them teetering on the edge of a rift. "Radios in the trucks . . . cameras in the vans. People have got to know something bad happened here."

"But there's no one down there. It's like everyone vanished."

Serpentine tracks between the breaks in the ground hinted at terrible possibilities. The monsters had risen and taken to the sky. No matter. Nothing she could do about that. Her destiny lay to the south, past the helicopter that was now circling back for another flyover.

"You'd think there'd be more than a few choppers coming to investigate," she said.

"Maybe they can't handle the wind."

"Right, but there's no one on the ground either."

"Flooded roads?"

"Could be." She looked south. "Or maybe there's something bigger happening beyond those hills."

"Windslow?"

"All that water had to go somewhere." She shivered, though not from the cold or the wind. This chill was deeper. "*And behold,*" she whispered. "*I bring floodwaters to remake the earth.*"

"What?"

"Just thinking . . . wondering how much of this has been planned for us, pieces moved into position, strategies set in place."

The chopper was trying to land, dropping slowly toward a table of slag a little ways back from the news vans. It drifted as it came down—lilting to one side, then the other—but the descent was steady. Two hundred feet . . . one hundred fifty. The engine changed pitch, racing as the blades spun faster. Then the craft dropped, straight down to crash against the rocks. It exploded. First a silent flash. Then a concussive boom.

"Jesus," Dalton said.

The chopper was just a starburst now, a smear of burning wreckage. If there were people amid the debris, she couldn't see them.

Dalton shook his head. "That's messed up."

"Yeah, but it's not our problem." She peered out over the edge of the spillway, gauging the climb down.

"It just fell out of the sky!" Dalton said. "Like a freaking stone!"

She felt Kasdeja watching, urging her on. "We need to get moving."

"Through the mine?"

"Yeah." She looked along the wall, toward a point where debris from an earlier rockslide angled down toward the base of the storm. There was other stuff down there too, deposits of pulverized earth and trees—remnants of an uprooted forest. Some of it was still shifting, settling around rocks that jutted like fractured bones. "You climbed this?" she said.

"Yeah. It's not so bad if you take it slow. Want to follow me?"

"No. I'll go first." She looked skyward. "He'll protect me."

"Who?"

"Kasdeja."

"The clay man?"

"Why do you call him that?"

Dalton looked confused. "Why wouldn't I?"

Perhaps he was still addled from his beating. Whatever. It didn't matter. She grabbed the edge of the spillway, swung beneath it and onto a foothold in the rock wall. Then she climbed, slithering down like a lizard until she reached a berm of dry slag that angled out onto the floor of the mine.

Dalton was right where she'd left him, staring in disbelief. "You got some moves."

"You coming?"

He started after her.

She looked toward the base of the storm, down to where a dome of localized fog marked the spot where she had seen a vintage Mustang burning just before dawn.

The mist rumbled. A strange sound, almost like a voice.

"You don't want to look at that," Dalton said, coming up behind her. "I did the last time I was here. It made me feel weird, like it was talking."

She looked away from it, feeling lightheaded—as if she'd been on the verge of falling asleep.

"It wasn't really words," he said. "But when I listened, part of me had this urge to walk into it."

"Into the mist?"

"Yeah. But then there was this other part of me that wanted to go back and find you."

"That's touching."

"Yeah. But there was still this other part that wanted to say 'screw it' and keep running."

"Which is what we need to be doing." She turned her back to the storm and stepped out onto the shattered floor of the mine.

Dalton followed. "You still haven't told me where we're going."

She pointed south, past the burning chopper, toward the sirens.

"Windslow?"

"Strip Mine Gentlemen's Club," she said. "Heard of it?"

"No."

"That's in your favor."

"Is it a stone fortress?"

"No. It's a steel-frame sex shop. But the manager might know something . . . if he's still there. Anyway, it's the only lead I've got." She was jogging now, moving toward a pass that would bring them out onto the lower bends of Cliff Mine Run.

29

A metal ladder led from the catwalk to a door in the strip club's ceiling. Fox pulled the release, pushed back the hatch. Wind lifted his Stetson. He grabbed the brim, set it back on his head, then reconsidered and dropped it to the floor at the base of the ladder.

He continued up, hair whipping as he passed through the hatch and out onto the flat roof. The sky swirled, dark as a bruise, rumbling like an angry god. Exterior ductwork surrounded him, branching from compressors and heat exchangers. He held his cell phone, hunting a signal. Nothing. He stepped out of the ductwork maze and onto a gravel plain bordered by a raised ledge. In the distance, the funnel rose from the mine like a proverbial whirlwind.

His phone's signal bar flickered and dimmed, then brightened again as he neared the edge of the roof.

On the hillside below, broken concrete and twisted rebars formed a jagged stair to the edge of the flood. Amid the debris, a broken sign:

SKY TOWER

Judging from the rubble, the fallen building couldn't have been much of a tower, let alone one that got anywhere near the sky.

Let us build a tower that reaches to heaven!

He stepped onto the raised ledge. The signal was stronger here. He thumbed the code for Ilya's Brooklyn office. The connection rang—once, twice, then: "We're sorry. All circuits are busy—"

He hit redial.

Another ring. A man answered. "Fox! You son of a bitch!" It was Ilya's advisor. Fox had never met him, but the voice suggested a no-neck thug with a bucket head. "Where the hell—" The connection failed.

Fox tried again.

The line rang.

"We're sorry. All circuits—"

The wind shifted, threatened to push him off balance. He jerked back, almost dropped the phone.

He hit redial.

One ring. Then another. Then: "Fox! You goddamn—"

"Give me Ilya."

"No. You talk to me!"

"I've got news about Kirill."

"Tell it to me."

Something droned overhead, the welling *whooomp-whooomp-whooomp* of a circling chopper. Fox couldn't see it, but it was up there, shifting in the wind, getting louder.

He covered his free ear, cupped the phone tight to the other. "Listen. First thing, Windslow's flooded—"

"No! That's not a first thing. First thing is Kirill! We need to talk to—"

"He's not here. Pavel Danilov says he's in Morgantown."

Silence. Broken connection? He checked the screen. The clock was still running, timing the call.

"Hey!" Fox said. "You hear me?"

"Morgantown?"

"Yes, that's—"

"He . . . Morgantown?" The signal was breaking up.

"The club manager gave me a hotel. Says it's where Kirill goes to hide out. Ask Ilya if he wants—"

"Goddamn *Morgantown?*"

The thumping helicopter was right overhead. Visible now, a news chopper swinging low over the roof, buffeting Fox with the wind of its blades.

"Fox? Are you there, Mr. Fox?" It was Ilya now, his demeanor a sharp contrast to the advisor's. "Mr. Fox?" His voice was smooth, inflected with Russian vowels. "Are you still there, Mr. Fox?"

Wind gusted, lifting the tails of Fox's jacket, threatening to tug him off balance. "I'm here."

"I barely hear you."

"Lines are down. There's been—"

"A flood. We hear that. On . . . radio." Ilya was too blind to watch TV. "You're at the office?" That was Ilya's name for the sex club. "You are . . . Mr. Fox?"

"I'm here. But you're breaking up. I can't—"

"You said . . . Morgantown?"

"Yes. That's straight from Pavel Danilov."

"Pasha tells you this thing?"

"Pasha?"

"Pasha Danilov . . . believe him?" Now there was an edge in Ilya's voice. "You want me to pay you . . . this information?"

Fox leaned forward. The connection seemed to be a little better when he did that, teetering on the edge 20 feet above the Sky Tower rubble. He didn't dare look down. "Danilov spoke with him before he left. Kirill made him promise—"

"You let Pasha lie to you, Mr. Fox?" Something crackled in Ilya's voice. Maybe it was the connection. But it seemed to come from a deeper place, from the words themselves—a crackling voice in a suddenly clear connection: "Kirill is not in Morgantown, Mr. Fox. I know this thing because Kirill called me from Gusky Tower. That was right before the flood. Gusky Tower, Mr. Fox. In Windslow. Do you know the place, Mr. Fox?"

Fox glanced down at the rubble, at the broken sign with its partial name. Not SKY TOWER, but GUSKY TOWER!

"Are you . . . Fox . . . listening?"

Fox leaned into the signal.

"Do not hang up, Mr. Fox. That's what Mr. Gusky did. I do not like being hanged up, Mr. Fox. *Vy ponimayete meniya?*"

"Yes. I understand."

"I think maybe Kirill is still at Gusky Tower. You can see the building if you go outside."

Fox considered the concrete slabs, twisted rebars, stagnant water. If Kirill had been inside that building when it fell, he was certainly dead now. But that didn't really matter. The real issue was that Danny Love had lied.

"Mr. Fox. I will give you some advices."

Advices! Ilya had been living in the States 20 years, but sometimes he talked as if he'd just gotten off the boat.

"Some advices, Mr. Fox. Forget Pasha Danilov. Go to Gusky Tower. Fifth floor. Call me from there."

"But I can't."

The wind blew harder, forcing Fox back from the edge.

"I can't do that. There isn't any fifth floor. Gusky Tower is gone."

No answer.

"Ilya?"

No one there. Perhaps the connection had failed, but more likely Ilya had broken it.

Danny Love was going to pay.

haro moved out of the forest and into the LED glow of battery-powered flares. A stretch of washed-out road lay before her, roped off with warning tape and sawhorse barricades. The police had come and gone, and now here she was, standing before a massive flood-carved trench that had once been a two-lane mountain road.

But not always.

Long ago, before being diverted by the powers of industry, natural waterways had flowed through these hills. Too large to be creeks, too small for rivers, they had been referred to as *runs*. Cliff Run had been one of them. Drained, filled in, and paved over, its course eventually became the site of a coal trail called *Cliff Mine Road*. But the name had never stuck. For the locals, it was *Cliff Mine Run*. And today the ghost of the run had reclaimed its turf, destroying the road as if it had never been, replacing it with water that for a short while had flowed with the force of a mighty river.

She ducked beneath the police tape and continued to where the pavement ended at a ledge of jagged asphalt. Then she climbed down, crossed the remnants of the flood, and ascended the other side. There she stopped before a break in the trees. The mine lay a hundred yards away, close enough to give a clear look at the funnel that rose just beyond a leaning guardrail.

Wind hammered her back, twisted her hair, tugged her rags. She walked on, paused at the guardrail. The crater below lay strewn with abandoned trucks and vans. Some seemed to be running. Farther to the south, a piece of fuselage rose from a mass of burning metal.

The place had been busy.

She descended the slope, picking her way along weedy rocks and crumbling scree, moving slowly until she reached the floor. Then she jogged to a place where the ground had opened and a news van angled over the brink. She paused beside it, knelt down, looked into the void. There was no bottom, just a layer of glowing ash. If she fell in, she'd never climb out.

But the rift was barely five feet across in some places. She found a narrow point, took a running jump, and leaped over. Her powerful legs did the job. She landed with inches to spare and continued across a section of ground gouged with serpentine trails. And there were other things here too—smashed camera, woman's flip-flop, wireless microphone affixed with a news logo. She walked past all of it, making a beeline for one of the fire trucks—engine running, voices crackling from the radio. She climbed onto the running board, slid behind the wheel. She knew the radio codes, the vocal shorthand that emergency dispatchers used for floods, fires, fatalities.

She listened.

"Sweet Jesus!"

She reached for the mike, then drew back. What good would reporting in do when her primary job—the only one that mattered—was getting home?

She sat back, gripped the wheel, looked past the truck's hood and toward the twisting funnel, so close now that she could see its swirls of churning mist folding together, colliding, flashing. Patterns formed. Strange shapes. They seemed to be looking at her.

She looked away, realized she was wasting time. And worse than that, she was sitting on a level plain beneath a gathering storm.

A Pittsburgh-6 news van idled a few dozen feet behind her, antenna fully deployed and begging to be the first thing struck once the storm broke. But if she could lower that antenna, and if there was enough fuel in the tank, that van was sure to get her to Windslow a lot faster than walking.

She climbed from the truck, back into the full force of the wind, and hurried toward the van.

The cargo door was open.

She climbed inside.

Twin monitors blazed in a wall of electronics. A chair waited, bolted to the floor, a backpack resting beside it. She sat. One monitor showed Windslow Mine—a wide, static view of the gated entrance. Nothing of interest there. But the other showed a flooded town. The sound was muted. She read the captions.

Live from Chopper 6, Windslow, Green County.

Casualty estimates in the thousands. . . .

Wind blew, rocking the van.

Watching the monitor wouldn't change anything. She could see the real thing when she got to Windslow. Right now, she needed to retract the 40-foot lightning rod.

Some of the editing bay's controls looked simple enough. There was a keyboard, mouse, handheld remote, joystick, telephone handset. But there were also plenty of things that meant nothing to her, mostly knobs and slides. Some of the things were labeled, but not in any way she could understand, nothing marked *antenna*.

She got up and returned to the cargo door, figuring her best bet would be to look for an emergency release on the roof, but she stopped when she saw something moving on the mine's western slope.

"No!" Her heart skipped. "My God! No!"

A moment later she was out the door, charging across the mine.

xle stood in a room with paneled walls, vaulted ceiling, hardwood floor, a four-poster bed beside an open window. Curtains blew inward, casting shadows over a sleeper in the center of the bed. Outside, windblown gardens sloped toward the marble deck of an in-ground pool. Clearly, this room did not belong in Yeyestani's trailer. It was part of the Frieburg Estate, and the person asleep in the four-poster bed?

That's me. Asleep. Dreaming all this . . . everything I'm doing now.

But the moment didn't feel like a dream. Nor did he feel entirely like himself. Before entering this room, he had been wearing a leather jacket, jeans, boots. Those things were gone now. In their place was a terrycloth robe, and the body beneath it was the kind that came from workouts rather than work. His hands were like that too, long fingers and smooth palms. He pushed them through his hair. It was thick and long, rock-star hair.

Bird?

But his thoughts were still his own, as if his true spirit—that of Axle the dreamer—were taking a ride in Bird's body.

I'm still myself, not entirely Bird.

He closed the shutters and sat down on the bed.

It's all me. Everything I dream is me. Everyone and everything.

The sleeper stirred, muttering. "Tell me. Tell me what to do."

He wondered what would happen if he woke his sleeping self. Would Bird go back to being just Bird? Would this crazy layering of dreams finally come to an end then?

Tell me what to do.

He got up to leave the room, but he paused again at the sight of Bird's reflection in the mirror above a bureau.

Of course it's his reflection. My dream . . . his body.

The moment of disorientation passed, and he continued out the door, into what should have been the interior of the Frieburg mansion, but which turned out to be the narrow hall of Yeyestani's trailer.

He was Axle again.

The living room stretched beside him, silent except for the barely perceptible clicking of the moth in the kitchen, still beating itself to powder against the light.

The table in the center of the kitchen was gone too. No hand file. No stone knife.

Did you bring it with you?

The storm door stood closed behind him. It was no longer dark outside. Evening light spilled through the screen, casting a wedge across the floor. And there was Yeyestani, standing within the glow, hand against the screen, pushing the door open. "Ready, Akeo?" She stepped outside. "Come on. Let's try this again!"

32

Danny still had to pee. It was his own fault for not having asked Prutko and Boone to take him to the toilet, and now Fox was coming back from the roof.

"You get a signal?" Boone said, calling from the open door where he and Prutko had gone back to keeping an eye on Danny from a distance.

"I did."

"Talk to Ilya?"

"I did."

"And?"

"It seems Kirill never left town." Fox glared at Danny. "And if there's one thing I hate . . . one thing I can't abide . . . it's being duped by a lie."

"But I told you what I knew. I swear to God!"

"Careful, son. What did I tell you about calling witness?"

"I'm just saying—"

"What you say is always second to what you do. Remember that, son. It's the deed that makes the book."

"The book?"

"It's not just me who's listening, if you get my drift."

Danny glanced at Prutko and Boone.

"Not them either." Fox turned his face toward the rafters. "I'm talking about all-seeing eyes."

Danny wished his ankles weren't zip tied. Maybe he wouldn't have to pee so bad if he could cross his legs. "Mr. Fox, listen. I still have to—"

"Listen? You want me to listen, Danny? Listen to lies?"

"Seriously, Mr. Fox. I couldn't tell you what I didn't know. I just work here. I take care of the bar. I manage the dancers and staff, not Mr. Vorarov."

"You don't manage Kirill?"

"That's right."

"You say you're not his keeper?"

"I'm saying—"

"Danny!" Fox said. "*Why is thy countenance fallen?*"

"Mr. Fox?"

"Shall I tell you?"

Danny really had to pee now, the ache spreading from his gut to his chest—a terrible weight that he couldn't hold much longer. Being scared didn't help. And he *was* scared, trembling, absolutely on the verge of letting loose the biggest vodka piss the world had ever seen, a flood that on a human scale would dwarf the one that had flooded the town below the hill.

But Fox was evidently past listening.

"Shall I tell you a story, Danny?"

Danny shifted.

"I suppose there's time," Fox said. "No one's coming, and we're not going anywhere." He started pacing. "It's a story of a man whose lies got him marked for life, marked indelibly, marked so irrevocably that all who saw him knew him for what he was!"

"Mr. Fox—"

"He was a keeper of cattle, son. A manager of livestock, schooled in the art of slaughter!" Fox glanced toward the bodies by the bar as if making a reference. "His name was Cain, son of Adam. One day he led his brother into the wilderness, and there he killed him with a club used for the slaying of sheep. Then, with his brother bleeding on the ground, Cain used that same club to dig a grave. Arduous work. Backbreaking! But he did it alone and did not cease until the body was concealed. And yet . . . even then . . . despite his efforts . . . evidence remained! It always does!"

"Mr. Fox, I—"

"Cain left the killing ground and travelled to the river. He knelt beside the water. Not to pray, but to wash his hands, scrubbing and rubbing until not a trace of blood remained. But no sooner were those hands clean than three travelers approached from a province east of Eden. The land of Nod, Danny. Ever been?"

"To Nod?"

"That's my question, son. Have you ever visited the Land of Nod?"

"I don't think so, Mr. Fox."

"Well, son. That's another thing you share with Cain. He'd never been either. Never even knew it existed. But the travelers were from there nonetheless. And on their way to the river they had passed the killing ground. They had seen the blood on the earth, and now they saw the same stains on Cain. Not on his hands, Danny. His hands were clean, washed in the river. But he had forgotten his clothes!"

"Mr. Fox—"

"Yes, I know. A terrible oversight, one that could only be solved with more killing. And that's what Cain did! With that same club, he slew the men from Nod, crushed their heads and made such a spray of blood that his skin and clothes were soon black with gore, so stained that anyone who saw him would know him for the killer he was."

Danny sat up straighter, trying to take some of the weight off his bladder. It didn't help. The piss just got heavier, the weight of the world bearing down on the pit of his groin.

"Am I making you uncomfortable, son? Because it's not over. The most important part is coming. You see, Cain was desperate, so frantic to hide what he had done that he dove headlong into the river and rode the currents until he came to a waterfall. And he grabbed the rocks that lay beneath that torrent, and when he was sure he must be clean, he stepped from the water . . . and behold!" Fox looked toward the rafters. "The sky opened, and the voice of Cain's maker called down: '*Thy brother's blood crieth unto me!*' And in that moment, Cain knew that no man can hide his crimes. No man, Danny!" He reached into his pocket, drew out his knife, clicked the blade. "Am I coming through clear, son? Do you understand? Guilt flows from evil deeds. It builds like a terrible weight, a heavy burden that no man can contain or hide! Heavier and heavier until—"

Danny gasped, loud and full of shame.

"Yo, Fox! You reached him, man!"

Danny slumped forward as the warm deluge spread through his too-tight jeans, over the leather cushion of the lap-dance chair, and down onto the floor where it pattered like rain between his flip-flops.

Boone and Prutko left their seats, stepped closer.

"What's he doing, yo?"

"Aw, man!"

"Smells like piss, yo!"

"Is piss!"

The pool widened, and still the urine flowed. No end to it. A terrible weight set free at last.

Fox stepped back.

"He's really going, yo. Jesus—"

"Mr. Prutko! Do not make me tell you again."

"What?"

"Shut up!"

"I was just saying—"

"Mr. Boone! I believe you said there was a bucket in the kitchen."

"Yeah, tripped over it when—"

"Go and get it."

"For the piss?"

"That's part of it." Fox jabbed the point of his knife into the floor and removed his jacket. The gun was there, holstered beneath a spreading sweat stain. He shook his jacket, picked a piece of lint from the collar, then draped it over the back of his chair. "First we'll mop the piss." He rolled his sleeves, slowly, staring at Danny. "Then we'll take care of the blood."

33

Near the edge of town, Dalton and Sam came to a mass of jumbled homes, uprooted by the flood and flattened against a hillside. In one of them, beneath a groaning gable that shifted in the wind, Dalton found a change of clothes. He stripped out of the yellow fire gear and put on a pair of sweat pants. He pulled on a T-shirt too, extra-large, not too wet. It hugged his shoulders but hung loose around his belly. It would do.

No one saw him. There were no people among the ruins. Just pieces of them, twisted and crushed, packed in like wattle amid the debris. He avoided looking at them as he climbed toward higher ground to rejoin Sam on the crest of a water-carved hill. Currents flowed below her, flooding a four-lane street, coursing beneath darkened traffic lights. She gave him a quick glance as he came up beside her. "Nice clothes," she said.

"Think so?"

She turned away and looked toward a fallen building, concrete slabs and twisted rebars. Some of the slabs lay like serrated stairs against a cutaway hill. And above the hill, a black-and-yellow sign atop a metal pole:

STRIP MINE!
GENTLEMEN'S CLUB

"That where we're going?" he asked.

"It's our first stop."

"How do we get there?"

"Swim?"

The water reeked of gas and sewage.

"I don't think so," he said.

"That's what I say." She hunkered down, tensed like a cat, dropped ten feet to the top of a concrete abutment. Then she leaped straight out and over the flood, landing on a jagged slab some seven or eight feet out in the racing current.

She was something to see. Strong legs, light frame, feline reflexes. Could he move like that? He contemplated the drop to the retaining wall while she leaped again, then again, picking her way along the bits of broken building until she reached the rubble-strewn hill. And with each jump the snake-skin face on her butt gave a little spastic nod. *Uh-huh!* It seemed to say. *Yes! Uh-huh! This is how you do it!* He really needed to tell her about that face, give her a chance to tuck it in or cover it up. But she'd probably just get mad if he told her now, after following her so long without a word.

"Hey!" Her voice rang like a pistol shot, cutting through the sound of roaring water. "You coming?"

He hunkered down, mustered his courage, and dropped onto the abutment. He landed hard, his weight working against him. By the time he straightened up, she was once again on the move, skittering along the remains of the broken building on the other side of the flood, stopping halfway up the hill to inspect something among the jumbled slabs. She crouched, tensed, then scrambled over a jutting I-beam to crouch again.

Had she found something?

He called to her. "What is it?"

She grabbed a rebar and swung toward what looked like a deep opening among the slabs.

"Did you find something?"

She glanced toward him. Her expression said it all: *Get over here! Now!* Then she vanished, dropping down into the concrete jumble.

Dalton considered the route across the flood. The closest piece of broken building waited nearly eight feet away, a piece of bearing wall rising like a shark fin from the reeking currents. If he didn't get a good hold when he landed, he'd be swimming in sewage before he could call for help. Not that calling would do any good. Sam was out of earshot.

But he knew what she'd say.

Just do it!

He crouched, fixed his gaze on the jagged island, and leaped. A moment of weightlessness, then impact. He landed, grabbed hold. The slab was cold, damp, slicked with mud from the waves breaking inches from his feet. He pulled himself up, leaped again, then again—following Sam's path until he came to the place where she had disappeared.

A narrow opening in the rubble led to an almost horizontal stairwell, metal treads and risers sloping sideways, zigzagging toward a diagonal space that had apparently once been part of a large office. Furniture lay jumbled against one wall. Upended desk, sideways file cabinets, chairs going every which way—it looked like an Escher drawing: straight edges at insane angles. Sam was down there too, crouching on the tilting floor, her ass-face staring at him as she tried pulling something from the crushing weight.

Dalton gripped the rebar, leaned into the well. "Hey!" His voice echoed, a metallic ring. "Hey, Sam!"

She waved to him. *Come on! Get down here!* But she didn't look around. Her attention remained fixed on the twisted thing in front of her—the body of a large man.

Dalton entered the shaft and descended the stairs, moving hand-over-hand along a metal banister as he negotiated the angled treads.

The office had a picture window. No glass in it now, just a broken frame tilted toward the sky.

The dead man was dressed in a black jacket, white shirt. A brace around his neck suggested he had been injured before getting pinned by the mass of furniture.

Sam had hold of his blood-stained lapel. "This is Kirill." She said it as if making an introduction.

"You know him?"

"Did. Sort of."

Dalton hunkered forward, getting a closer look.

Kirill had broad shoulders, crushed head, half a face. His lips and eyes were gone, the skin around them cut away in ragged snips. A deep gash on the side of his head had drained through the neck brace, into the carpet.

Dalton had to watch where he put his feet. The carpet was soaked. "A friend of yours?"

"I worked for him."

"In this office?"

"No. I don't do offices." She tightened her grip, tried pulling him free. "Help me, Dalton!" She pulled harder. "Lift that desk!"

But it wasn't just the desk that had the body pinned. There was a ton of stuff heaped on top of it. Steel cabinets, projection screen, sofa, ceiling tiles, ductwork. And there were other things massing in the shadows—living things with beady eyes, hunched bodies, twitching tails.

Rats?

That explained the condition of the man's face.

Freaking rats!

"The hell you waiting for, Dalton? Lift it!"

He considered the task. To lift all that weight, he'd need to plant both feet in the wet goop that saturated the carpet.

"Dammit, Dalton! Now would be nice!"

And the goop wasn't just blood. The carpet was covered with all the things you got when you squeezed a man like a grapefruit. No wonder the rats were hanging around.

"Dalton?"

"Give me a sec." He scuttled sideways, close to where a corner of the desk lay against an intact wall. The carpet squished between his toes as he got into position.

"Lift it!"

He gripped the desk, heaved.

The weight moved. Not much. An inch maybe.

Sam pulled.

"Pull him with two hands!" Dalton said.

She ignored him, tightened her one-handed grip, tried again. But it was futile. The man weighed 300 pounds easy. Maybe more. And what was she? A hundred pounds? Less? What chance did she have using one hand against so much deadweight? And the floor was slanted, forcing her to pull uphill!

"Lift, Dalton!"

"But you're—"

"Don't argue, Dalton. Lift!"

He gave it his all, straining. The stuff atop the desk shifted.

"You're getting it!"

Another heave. The desk rose.

She pulled, toes splayed, muscles flexing like steel cables. No body fat. Was she that way naturally? Or was it part of her transformation? She closed her eyes, concentrating, face strangely serene. And then . . . miraculously . . . the body slid free, smearing a slug-like trail as she hauled it out.

Dalton let go.

The desk fell, landed with a bang. A rat dropped from the ductwork, skittered along a file cabinet and up onto a dangling cable. It dove behind a wedge of ceiling tile, hiding as Sam caught her breath.

The dead man's legs looked all screwed up. The bones hadn't just been broken, they'd been crushed, hips splayed like the wings of a manta ray. It hurt just looking at them.

Sam pressed her hand to the man's head. It was a strange gesture, palm down as if feeling for a temperature.

Dalton moved up beside her. "What're you doing?"

"Same thing I did to you." Light shimmered beneath her palm, pink through her fingers, the color of a hand cupped across a flashlight. The man's face twitched. Not much, barely noticeable, possibly imagined.

"You did this to me?" Dalton said.

"Like I told you. I brought you back."

"To life?"

"Maybe. I don't know. Are you alive?"

"What?"

"Maybe you're something else. Maybe we both are."

"Like what?"

"I don't know." She raised her hand, hiding the glow in her fist. "You need to stay with him, Dalton."

"With this guy?"

"Yeah. I need you to be here when he comes around. When he's able to talk."

Dalton considered the man's ragged mouth. "How long will that be?"

"Don't know. I wasn't—" She turned suddenly, looked back at the wedge of ceiling tile, cocked her head, listened.

"Yeah," Dalton said. "There' a rat back there. I saw—"

She spun, lunged, left hand blurring. She grabbed something, brought it out, swinging it into the light. It was the rat—eyes wide, teeth bared, tail swinging.

She held it by the neck.

"What the hell?" Dalton said.

The rat gave a long, breathy squeal.

"A drawer!" She pointed to the desk. "Get one. Pull it out. Come on!"

He grabbed one of the handles, tugged hard. Papers spilled over the floor.

"All the way, Dalton. Yank it loose."

He tugged again, ripped it from its track.

"On the floor!" She gestured with the rat. "Right there! Top down. Make a trap."

He did as she said.

She pushed the rat under it, slammed it down. Then she sat on the drawer.

"There's more of them, you know."

She ignored him, looked down at her hands.

The rat moved inside the drawer, feet drumming the carpet, running in circles, hunting an exit.

"Catching one rat isn't going to make any difference."

"It's not about catching."

"What then?"

"It's an experiment. I need to know what happens, how long it takes." She had her right hand balled into a fist, the left one open, looking at the dark gash in the center of her palm. It was like a bruise that had been sliced open, blue along the edges, red in between. It looked faintly like a mouth. No teeth, just bruised lips around a throat that seemed to curve back through the core of her wrist, into her arm. She seemed to be staring into it . . . or maybe she wasn't looking at it at all. In a way, her gaze seemed more inward than outward.

"You all right?" Dalton asked.

She made a fist, folded her arms, slumped forward.

The rat was going crazy now, banging around inside the drawer, clawing at the wood beneath her ass. She ignored it, looked at Dalton. "I got a question for you," she said. "It's about that thing you asked me before, when you came back to find me after trying to run away. You asked me what you were, what you'd been changed into." She looked away. "I'm wondering the same thing about me."

"About what you are?"

"Yeah. If we're really alive. I can't figure it out."

"So you're asking me what?"

"I'm asking—" She opened her fists, then clenched them tighter. "Do you think we're really alive? Or are we maybe something else?"

"Like what?"

"I'm asking you, Dalton."

"I don't know. I mean, we're not dead. So we've got to be—"

"But what if there's something other than life and death. Something more than just being alive? Do you know what I'm saying? Do you feel it?"

"Yeah. I guess."

She hugged herself with her fisted hands. "Me too." She looked at the dead man. "I wonder if it'll be the same with him."

"Why wouldn't it be?"

"Because we're different. You and me . . . we died in the flood. I think that matters."

"Waterborn?"

"What?"

"It's what I thought when I saw you," Dalton said. "You were beaded with water, drops that hardened into scales. And I was the same. I don't know what it means, but when I saw you it was like I heard a voice. It said, 'Waterborn.'"

"Voice of an angel, maybe."

"I don't know," he said. "What do angels sound like?"

The rat slammed the drawer, a loud bone-cracking thud followed by a frantic drumming of paws . . . running in circles, picking up speed for another try.

"So what's with the rat?" he asked.

"A test. I sort of know what my right hand does. I figure it's time I learn about the left."

The rat screamed, low and feral, then resumed its clawing.

"The left hand's supposed to do something terrible," she said. "Some kind of terrible death."

"Seems to be taking a while."

"Yeah. It's like that with both hands. I wasn't around when you came to. So I don't know how long that takes either."

The rat screamed, high and piercing. And then—WHOOMPH!—the drawer lurched as if something had ignited inside it.

Then silence.

Sam got up, lifted the drawer. Smoke wafted out, sharp and acrid, the stink of burnt flesh and hair.

"Aw, man!" Dalton covered his nose.

A blackened smear covered the floor. Around its edges, portions of the carpet sputtered and smoked. But there was no rat, no hint of where it had gone until Sam turned the drawer right-side-up.

"Aw, shit!" Dalton turned away, then looked again. It was as if a bomb had gone off inside, coating the wood with bits of smoking rat. "What the hell?"

"Looks like it exploded."

"How?"

She turned the drawer over again, returned it to the floor. "Too many questions, Dalton." She sat back down. "At least I know that it works . . . how long it takes."

"How long it takes on a rat, you mean."

"You think a person might take longer?"

"You're asking me?"

"How about a demon master?"

"A what?"

She leaned forward, chin on her fists, studying Kirill. "Anyway, life takes longer. Kasdeja told me that much." She got up, turned toward the stairwell. "Stay with Kirill, OK? Don't let him wander off like you did. When he comes around, ask him where Bird lives."

"Bird? Is that a person?"

"Yeah. His business partner. If he tells you, you come tell me."

"And you? You're going to be—"

"Top of the hill." She said it like it was the last place in the world she wanted to go, then she climbed onto the twisted stairs, leaving Dalton alone with the dead man.

34

Fox waited for Prutko to finish mopping the floor.

"Missed a spot," Boone said.

"Kiss my ass."

"I'm serious. Over here."

Prutko ignored him, pushed the mop into the bucket, and removed the rubber gloves that Boone had found for him back in the kitchen. "Done as far as I'm concerned." He placed the gloves on the rim of the bucket.

"Prutko," Fox said. "I'll be needing those."

"The gloves?"

"Hand them over."

Prutko picked them up, shook them dry, gave them to Fox. "You going to do some cleaning?"

"No." Fox pulled them on. "I'm about to make more mess." He picked up the knife. "Boone! A little help please. Stand beside Danny."

Boone hopped to.

"Prutko!"

"Yo."

Fox dug in his pocket, pulled out the zip ties. "Take a couple."

Danny watched, eyes wide, color gone from his face.

Prutko took the zips.

Fox put the rest of the ties back into his pocket. "Boone! Take Danny's arms. Hold them high."

Danny tried getting up, moving as if he thought he might hop away on his zip-tied feet.

Boone grabbed him, pulled him back into the chair.

Danny struggled.

"Don't fight it, son. It'll only get worse if you fight."

Boone held Danny's arms.

Fox pushed the blade between Danny's hands, drew it up and back, slicing the nylon zip with a decisive *snap!* "Arms behind his back, Boone. Behind the chair."

Danny tried pulling away.

Fox leveled the blade, held it close to Danny's face. "Hold still, son."

The lap-dance chair had a wide back. Danny gasped as Boone wrenched his arms around it.

"Prutko. Use those zips. Bind him good."

Prutko knelt beside Boone, turning his head away as he worked. "Piss stinks, yo!"

"Like I said, you missed a spot."

"Ain't no spot, yo! It's the chair. It's soaked through." He used one of the zips on Danny's wrists, pulled it tight, backed away.

"Did you bind him tight, Prutko?"

"Tight enough."

"Both zips?"

"Shit, man! One will hold him."

"Let's hope so." Fox pressed the blade to Danny's forehead. "The mark of Cain, son. I believe that's where we left off."

"Yo! Hold up!"

"Quiet, Prutko. Let me work." Fox lifted the blade, set it down again between Danny's eyes, on the tender spot left by Boone's head-butt. "The mark of Cain, Danny. You listening? The Lord put a mark on Cain so that—"

"Yo, man, check it! I'm trying to tell you. *We got company!*"

Sam had ascended the slope, climbing on the twisted beams and broken glass of Gusky Tower, finally reaching the wide cutaway ledge that held the Strip Mine Gentlemen's Club—the steel-frame box that contained all the things she detested about the world. Yet, thanks to Kirill, that place had also been central to her life, a source of income that made so many of her freedoms possible.

The parking lot looked much as it had the last time she had seen it from the highway overpass, when she had returned to Windslow a couple hours after delivering her dose of justice to Jason and his friends. Even then, the bodies and blood had been cleared away. The truck too. She had to hand it to Danny Love. He was good with cleanup.

Nevertheless, while walking through the lot, she had made out a few errant stains, patches of blood drying on the pavement, smears that looked no more incriminating than oil or transmission fluid—the kind of stuff you'd expect to find in any parking lot. And even the gouges in the pavement, places where her stray shots had scored the asphalt, probably wouldn't get a second look from anyone.

Danny's car, a blue Nissan, was still in the lot, parked beside a black Hummer with Ohio plates. She had no idea who that Hummer belonged to.

The club's door was propped open with a chair, a half-gone vodka bottle on the floor beside it. There was a sandwich there too, partially eaten, half-wrapped in plastic. She remembered what Kasdeja had told her about eating, about how important it was to fuel the changes in her body. She would see to that soon, after she talked to Danny.

She stepped inside.

Then she stopped.

The place was a mess of broken glass and toxic smells. Three bodies lay beside the bar. She glanced at them, recognized the boys from the parking lot, then turned her attention to the men in the center of the room, strangers standing around a lap-dance chair, acting as if they owned the place.

One was a skinny white kid with dreads and baggie jeans. Another was built and dressed like an off-duty marine. The third wore a Stetson, dress shirt, plastic gloves, and a shoulder-holstered Colt. He stood before the lap-dance chair, holding something to the face of a woman in a pink kimono. Her arms had been tied behind her, forced around the back of the chair. The man spoke to her. "The mark of Cain, son. I believe that's where we left off."

Son?

Sam drew closer.

It's not a woman. It's a guy!

"Yo! Hold up!"

"Quiet, Prutko. Let me work."

What's happening here?

"The mark of Cain, Danny. You listening?"

It's Danny!

"The Lord put a mark on Cain so that—"

I know that voice!

"Yo, man, check it! I'm trying to tell you. *We got company!*"

The Stetson man looked up.

They were all staring at her now, all except Danny who couldn't turn to look at her.

The Stetson man stepped back, and now Sam saw the knife in his hand, a stiletto-thin automatic. He'd been holding it to Danny's face, talking about the mark of Cain.

What the hell was going on?

"Do you work here, sister?"

She considered how she looked, a small woman in a halter, snakeskin skirt, bare feet.

He thinks I'm a dancer, a stripper reporting for work.

"Sister, do you work here?"

She didn't say anything. Just stood. Staring. Noting everyone's position.

"Hey!" Danny struggled, shifting in the chair, finally seeing her out of the corner of his eye. "Sam?" He struggled, kicking at the floor, trying to turn the chair. "Sam!"

"Stay out of this, son."

"Sam!" He shrieked louder. "Get me out of here!"

Prutko laughed.

The jarhead joined in. It must have seemed pretty funny to them, Danny calling for help from a barefoot stripper.

"Easy, son," the Stetson man said. "I don't think this little whore is the cavalry you're hoping for."

But Danny was frantic now, kicking and screaming. "Sam! Jesus Christ, Sam. He was going to—"

"Stay out of this, son."

She started forward.

"Hold it right there, sister!"

She kept walking.

"Boone! Get her!"

Boone came on fast to her left. She spun, acting on reflex, using her right hand to deflect his reach. *No! Not that hand!* She checked herself, pivoted, grabbing his wrist with her left, held on.

Boone yelled, pulled free, then shoved her with so much force that she almost landed on her ass.

"Shit!" He cupped his wrist, studied the point of pain. "She's got something!"

"Something?" the Stetson man said.

Boone looked amazed, maybe a little frightened. "Something in her hand!"

The dreadlocked guy came up behind her now, grabbed her arm and wrenched it hard across her back. She countered, tried using his thrust against him, but now Boone was on her again, holding her while the little guy slipped something over her wrists.

Zzzziiippp!

"Got her, yo!"

Boone backed away, fumbled in his waistband, and pulled out a Makarov. Not a standard issue, but one with a leather grip, gold plating, engraved markings—probably pilfered from Kirill's collection. She had only a moment to notice these things before he swung it hard, striking her face.

Thooonk!

She felt the force of it, heard the snap of breaking cartilage. She went down.

The men closed in.

She coughed, gagged, rolled facedown to clear the blood from her mouth.

"Check her hands!" Boone said. "She's got something. A Taser maybe!"

Her face spasmed, pain so deep and maddening she wanted to scream. But she held it in, clung to her wits.

The little guy knelt beside her.

She balled her fists.

But the little guy wasn't looking at her hands. "Hey!" he said. "Look at her ass, man! Check it out—"

She spun around, blood flying as she head-butted the dreadlocked bastard, throwing him back against Danny's chair.

The little prick screamed. Strange words.

Russian?

She fell back to the floor, the pain in her head worse than ever now. But it had been worth it.

The little guy switched back to English. "Fuck! She broke my nose. Damn, Fox! My nose!"

Fox!

The name echoed inside her, reverberating with the pain.

Where do I know that name?

"Pick her up," Fox said. "Put her in the chair."

They grabbed her under the arms, lifted her, slammed her down.

"Bind her feet!" Fox took a bundle of nylon zips from his jacket, gave some to the little guy. "Bind her good."

"And check her hands!" Boone said.

"There's nothing there, yo!"

"Check them, Prutko!"

Prutko grabbed her hands. She kept them closed, clenched tight.

"Come on, bitch! Open—"

She moved fast, grabbing him, laying on the touch and squeezing hard. Prutko screamed, pulled away. "Fuck!"

"Told you!" Boone said. "She's got something." He was sweating now, drops coursing along his forehead, gathering in his unibrow. He wiped it with his arm, smearing the sweat. "I'm telling you, Fox. She's got something. In her hand!"

"Which hand?"

"Left one, yo! She got me too."

Fox stepped in front of her, keeping his distance.

She tensed, leaning forward, feet splayed against the floor.

"I told you to bind her ankles, Prutko."

"Fuck you, Fox! You bind them."

Fox drove his knife into the floor. Then he drew his gun, pearl handle, engraved barrel.

Who is this guy?

"She's got something, Fox." Prutko moved behind her, keeping his distance. "A Taser or some shit. But it's, like, embedded in her hand!"

She opened her left fist to give Prutko a better look. No point hiding the palm now. It'd done its work, and Prutko wouldn't be around much longer to do anything about it.

"Damn, Fox! You need to look at this."

"A Taser?"

"No. It's not a Taser. It's like I said . . . it's part of her hand!"

Sam's face spasmed, the pain in her nose becoming a maddening itch . . . as if the wound were mending.

Your body is strong . . . if it breaks, it will heal.

Fox raised the gun, barrel toward the ceiling. "Your hands," he said.

"What about them."

"Can I look at them?"

"Help yourself."

Fox stepped behind her.

"*The keys of hell and death,*" she said.

He walked in front of her again, met her gaze as something snapped behind her nose, bone and cartilage moving back into place.

"I'm healing," she said. "You see it, don't you?"

He crouched again, resuming his place beside the knife he had driven into the floor.

"Who are you?"

"*One who lives and was dead.*"

His gaze darkened. "You're quoting Revelation?"

"Yeah."

He took off his hat. The hair beneath was pressed against his forehead, flattened with sweat. He set the hat atop the knife, on the upright handle so that the brim didn't touch the floor. "You know the Book, sister?"

"Fucking hot!" Boone said. "I'm fucking burning up!"

Fox glanced at him, then back at Sam.

"What are you?"

"Tell you the truth," she said, "I'm still trying to figure that out."

"What're you doing here?"

"I work here."

"A stripper?"

"No. I do other things. But what about you? What are *you* doing here?"

"He wanted me to tell him about Kirill," Danny said, voice brittle, lips white with spit. "I told him what I knew, but he said it wasn't enough. I think he was going to cut me."

"Yeah," she said. "I heard." She stared at Fox. "The mark of Cain. With a switchblade? That's just twisted. I ought to do you just on principle."

"Fox!" Boone sat on the edge of the stage. "I don't feel right, man!" Sweat slicked Boone's face, gathering on the end of his nose as he looked at his hand. It was clenched now, fisted tight . . . and maybe it was a trick of the light, but that fist seemed to be glowing, turning pink beneath the skin. "Can't move it." He held it up. The glow brightened.

"That's fucked up, yo."

Fox kept staring at Sam. "Don't suppose you can stop it, can you, sister?"

"Not that I know of. Not that I'd want to."

"How long have you had it, the touch?"

"Not long. Truth is, I'm—" She flinched as her nose gave a sharp crack, part of a sudden realignment that extended back through her face and into her mouth. Fluid drained from her sinuses, hot and salty. She coughed and spit between her feet. Then she sat back. "Truth is, I'm kind of new at this."

"Aw fuck!" Boone sounded ready to cry. "I'm burning up!" His face was flushed, glowing with a fainter version of the light that now blazed from his hand.

"Get him out of here, Prutko."

"Out of here? Where to?"

"I do not care! Just get him—"

Boone stood up, took a step, and dropped to one knee. He fell, catching himself on both hands: one slapping the floor, the other bursting into flame. He didn't scream, just raised the flaming hand, sizzling like a sparkler. And now his eyes were glowing too, his head burning inside.

Prutko ran toward the stage, pulled the mop from the bucket, and hurled the soapy piss-water at Boone. The move was instinctive and logical, but the fire wasn't that kind of fire. Boone exploded as the water struck him, shattering into a storm of flame, pieces raining through the room to sizzle where they landed. Most of the fragments hit the floor. A few hit Prutko, burning his skin, igniting his dreads. He screamed, smacking himself to knock the pieces away. But they clung, burning deeper . . . and one of his hands, the one that Sam had grabbed, was starting to clench and glow just like Boone's.

"Fox! Help me!"

Fox leveled his revolver.

"Yo, Fox! Jesus, don't—"

Fox fired.

The little guy's head exploded, blond dreads streaming. The rest of him collapsed, smoldering atop Boone's ashes. A terrible burnt-liver stink filled the room. Fox took a handkerchief from his pocket, folded it over his nose. Then he aimed at Danny.

"No!" Sam flexed against the nylon zips. Once, twice—*snap*! Her hands swung free.

Fox fired.

She leaped, lunging as Fox fired again—this time at her, striking low in the gut. She lost balance, hit the floor, grabbed the wound. Blood spilled through her fingers, hot and black.

Fox raised the gun, seemed to consider shooting her again, then turned and bolted toward the door.

She got up and stumbled after him, slipping in her own blood, her side cramping as she pushed on—through the door and out beneath the angry sky.

Fox stood beside the Hummer, looking as if he had forgotten something. His hat? Jacket? Ignition keys?

She started for him, stumbling as the pain burned hotter. Two more steps and she was on her knees, clutching her side, making an easy target.

He walked away from the Hummer, aimed at her eyes. A headshot! That would take her out of commission for a while, maybe for good. But he was almost within reach now, almost close enough to touch.

Keep coming, you son of a bitch!

She couldn't stop the bullet, but she could kill him all the same, lay on the death hand so that when her body healed—*if* her body healed—he would be nothing more than a Rorschach of ash.

He took another step, overconfident.

She lunged, grabbed his hand, held on tight.

His expression changed, momentarily startled. Then he relaxed as they both realized she hadn't touched him at all. Just his glove. His yellow, skin-tight glove, now smeared with blood from her palm.

He smiled.

Then he shot her in the face.

36

After securing the caretakers in their bungalow, Bird returned to the mansion's dark and shuttered first floor. Candles burned in the dining room, flickering over a dozen square feet of leftovers. He paused in the archway, considered the sensations waiting for him at the table, then looked toward the dark hall and wondered if he really wanted to give up his skyborn senses. For what? Saving the earth? But that wasn't really what he'd be doing. If he succeeded in shielding Axle from whatever was coming, humanity would still be doomed, and both he and Axle would go back to being human. Nothing more.

He entered the dining room and sat in the captain's chair.

If he abandoned his post right now, the *U'këë Ushaista* would burn themselves out on their own, and the human race would continue on its path to eventual extinction. Atmospheric temperatures and sea levels would rise, lakes would die, forests would be paved over or plowed under, human population would rise into the tens of billions, and then—maybe—in 50 years, possibly more, the ecosphere would fail. The earth would die, never to be reborn.

Fifty years.

He'd be 77. His own father had died of a stroke at 53, and what had he experienced?

A plate of roast beef sat before him, cut and glistening in the light, red in the middle, dark around the edges. He peeled off a piece, a small thread of char from the outer edge of a single slice. He put it on his tongue, sat back, gripped the chair.

Oh . . . my . . . god!

There were more flavors in that crumb of beef than in all the roasts he had ever known. And if food could pack such a punch, what about life's other pleasures? The sound of the London Philharmonic performing in Symphony Hall . . . or the colors and smells of the Boboli Gardens on a golden evening . . . or sex.

He swallowed.

The flavor of the beef lingered, the intense aftertaste filling his head as he pushed away from the table.

He moved deeper into the house.

The main hall was darker than the dining room, lit only by intermittent flashes from the skylight above the mezzanine. He thought of Axle, searching his dreams at the far end of the second floor.

Can I just leave him up there?

Without someone standing guard, Axle would be easy prey. But what if Axle concluded his search before the adversaries arrived? In that case, Bird would still find himself back at square one. No more skyborn senses. Just a man.

The solution was clear enough. Unpleasant but doable. After all, it wasn't as if Bird hadn't shot Axle once before. But that had been in a moment of justified rage. Could he do it again while Axle slept? And more to the point, how many bullets in the brain would it take to kill a skyborn man?

Maybe I should just wake him up, take him with me.

And then what? Hold the dream-spirit powers at bay by keeping Axle awake for the rest of his life?

He paused in the center of the hall, listening as the sealed house echoed with the muffled sounds of the rising storm. Perhaps the best thing would be to simply open the shutters and get the hell out of Dodge, trust the adversaries to do the rest.

So many options, and they all had one thing in common. He was incapable of seeing any of them through. His imperfections might be legion, but treachery wasn't one of them.

He looked back at the table again.

Screw it!

Even if he managed to outrun the storm and settle into a life of earthly delights, what were the chances he wouldn't soon become bored with his new normal? How many heightened symphonies and sunsets could he experience before he found himself wanting something more. How long before even amazing sex became blasé? Well, maybe that would be the exception. But in any event, there would come a day when it would all be over. When that happened, it would be good to know he hadn't abandoned the one person who had actually needed him.

Lightning flashed, booming beyond the skylight, rattling the locked shutters as he looked toward the second floor. "All right, Axle. I got your back." He turned and headed for the basement. If he was going to stand guard, he had better make sure he was armed with more than a sense of moral obligation.

37

haro raced across the mine, leaping over the jagged chasm where one of the news vans balanced on its frame, continuing toward the three-legged boy who was now halfway down the slope.

She called to him, telling him to stop, wait for her.

But he kept coming, having trouble now, stumbling.

"Benjie, hold on!"

His good foot slipped on crumbling dirt. He skidded, dropped his crutch, fell to his knees.

"Benjie!"

His hand had been rubbed raw from the improvised crutch that had never been intended for cross-country hiking. How had he navigated the washed-out road? What was he doing here at all?

He tried getting up.

"Benjie! No!" She climbed toward him. "Stay there! I've got you!" She reached for him.

He recoiled, shouting now, babbling crazy stuff. "You can't," he said. "Can't be here!"

"Calm down."

He put up his arms, blocking her as if he didn't want to be touched. "You can't be here!"

His improvised ankle brace was gone. The exposed foot looked worse than before—cut, bruised, twice normal size. And his knees were bleeding, jeans torn, skin laid open. He wouldn't be going any farther on his own, and the storm was building, ready to let loose at any moment. He needed to get to shelter. They both did.

"Benjie! Let me help you."

"Can't be here."

"I know! It's why I want to get you someplace safe. Please, let me help you." She reached for him again.

He closed his eyes, balled his fists.

She put her arms around him. He felt small, trembling and scared, a baby caught in a terrible dream. But the dream was outside him, nightmares all around. And she was one of them, cradling him in giant arms, pressing him to her massive shoulder. He resisted at first, then went limp in her grip, tension draining away until a clap of thunder brought it back. He looked skyward. "No! We can't be here!"

"You got that right." She shifted his weight, slipping one hand under his shoulders, pushing the other beneath his knees. "I'll get you someplace safe." She picked him up.

"Where're we going?"

She started down the slope.

"No!" He struggled. "Not here!" He looked toward the dust cloud at the base of the funnel. "We can't be here!"

"Why?"

"Monsters."

She gripped him tighter.

"They're here," he said. "All over. I saw!"

It wasn't frightened babble. Such monsters were real enough. She'd seen one for herself right before the ambulance carried her from the forest clearing behind the mine, a monster snake that moved like a whirlwind of twisting dust and flashing static. But she had seen no such monsters here, nothing moving but the clouds, racing wind, jagged lightning.

"They're gone, Benjie."

"You saw them?"

"Yeah. One of them. But it flew away. They all must have—"

"They might come back."

"Maybe. But we won't be here."

"We're leaving?"

"Yes. Relax . . . and trust me."

The tilting van lay straight ahead, communications mast slanted 20 degrees out of plumb, front end dangling over a deep break in the ground. Could she jump the rift with him in her arms? Did she have a choice?

"Close your eyes, Benjie."

He did.

She walked along the rift, coming to a point where the other side was barely five feet away. She had jumped it before. But this time she had Benjie, a young man shivering like a frightened child.

"Trust me, Benjie." She backed up three steps, summoned her strength. The sky flashed, brightening as she entered her run, rumbling as she leaped. The air crackled. A charge went through her, bristling her skin as she cleared the center of her jump. She was going to make it.

That's when the lightning hit, striking the communications mast 20 feet away. Thunder crashed—a hot, metallic shriek that rocked the ground as she landed.

Benjie screamed.

She fell, her shoulder slamming solid rock as blue light engulfed the van and fanned across the ground. A rear tire exploded. The van angled forward, grating against the rock.

Benjie squeezed her tighter, every muscle locked in a silent scream, and she gave it right back as the van fell . . . and then stopped.

BAM!

Its mast struck the opposite wall.

She backed away, the rear axle looming like an industrial monument until the mast snapped and the van resumed its downward slide, clanging and banging into the glowing depths.

Benjie held her tighter.

She got up and ran.

The Pittsburgh-6 van's antenna was still up too, shaking in the wind, ready to catch the next bolt from the sky. But they'd be safe once they got inside. A direct strike would deflect around the panels, disperse through the ground. Nevertheless, she couldn't drive with that thing fighting the wind. She needed to get it down, do it fast.

She reached the cargo-bay door, slumped forward, set him on the carpet beside the floor-bolted chair. And now he wouldn't let go. His entire body seemed locked in place, arms gripping her shoulders, legs clamping her hips.

"No, Benjie!" She tried prying him free. "Please!" She was getting angry now. She didn't need this. She had a real baby to get back to. "You have to let me go, goddamnit!" She regretted that instantly, but it worked. He pulled away, drew his legs to his chest, wrapped his arms around himself, buried his face in his knees.

"Benjie. I'm sorry." She climbed in, crouched beside him. "I didn't mean to yell."

He looked up. No tears. He was beyond them.

"You sit here. You'll be—"

He wasn't looking at her. There was something far more compelling beyond her shoulder. The editing bay monitors were on, one of them blazing with footage of the flooded town, emergency workers pulling bodies from the muck.

"Don't look at that." She got up, crossed to the bay, started pushing buttons at random until the broadcast screen went dark. An instant later, something thumped against the roof.

Benjie screamed.

The sound repeated—banging and hissing as if a giant snake was settling onto the roof. She leaped outside, looked up, and there it was, the 40-foot antenna collapsing, telescoping into itself as pressurized air bled from its base.

Thank you, Jesus!

Benjie screamed.

"Benjie, listen." She climbed back inside, crouched beside him. "Hey! Everything's going to be fine." But it wasn't really. She still needed to tend to his bloody hand and swollen leg. "It's just the antenna. Be over in a second."

He covered his ears, smearing them with blood from his hands. She needed to clean and dress those wounds, find something to calm him down.

It was time to start scavenging for supplies.

She grabbed the backpack from beside an editing-bay chair and emptied it onto the floor. If police work had taught her one thing, it was that personal gear held all manner of pharmaceuticals.

"That your bag?"

"Is now."

She sorted through the stuff. Notebook, thumb drives, rumpled T-shirt, iPod wrapped in ear-bud wire. She pushed these aside and searched the pockets. Contact-lens solution, tissues, gum, pack of condoms, part of a Hershey Bar.

Keep looking.

The editing-bay was shorter than the length of the van, ending at a foamcore wall with a closet door. She looked inside. Not much there, just cables and electrical gear. She rummaged through some of it, then gave up and turned to Benjie. "I need to go outside for a few minutes." She gave him the half-gone candy bar from the backpack. "Here. Eat this."

"Don't want it."

"It'll raise your blood sugar."

"Don't want blood sugar."

"Eat it!" She was sounding angry again. "I'll be back by the time you're done . . . or pretty close."

She stepped outside.

The wind was stronger now, whipping in her hair. She closed the door and ran to the closest fire truck, climbed into the officer's seat to retrieve a medical kit from beside the radio. It contained gauze, tape, pads, bandages, splints—basic first-responder stuff. Nothing for pain. She took it with her, climbed from the cab, and moved toward the rear of the truck, past the pump controls to a compartment where she found a shrink-wrapped flat of water bottles. She tore the plastic along one side, pulled out all but four of the bottles and replaced them with the first-aid supplies. Slung beneath one arm, the plastic-wrapped flat made a serviceable carrying case, keeping everything together as she continued her search.

A Ford sedan waited beyond a chasm to her left. It was a standard-issue Crown Victoria customized with lights and radio. She put her scavenged supplies on the ground, leaped across the void, and checked the car. There was an extra back-support cushion on the driver seat and a jacket on the backrest. She went through the pockets, then checked the glove compartment. "Bingo!" Oxycodone. Strong stuff. One tablet would take care of Benjie's pain. Two would knock him out, let him rest while she got him to safety.

She left the car.

Thunder was constant now, roiling overhead like breaking waves. She jumped the crevice, gathered her things, and returned to the van. But when she opened the door, Benjie was gone.

Everything else was there, all the scattered gear, the empty candy wrapper lying right where he'd been sitting. Then she noticed the door to the rear compartment. She'd left it open. It was closed now. She looked inside. There he was, scrunched tight amid the gear. "Benjie, what're you doing?"

"Hiding."

"From me?"

"The storm."

She didn't argue.

She cleared out some of the cables, tossing them outside before sliding the cargo door back into place. Then she joined him in the tight compartment. He didn't seem to like that at first. He covered his head, started to moan. She cleaned his cuts, dressed his hand, bandaged his ankle. When she finished, she opened the oxycodone. "I need you to take these."

"Meds?"

"Yeah."

"Mine are at home."

"Then these will do for now." She shook two of the caplets into her palm, handed them to him.

"I only take one."

"These are different." She cracked open a water. "Here. Wash them down."

He popped the pills, drank half the bottle, tried giving it back.

"No. You keep it." She moved back into the cargo bay. The closet was all his now. "Lie down. There's room—"

He settled into a corner, still sitting, arms about his knees, hugging himself. "I like it this way."

Thunder crackled—loud and close.

"I'm going to drive us out of here."

"OK."

"I'll be right up front. I'll leave the door open so you can—"

"It's supposed to be closed." He said it as if it were a rule he'd settled on long ago, as if this were not the first time something frightening had forced him into a closet.

"You want the door closed?"

"It's supposed to be closed."

"Fine, Benjie. But call me if you need me." She eased it into place, listened for the clicking latch, and returned to the cab.

The center of the storm was spinning faster now, flashing with a ruddy light that was too close to the ground to be proper lightning. It seemed to tug at her. She blinked, rubbed her eyes. When she opened them, she was no longer in the van.

am never heard the shot that put her down. Never saw the flash of the barrel. All she knew was that one moment she was gripping Fox's gloved hand, and the next she was looking up at the angry sky, churning clouds, and silent lightning.

There was no pain. No fear. No senses other than sight, and that seemed to be fading. She had healed before, her nose snapping back into place after Boone had broken it. But misaligned cartilage was one thing. A bullet in the head was another game altogether.

I must be dying.

Fox appeared, bending close, looking down. He removed his gloves, folded them inside out, dropped them on her chest. Then he drew his gun and aimed again at her face.

Kasdeja! She filled her mind with his name, offering it as a silent prayer, certain that he would come for her, make everything right.

Fox cocked the hammer. The chamber turned. But he didn't fire. Instead he looked toward the northern end of the lot. His lips moved. She read the words: *Oh, shit!*

A hand appeared. Fat fingers. Gold ring. It grabbed Fox, yanked him up and out of view.

Kirill!

Fox returned a moment later, falling past her, vanishing from view before he struck the ground. It was the last thing she saw before her vision failed. Darkness closed in, and with it searing pain. She convulsed, took a breath, gagged.

Kasdeja! Help me!

Someone moved beside her.

Kasdeja?

"What the fuck?" It was Kirill. Her ears were working now. "She's still alive?"

Her heart clenched, then relaxed and clenched again.

The darkness lifted. Kirill's face appeared above her. She tried saying his name. No good. No voice. Just blood and pain.

"She doesn't look so good," Kirill said. "Shot in the face. Shot in the gut. All fucked up!" His eyes and lips had grown back, and the general contours of his face were much as she remembered. Head like a granite slab, chin like a mallet. But his old scars were gone, as were the spider veins that had webbed his cheeks and nose. This new face was some kind of sculpted version of Kirill Vorarov.

She reached for him, then stopped, not sure what would happen if her healing hand touched him again. Another hitching breath, and this time she found her voice. "Kill!"

"Kill?" Kirill frowned. "Kill who?"

She tried again. "Kirill!" She felt cold and wet, probably lying in her own blood. She tried getting up. Dalton helped her, and soon she was sitting, hunched forward. She swallowed, then spoke, her voice reverberating through her ruined face. "BIRD'S HOUSE!" She sounded like a demon in a horror movie. "WHERE . . . BIRD'S HOUSE?"

Kirill just stared, looking as if he didn't understand a word. Or maybe it was more a case of not understanding how a person with a gunshot face could be alive and talking . . . or maybe he was just grossed out by the way she looked.

Her face popped, bone realigning. She gasped and tried again. "Birth houth!" She was slurring now, and the pain was huge. How could she do anything with so much pain? How could she even think? She kept hoping it would pass, but instead it got worse, pressure building until something snapped between eyes and mouth. Her cheeks pushed forward. More blood spilled from her nose. She let it fall, coughing. "Bird's house, Kirill! Take me there!"

Kirill seemed to consider it, or maybe he was just disoriented. "Bird?" he said at last. "You want to see Maynard? Maynard Frieburg?"

She coughed, spit, wiped her mouth with her hand. "Yeah."

"Now?"

"Yes."

"No. I don't think so," Kirill said. "Maybe you lie down for a while."

"I'll be OK."

Fox groaned, shifting on the pavement beside her. His broken Colt lay nearby, barrel snapped from its frame as if Kirill had broken it in a rage.

"This guy," Kirill said. "Why'd he shoot you in the face?"

"Guess I scared him."

"Who is he?"

"His name's Fox. He came here . . . looking for you." She tried standing again, succeeding this time, rising through a moment of dizziness to claim her balance. There was blood everywhere, on her skin, halter, snakeskin skirt, pavement. Whatever she had become, she still ran on blood. She took a step. Her side spasmed, clenching around the path that Fox's first bullet had plowed through her gut. She dropped to one knee, hands to the ground.

Dalton grabbed her.

She made a fist, pushed him away. "I can do this. I'm OK." But she wasn't. Not yet. The bones of her face had reformed, but pain lingered—sharp and throbbing behind her eyes. And her gut . . . that was ten times worse, cramping each time she moved, as if her organs were adhering in ways that made it difficult to stand.

Fox rolled over, coming too.

"We need to tie that bastard up," she said. "Dalton. Go into the club. There's a jacket. It's on a chair."

"You want his jacket?"

"No. Check the pockets. There're zip ties. Get them."

Dalton started away.

Kirill studied Fox. "This guy was looking for me?"

"Yeah. Apparently. That's what Danny Love said."

"Danny Love? He's still here?"

"Not exactly." She caught her breath, then called to Dalton. "Hey! It's pretty ugly in there."

Dalton paused by the door, looked inside, then pushed on.

Fox rolled onto his side.

Kirill walked over to him, put a foot on his chest, held him down. "This bastard. He trashed my club?"

"It wasn't all him," Sam said. Indeed, with the exception of Danny Love, all the death inside was her doing. And the rest of the mess—everything from the backed-up sewers to the broken disco ball—that was her too. After all, she had released the flood. "He killed Danny. Tried killing me. The rest was collateral."

"What? My club is collateral?"

"It's all beside the point, Kirill. Finding Bird. That's what matters. Where's he live?"

"Bird?"

"His house, where is it?"

"North. Up Windslow Road." He took his foot from Fox and turned around, staring past the rubble of Gusky Tower, over the flood, toward the mine where he had once planned to build his resort. His gaze lingered on the storm, brooding until Dalton returned.

"It's not a mess in there," Dalton said. "It's a freaking disaster. What happened?"

"Long story," Sam said. She still felt out of it, and it wasn't only the pain. She felt dizzy, lightheaded, incredibly weak. "You got the zips?"

He held them up, letting her see them.

"Let's tie this bastard."

Fox's eyes were open but dazed.

She leaned over him, bracing herself against the Hummer. "You really hit this guy, Kirill."

Fox roused at the sound of Kirill's name. He tried getting up, but Dalton pushed him down, flipped him over, drew his hands behind him. He bound Fox's wrists, then his ankles. Fox flinched as Dalton tugged the last loop.

"Too tight?" Sam said.

"Yeah."

Sam gave the tie another tug.

"Ow!"

"Hey, Dalton," she said. "You happen to find any keys in that jacket?"

"No."

She sat down, her back to the Hummer, looking at Fox. "The keys. Where are they?"

"I think Prutko had them."

"Prutko?" Kirill said.

"Yeah," Fox said. "Snoop Dogg."

"Oles?"

"He's in the club," Sam said. "What's left of him."

"Oles Prutko?"

"We need to get those keys," Sam said. "Get in the Hummer and drive out of here."

"How?" Fox said. "Humvees don't float, you know."

She rose to her feet. Pain flared again in her side. She leaned against the Hummer, looked toward the overpass.

The traffic had been cleared. Nothing there but an empty stretch of highway and—beneath it—an unpaved hill leading down through a ravine and up onto a two-lane road. The ravine and road weren't visible from the lot, but she'd seen them both while sniping from the hill beyond the interstate. If the Hummer made it to the road, they could drive north to Windslow Road, get to Bird's from there.

"We'll go that way." She pointed. "Down the slope, under the highway—"

"Forget it," Fox said. "The way's blocked by runoff. We checked."

"A Hummer's got three-foot clearance."

"No," Fox said. "Not quite three. And that water looked a lot deeper than—"

"A lot deeper when?"

"I don't know. Two hours ago. Maybe—"

"Water level's falling. It'll be lower now."

"Waste of time."

"Faith, Fox. Sometimes you got to have faith."

A drop of rain thumped the Hummer's roof. Another followed.

"We should get inside," Sam said. "Find those keys. Make plans."

"Fox too?" Dalton said.

"Yeah. Drag him if you have to." She turned to Kirill. "You should go ahead of us. Take a look. We'll be right with you." She figured it would be best to give him a moment to get his head around the condition of the place.

Kirill stepped toward the entrance, looked inside. He put a hand on the door frame, muttered something in Russian, then lumbered forward, into the darkness.

Sam pushed away from the Hummer, took an uneasy step, then another.

"You OK?" Dalton said.

"I don't know." The dizziness came in waves. She looked toward the club's open door, still propped by a chair. She could probably make it that far.

"You don't look so good," Fox said.

"No thanks to you, you prick."

"I'm just saying—"

"Drag him inside, Dalton."

"What about you?" Dalton said. "You need help—"

"I can take care of myself. Just get him out of my way."

Dalton did as he was told.

She gave them a head start, then followed as far as the door. The strength went out of her legs. She plopped into the chair, clutching her side.

In the center of the club, Kirill stood by the lap-dance chair, silently pondering the remains of Danny Love.

39

Axle followed Yeyestani through the screen door and out into the slanted light of an August afternoon. Shadows bled across the lot, spreading from trailers whose western walls glowed with golden sun. It was all as he remembered from the day they had taken their last walk together. And yet it seemed different. Perhaps that difference resulted from seeing it through older eyes, overlaying it with the sensibilities of a man who had put nine years of disillusionment between the experience and now.

Her white eye flashed as he pulled beside her. "True," she said, reading his thoughts. "It isn't the same. Not exactly." She turned toward him, walking backward, her hemp moccasins kicking dust as she veered onto the road's gravel berm. "You've thought about this too often, Akeo. Over and over. And each time you change things just a little, add a detail, forget another. It's always that way. Remember a thing often enough, it becomes a waking dream."

"Except that this walk really happened," he said.

"Did it?"

"It's a memory. It has to come from somewhere."

"But what if all of it comes from something you dreamed last night, imagined as you sat dying in the pressboard shack?"

"No. I don't think so. We walked. I know we did."

"But how do you *know*? How do you truly know anything, Akeo?"

She had him there.

"No matter," she said. "The point is you're experiencing it now. Open yourself to it. Learn from it. It might just save your life."

They came to a point where Cliff Mine Run veered sharply, away from a weedy slope that descended into a wall of trees. She went that way, through the weeds and onto a wheel-rutted path nearly hidden in shadows. The path was much as he remembered, but the air was different. A stiff wind blew along it, raising whorls of dust and leaves, growing stronger as they approached the highwall. She drew him close, pulling him into a one-hand-ed embrace. "Stay close," she said, leading him through the trees. "The last time we came here, we sat on the brink and looked out at two columns of light. Do you remember? They were the spotlights Kirill Vorarov used to advertise his business."

"I remember."

"Talking about the sex-club embarrassed you then."

"I think I can handle it now."

"Yes," she said, still leading him through the windblown trees. "But can you handle this?" The forest opened before them, branches parted by a violent updraft, and there was the funnel, rising like a black weed from the pit of Windslow Mine. "The last time we looked across this mine, we looked at distant lights and spoke of the future. But the lights are gone, Akeo. This time, we look out at a column of darkness. This time, we need to talk about the past."

The column twisted as if alive, conscious, trying to break free.

"Another storm rages beneath it," she said. "Equal but opposite."

"Two storms?"

"Opposing forces, each balancing the other, each struggling for domi-nance. But the balance won't hold, Akeo. Not this time." She released his shoulder, stepped to the edge, and sat with her legs dangling over the abyss. "Sit with me, Akeo."

He held back.

"You were braver last time," she said. "Is it the storm? Does it frighten you? Or maybe it's the sound of the wind. Does it speak your name?"

He listened. No voices. Only the hiss of flying dust, the intermittent crackle and roar of flashing static.

She looked out at the storm. "Nine years after I brought you to this mine, you parked your car in the center of Windslow Road. Your friends got out and hid in the trees while you blocked the downhill lane."

"They weren't my friends."

"Call them what you like."

"I hardly knew them."

"You hardly knew yourself, Akeo. But whatever they were—whatever *you* were—you were all three together, partners in crime. They hid, and you stepped from your car, ready to flag down and rob the man who now guards you as you sleep."

"I remember."

"And you heard a rustling wind, the whisper of the earthborn guardian."

"I remember that too."

"Did those sounds speak to you?"

"No."

"No words? No meaning?"

"No. Not that I remember."

"But when you heard the wind, you thought of me, of the things I had told you about yourself, about your destiny. Those things almost made you change your mind. Do you remember? That twinge of regret? The realization that you were at a crossroads, about to follow a path that would change your life forever? Remember?"

He shivered. The wind was getting to him. He wanted to wake up, wrap himself in a blanket, get warm.

"Stay with me, Akeo. We're not finished. The most important question comes next." She looked back at him, fixing him with her good eye, the one that saw him as he was. "What if, at that moment of choice, you recalled a truth so powerful that it sent you racing back into your car, forced you off the terrible path, directed you onto a course that did not lead to the place you are now."

"This place? The brink of this mine?"

"Yes. And to the room where you lie dreaming this dream, shivering in a cold sweat while the man you robbed stands guard against forces that want you dead. What if a memory could have put you on a path to a different place, a safer place?"

"What kind of memory could do that?"

"You tell me."

"I don't know," he said.

"Maybe you do. Maybe inside you there is a truth that you have never let yourself remember, something unaltered by remembering and re-dreaming."

"Are there such things?"

"Oh, yes," she said. "Lots of them. Most are too insignificant to recall, but others get buried by fear."

"We're talking about a specific thing, aren't we?" He moved closer, fighting the wind. "You're saying I need to remember it. Whatever it is, I need to retrieve it." He sat beside her.

She put her arm around him.

"It's something terrible, isn't it?" he said.

"To you it is, but the terror may only be a screen. The memory itself, the thing you need to know . . . it may be something good, a revelation that changes everything."

"But you can't tell me what it is?"

"No."

"But you know what it is?"

"Yes," she said. "And you do too. It's just locked away."

"And if I can remember it, everything will change? Just like that?

"No. Remembering is a step, not a destination. Remembering it *now* won't help. You need to remember it *yesterday*. It needs to come to you as you stand on the road with your friends. It needs to force you to change your mind, get you back into the car so you can drive away from the dead-end path."

"And how do I do that?"

"I'm not sure." She released his shoulder. "But I think it begins with you going back home."

"To the trailer?"

"Yes."

"You think this time I'll remember—"

"No. This time it won't be about remembering. You need to *see* what happened, not *remember* it."

"How?"

"By going in spirit."

"Into the past?"

"That's where the answers are."

"Back to that night?"

"Yes. The night of my death."

"I already tried that."

"Yes, but this time you go without Kwetis."

"That will make a difference?"

"I think so."

"Will you come with me?"

"No. This is a journey you must make alone." She faded as she spoke, voice merging with the racing wind.

Thunder boomed.

He was alone now, just him and the raging storm, dust and wind expanding before him, swelling until it seemed to fill his dream.

40

A flight of unfinished stairs led to the mansion's basement. No light down there, too much darkness for even skyborn eyes. Bird took the candelabrum from the dining room, carried it down toward the hot-water tanks, furnace, and circuit breakers. He moved past these, along a dirt-floored space lined with piles of cast-off junk, much of it arranged in layers, his things stacked atop rows of sealed crates inherited from his father.

A door beyond the piles led to his climate-controlled gun room and shooting range. Before meeting Kirill, Bird had never thought much about guns. Now this space held a collection considerably larger than the one in Kirill's strip-club office. Not that all the guns belonged to Bird. Most of them he was simply storing for Kirill, who—having grown up in a country where few people owned guns—was now bent on exercising his inalienable right to bear arms.

Some of the weapons weren't exactly legal. But who was ever going to find out? And if they did, Bird and Kirill had enough influence between them to make sure no one cared.

Bird took a Kalashnikov from its rack, fitted it with a magazine of tracer rounds, and carried it back through the junk-filled corridor, stopping when he noticed something potentially useful wedged between a pair of bookshelf speakers. Its screen reflected the flames from the candelabrum, growing brighter as he stepped nearer. It had been a piece of state-of-the-art technology back in his youth, a black-and-white television with a five-inch screen.

He put the candelabrum on the floor and pulled the fossil free. Perhaps, if Kwetis wouldn't tell him exactly what was coming, broadcast news would.

The set ran on batteries. The old ones were still in the power compartment, dead and coated with crud. He pulled them out, carried the set to the kitchen, and cleaned the terminals.

Then he went searching for batteries.

He found two in a flashlight, three more in a cone vibrator left behind by a former girlfriend. The ones in the vibrator were nearly dead, but after some rearranging he managed a combination that worked. The tiny screen flickered, filled with static.

He extended the built-in antenna, tried dialing in a local station. The snow coalesced, took shape. It looked like a snake. He moved the antenna. The image fluttered. No snake. Just a man standing before a weather map.

He tried dialing in the sound. Static popped like heavy rain.

This is taking too long.

He carried the set upstairs.

The elevation seemed to help. The weatherman returned, his image becoming clearer as Bird entered his bedroom and stood beside a shuttered window. There still wasn't any sound. He hit the off switch, put the TV on the bed, considered his options.

The house had an old roof-top antenna on the east-wing tower. Back in the day, that antenna had been connected to sets all through the house. He remembered his father lying in bed, watching a 20-inch Zenith in a wall-size entertainment center. The wall unit was long gone, replaced by a dresser that Bird had moved in from his mother's room. But the antenna connectors? They were probably still in the wall.

He moved the dresser and found the wall plate. Then he worked the screws with his thumbnail, connected the set, turned it on. This time he got two news anchors seated at a desk. Text scrolled beneath them, flashing a list of cities and towns: *Monroeville, Irwin, Greensburg. . . .*

He cranked up the sound.

". . . following a northeast path through—"

Reception cut out as wind struck the house.

He cupped the set in his hands, waited, considered trying another channel.

The image cleared. No sound this time. Just a grainy shot of something soaring above a wood-frame house. Cell-phone footage, handheld and shaky. The image played for a couple seconds, then repeated. It looked like a glider. Long body. Curved wings. But the wings glowed . . . and the cockpit had eyes. It was there for a moment, then the image cut out.

"Come on!" He shook the set. "Piece of crap." He slapped it hard. The image returned.

The weatherman was back, standing before his map and running a hand along a path that extended through Green County, north along the I-79 corridor, veering east. No sound, but the guy didn't look like he was giving the weather.

Bird put the set on his knees, stared at the screen.

Monster snakes with glowing wings.

Just like in his dream, the snakes weren't snakes. They were vectors, heralds of renewal that had been part of myths and legends since the beginning of time, creatures such as *Quetzalcoatl, Gukumatz, U'këë Ushaista.* . . .

The image dimmed, cutting out as the batteries died. The last things he saw were serpentine shapes coiled atop a pair of flat-roofed buildings. Their mouths glowed, spitting static fire.

The TV went dark.

He set it down, considered the Kalashnikov leaning by the bed, and wondered if it was going to be enough.

41

A half-eaten sandwich lay on the floor beside the chair. It was some kind of hoagie, partially wrapped in plastic and stuffed with deli meats and cheese. Processed food. Sam hated that stuff. But she studied it nevertheless.

You'll need to keep eating to sustain your powers.

She picked it up, peeled back the plastic, took a bite.

The flavor hit her in a rush. She dropped the sandwich, gripped the chair.

Dalton had been tying Fox to a barstool. Now he looked at her.

"I'm fine!" she said.

Dalton went back to work.

Fox kept staring.

She looked away, back at the sandwich. Some of the meat had spilled from the bun, pink and glistening on the floor. Maybe if she ate it fast, she wouldn't notice the taste.

Maybe.

She picked it up, gave it another try, biting off hunks and forcing them down with as little chewing as possible. After a couple mouthfuls, her dizziness lifted. A few more and the pain in her side eased. Her body grew stronger, but so did her waterborn senses. It was getting harder not to give into them and savor the pleasure of the final bites. When she finished, she retrieved the bits of spilled meat from the floor, then forced herself to stop.

Enough!

She dropped them, stood, stepped away from the chair.

No need to go overboard. She felt better now, stronger, more alert.

Dalton, Fox, and Kirill were all staring now.

"The hell you looking at?"

"Guess you were hungry," Kirill said.

She ignored the comment and stepped toward him. Her strength and balance had returned, but so had her other senses. The room reeked.

Focus. Tune it out!

She joined Kirill beside the lap-dance chair where Danny Love seemed to be reclining, legs extended, head back, mouth open in a bloody scream. Fox's Stetson hovered nearby, brim suspended an inch from the floor, crown resting on the handle of the knife that Fox had left stuck in the boards. She picked up the hat, tossed it away, dislodged the knife. Then she slipped behind Danny and cut the nylon that bound his wrists.

"Who did this?" Kirill said. "Who killed my manager?"

"Who do you think?"

"Fox?" He pronounced the name *Fucks*. "*Fucks* trashes my club and kills my manager?" He looked across the room to where Fox sat bound to his barstool.

"He forced my hand," Fox said. "All he had to do was tell me where you were."

Kirill ignored him. "Maybe I should kill *Fucks*, Sam."

"Not yet. First we take care of Danny."

"Take care of him?" Kirill said.

She set her palm on Danny's head, administering the touch. Her skin glowed.

"What is this?" Kirill said.

"Healing touch."

"So you fix people?" he said. "You get shot in the face and fix yourself. Then you fix other people?"

"That's part of it."

"And me? You fixed me?"

"Yeah. And Dalton."

Kirill pushed his chin forward, nodded as if to say *very cool*.

Across the way, Dalton and Fox watched too.

Danny just lay there.

Sam took her hand away.

Kirill frowned. "Still dead."

"For now. It takes time." She left the chair, crossed to the trash-bagged bodies by the bar.

"Them too?" Kirill said.

"He said I need seven of you. An army of seven."

"Who said?"

"Kasdeja."

Fox stared, taking it all in, his expression a blend of amusement and wonder.

"What is Kasdeja?" Kirill said.

She ignored the question. She had work to do.

"A clay man," Dalton said.

Why does he keep saying that?

"A clay man who gave her powers," Dalton said.

"How?"

"Long story," Sam said. "We'll talk about it later." She set her hand on the tallest of the three boys. In life, he was the one who had come across as the group leader, the alpha dog. She'd had no beef with him. He'd simply been in the wrong place, catching a bullet that had been meant for Jason.

"You know these guys?" Kirill asked.

"Not really."

"*Fucks* killed them too?"

"No. This is my work." She raised her hand, moved on to the kid with the overbite.

"So now you bring them back?" Kirill said. "Make them your army?"

"Yeah. That's the idea."

"And him?" Kirill pointed toward Dalton. "That guy? You brought him back?"

"My name's Dalton."

"Eh?"

"Dalton."

"*Dolboeb?*"

Sam had spent enough time around Kirill to pick up some of his Russian expressions. *Dolboeb* was one of them. It meant "dumbfuck." The revived Kirill might be bigger and stronger than he'd ever been in life, but his attitude remained intact.

"It's *Dalton!*" Dalton said.

"That's the way you say it." Kirill turned his back to Dalton, stepped closer to Sam. "*Dolboeb* is in your army too?"

"He is now."

"And me?" Something in Kirill's tone suggested that he knew the answer. "We are your soldiers? The soldier's soldiers?"

"Maybe," she said. "Something like that." She kept her hand on the second kid's head. Like the first, he had been collateral damage. Her only real target in the shooting had been the big one, the rapist—Jason. Did she need to revive him too? How many people did she really need to force her way into Bird's home?

"So you enlist us—these guys, me, *Dolboeb*—"

"Dalton!"

"And we all go to Bird's house and do what?"

"Wake a sleeping demon."

If Kirill thought there was anything odd about that, he didn't let on.

"And Bird?" Kirill said. "You think he will be there? He could be already dead. After last night, he could be—"

"He's alive. He serves the sleeping demon."

"You know this?"

"Yes. I know it."

"But you don't know where Bird lives?"

"No. That's why I need you. You're going to take me there." She pulled her hand from the scrawny kid and moved on to kneel beside Jason. His eyes were open, rolled back, swollen. She remembered how he had looked when he'd attacked her. It had been just outside this building, in a narrow extension of the main lot. She had been changing a tire on her Jeep when he came up behind her, clobbered her with a pry bar, then raped her . . . or tried to. She still didn't know for sure.

She hesitated, considered staying her hand, then she touched Jason's head, wincing at the cold feel of his skin. She almost let go, but what she gave with her right hand could always be taken away with her left. If it came to it, she could let Jason feel the fire of her rage.

Her hand glowed.

Jason just lay there, a slab of meat . . . for now.

She wiped her hand on her skirt and crossed to the embers of Boone and Prutko. Metal fragments lay scattered amid the debris: fillings, belt buckles, a gold grill.

"Oles Prutko?" Kirill said. "You brought him back too?"

"Not me," Sam said. "I killed him."

"But first you brought him back, eh? He died in New York. He was a good soldier."

"He never died," Fox said. "That was a cover. He's been living in Youngstown, taking care of business."

"You knew him?"

"We worked together sometimes. For Ilya."

Sam knelt beside Prutko's remains. They were still hot. She picked through them. "Here we go." She pulled something from the char, shook it.

"Key chain?" Dalton asked.

"Yeah. Hummer keys."

"So we drive to Bird's house?" Kirill said. "And then what? He invites us in?"

"I don't think so. He'll see you've changed and know something's wrong. We'll need to use force."

"Break down the door?"

"Maybe. If it comes to that." She looked toward the upstairs office. "Don't suppose you'd mind letting us borrow your guns."

"You think maybe we shoot Bird's demon?"

"No. The guns would be for getting inside." She raised her death hand, showing her palm. "This is for the demon."

"That?" Kirill frowned, a look of disgust. "The clay man gave you that too?"

"Not a clay man. An angel."

"An angel did that to your hand?"

"Yeah. It's a death hand."

"For killing?"

"Yeah," Dalton said. "I've seen it work."

"So you will need to get close," Kirill said.

"Very close."

Kirill grinned.

"Something funny?"

"I am thinking there is a better way than guns."

"A better way to get inside?"

"A better way to get close to Bird. An easier way." He started for the stage. "Come on. You won't like this, but it will work." He waved and continued walking. "I'll show you a different kind of magic."

42

Sharo was no longer in the van.

She stood below the spreading funnel, a whirlwind of dust and mist that seemed part of something larger than the earth, wind, and sky—a force beyond the scope of knowing. And it seemed to speak to her, rumbling with a voice lower than sound.

Come closer!

The wind blew straight up now, whipping her hair in tangles, tugging at her ragged uniform. Yet the fog at the base of the storm seemed unaffected, its currents turning in on themselves, flowing in patterns that had nothing to do with the surrounding wind. It looked almost solid, more like a curtain than a cloud. She reached out, touched it with the flat of her palm. The currents responded, glowing. Her arm bristled, hairs spiking like the hackles of a cat. The sensation was strange but not unpleasant.

Closer!

It took her hand, drew her in, enfolded her.

Keep coming.

She pushed on, advancing into grayness, unable to see anything but a patch of ground at her feet, a stone berm rising atop the mud, a straight path leading deeper into the mist.

Thunder crashed, pulsing like breakers—surging, shattering, receding.

Don't stop.

The berm angled upward, became a stone arch, a bridge rising through the haze. She climbed, and soon the crashing came from below, rising around her, reverberating with vastness and depth. And still she climbed, the stone cold now, slick with condensation, tapering with each step until she could no longer place her feet side-by-side. Yet she felt secure in her balance, as if the air or possibly the stone itself were protecting her, holding her steady, urging her on.

Come home.

She kept climbing, cautiously now, an acrobat on a rope of stone. . . .

The wind shifted, an upward blast, and then the mist opened, pulling back to form a cylindrical wall of spinning fog. She had reached the funnel's eye, a column of clear air in which she found herself standing not on a stone arch, but on a ledge. The path was a dead end, a road to nowhere, a needle of stone suspended over a flooded pit. Water roared beneath her, misting as it plunged into a maelstrom that seemed larger than the crater of Windslow Mine . . . possibly larger than the world itself. And deep within its core, the waters burned, glowed red, thundered. . . .

Closer.

But there was nowhere to go. One more step and she'd move from the needle of stone, into empty air.

Return to me.

The words reverberated inside her, roiling with the sounds of falling water and rising air. Not one voice, but two. Both called to her, urging her on.

Another step and one of them would take her. She would fall into the abyss . . . or rise into the air. Either way, she would shed the weight of the world, achieve the inevitable end that awaited everything that had ever lived.

I am your destiny.

They spoke in unison. Not in harmony, but in balanced discord. And it was then that something new caught her eye, a dark line at the point where rising mist became plunging maelstrom, the demarcation between opposing spirals. But there was something wrong about those spirals. They seemed to be spinning counter to each other, mist swirling to the right, water to the left. Impossible, yet there it was. She was in the center of opposing forces, each momentarily holding the other in check, each calling out to claim her as its own.

Return to me!

It would be so easy. One more forward step and she'd join one of them. It didn't matter which. Either way, she'd shed the weight of life, become part of something vast and eternal.

It was tempting. And yet. . . .

She had promises to keep.

To herself.

To Jordan.

Closer!

She stepped back from the brink.

The wind pulled. Water roared.

She turned and ran, back along the widening cliff, back to solid ground, and then. . . .

She was in the van, staring out the windshield.

She felt stiff, as if she'd been sleeping for hours. But that was impossible! She hadn't slept. The experience couldn't have been a dream.

She looked at the dome of mist, felt the rumble of falling currents and rising air.

Return to me!

She looked away, put the transmission in gear, and spun the van around toward the southern end of the mine. There was an easement there, an unpaved trail that would get her to Coals Hollow and then to Windslow Road.

Fire and lightning flashed in her rearview, calling, urging her back.

She kept driving.

43

R ain hammered the club's roof as Kirill led Sam to a passageway behind the stage. No lights or ventilation. Kirill stepped into it alone, becoming a pale shape in the darkness.

Sam held back, waiting to see what he was doing.

Dalton came up beside her.

"You should stay with Fox," she said.

"He's not going anywhere. I tied him to the stool."

"I don't care. You should go back. Keep an eye on him. Just in case."

"What? And miss this?"

"Miss what? You know what's going on?"

"I can guess."

Kirill leaned against a steel door. A latch disengaged, then came a gust of wind as he pushed open a fire exit. Dim light and gray rain angled in, breaking against the floor. He propped the door, then turned and waved for Sam to join him in a narrow dressing room.

Kirill crossed to a sink. "You can wash up." He tried the faucet. Pipes banged, but the water was clean—at least for now. Kirill turned it off and stepped toward a rack of clothes slung across metal hangers. Robes, blouses, slacks—odds and ends left behind by the strippers who worked the stage.

There were lockers too. Some had locks. He opened the ones that didn't, encouraged her to pick through their contents. "It's all crap, but better than an ass-face skirt."

"What?" *Ass-face* didn't sound like one of his Russified expressions. "Ass-face skirt?" It dawned on her then. From the front, the snakeskin looked OK, but from the back? She glared at Dalton. "You son of a bitch! Why didn't you say something?"

He gave a shrug that might have looked innocent before his transformation.

A full-length mirror stood beside the clothes rack. She crossed to it, stopping the moment her reflection appeared. Like Dalton and Kirill, she had changed. Unlike them, she was beautiful.

No. Not just beautiful.

She resisted the thought even as she stepped closer to the image. Heart-shaped face, luminescent teeth and skin, hair like strawberry fire. She had never considered herself homely, but there had always been something pre-pubescent about her looks, as if her growth and development had stopped somewhere between 12 and 13. But the figure before her was definitely that of a woman, small boned but muscular, thin but full. She pushed back her shoulders, turned to the side.

Damn!

Even with the blood from her healed wounds crusting her hair and skin, she was something to see. It gave her chills that she didn't want to feel, but there they were. She felt them, and they felt good.

Dalton and Kirill came up behind her, faces strong and bright as polished marble—like apes reimagined as gods. Yet their transformations were different, with Dalton's features conveying a sense of the angelic as opposed to Kirill's, which had a marked brutishness. And as for her? What had Kasdeja told her?

Fire and water. Tempered flesh. Very rare. You'll be a reckoning force, Samuelle!

"Shit-damn!" Dalton said. "Look at us!" There was wonder in his voice.

She gave another quarter turn, looking at herself from behind now. And there it was, a flaccid face hanging above the skin's knotted arms.

"I would have told you," Dalton said. "I just didn't know how. It wasn't like—"

"Forget it." She turned again, head back, hands on her hips.

This is me!

But Kirill hadn't brought her there to look at herself. The storm was raging, the clock ticking. "So what's your plan?" she asked. "How does coming back here get us closer to Bird?"

"Yeah. OK. About Bird." Kirill stepped away from the mirror. "Bird is a smart man. Head smart. Like a chess master. You cannot trick him when he thinks with his head. Your job is to make him think with his balls."

"Me?"

"Yeah. Should be easy."

"How?"

"Be sexy."

"Me?"

"You go to his door. Just you, nobody else. He looks out and sees a woman . . . a pretty woman. Maybe this woman says she broke down on the road. 'I'm cold and scared,' she says. 'You're a big man. You protect me.'"

"A woman?"

"You."

"I say those things to Bird?"

"Something like those things. I don't know. Whatever girls say to big strong men to make them think with their balls."

"I don't know those things."

"Yeah. Well, maybe you'll think of something."

"Suppose I do. I go to his door and say it. Then what? He believes it and lets me in, just like that?"

"Maybe. Probably. I know Bird. All you have to do is look pretty . . . act sexy. He thinks with his balls."

She checked the mirror again.

Look pretty.

She could wash the blood from her skin and hair, change her clothes. That might take care of looking pretty. But the other?

Act sexy?

"I don't know," she said. "What if it doesn't work?"

"We will be there, hiding, watching. We will be Plan B, but I think the A-plan gets you inside."

She stared at herself.

"Trust me. I know this man."

Act sexy.

She crossed to the clothes rack, grabbed a couple hangers, dropped them on the counter beside the sink. "Give me five minutes." She turned on the water, filling the sink. "Go on! I'm not getting dressed with you guys here. Get out."

"We'll check on Danny and *Fucks*."

"Yeah," she said. "And the others too. If they're up, make them eat. All of you need to eat."

"I'm not hungry," Dalton said.

"And you're not going to be, but you'll like it once you start. Raid the kitchen. Trust me. I'll be out when I'm ready."

The water flowed slowly now, darkening as the pressure fell. The sink was nearly full. She shut off the tap and waited until Kirill and Dalton were out of sight. Then she peeled off her scorched halter and snake-skin skirt, kicked them under the sink, and cleaned herself with water and antibacterial hand soap. There was no washcloth, but a stack of paper towels on the counter worked well enough at first. She dabbed them in the water and soap, wiped them across her skin. It was slow going. She worked until the sink was dark with blood, until dabbing herself with the dirty water became a zero sum gain.

What now?

Her arms and legs were still a mess, and she hadn't even started washing her hair.

Rain sheeted in from the open exit, spattering on the floor.

Shower in the rain?

The back of the club opened onto the face of a cutaway hill. It wasn't as if anyone would see, but just the thought of going naked in the world frightened her.

Just do it!

She pumped the hand soap into her hair, worked it in with her finger tips, then did the same with her arms, legs, and feet. Her hands came last. She soaped them slowly, relying mostly on fingertips and knuckles to spread the foam.

She checked herself in the mirror, a pillar of lather in the dim room. Then she glanced toward the door to the stage. Still no sign of Kirill or Dalton, but if either returned to see her like this—

Shit!

She didn't want to think about that.

The outside door waited, shifting against the chair Kirill had used to prop it open.

Go!

She stepped outside, braced against the hammering chill, and let the rain wash her clean. A minute later, cold and tingling, she returned to the dressing room. With the blood gone, she could finally inspect the state of her healing body. Remnants of bullet holes dented her belly and forehead, hardly noticeable. The site of the exit wound in the back of her head was in good shape as well, with the hair nearly grown back and the bone only slightly pliable, like the soft spot on a baby's head. To the untrained eye, there was nothing unsightly about her.

She dried off with the remaining paper towels and pulled on a gray skirt and blouse, simple clothes, but the result startled her when she checked the mirror.

Sexy.

"Hey?" She stepped closer, imagining Bird looking at her, standing before her in an open doorway. "Let me in, OK?" She remembered how he had looked when she last saw him, tall and strong, hair blowing as he bent over her. He had scared her then. Men always did when they got close.

"It's wet out here. I need to come in. OK?"

She wondered if he would recognize her. Probably not. She had been different then. But he would be much the same—a flesh-and-blood Kasdeja with rock-star hair.

"Can I come in?" She coughed, swallowed, tried pitching it a little higher.

"Can I come in?" She would need to work on that, but everything else seemed right. She was ready.

Kirill reappeared, sandwich in one hand, Coke in the other. "This is good shit!"

"What is it?"

"Some kind of egg salad," he said. "But it tastes like . . . I don't know. Really good stuff." He pushed the rest of it into his mouth, looking her over as he chewed. Then he swallowed hard, shook his head. "No," he said.

"No? What's *no?*"

"You." He drained the Coke, then looked at the can. "These are really good Cokes." He put down the can. "But you're not finished."

"What do you mean?"

He opened a drawer, pushed aside a mass of tassels and strings, lifted out a latch-box case and set it on the counter. "Here." He pulled out a chair. "Sit."

She did.

He pushed the case closer. It looked like a bait box. "Finish, OK? Look like a woman."

"What the hell, Kirill? I look fine!"

"A woman needs these things." He opened the box. It was a makeup case.

"No." She started to get up. "I don't do that."

"Not for you." He pushed her back down. "For Bird."

Dalton returned to the room, eating from a tub of cold chicken wings, munching them like popcorn, bones and all.

She took a black tube from the makeup case, removed its lid. There was a brush inside, like a scrubber for some kind of tiny toilet.

"That's for your eyes," Kirill said.

"I know what it is."

"For sexy eyes."

She pushed the brush back into the tube, threw the thing into the case. "No. You don't understand." She pushed the box away. "I don't know the first thing about using this crap. I've never used—"

"I have," Dalton said.

Sam met his eyes in the mirror. "You?"

"Face painting and body art mostly." He put down the empty tub and wiped his hands on his T-shirt. "Like I told you. In my previous life—"

"You can make her look good, *Dolboeb?*"

"I can give it a—"

"Hold on!" She wasn't sure she wanted anyone touching her face, let alone smearing it with makeup. "Don't I look good enough already?"

"We need to be sure." Kirill pulled out another chair, gestured for Dalton to sit. "We'll get one shot at this. One chance to make Bird think with his balls."

Dalton sat.

"Use this too." Kirill picked up a bottle, unscrewed the cap, held it to his nose. "Good Russian perfume." He sniffed it again. "This is really good shit!"

"I don't want to smell like a strip-club whore."

"I buy it for my girls. Special formula. With pheromones. Make Bird think with his—"

Something banged out in the club.

"What's Fox doing?" she asked.

"Sitting in a stool," Kirill said. "He says we're all going to hell. Says he's seen the signs."

"What about the other ones? They coming around yet?"

"Twitching," Dalton said. "We left food out for them."

"Someone should stay with them. Kirill?"

"Yeah, OK. I'll get another egg salad and Coke too. You have one of those Cokes, *Dolboeb*?"

"Dalton!"

"They're fucking good." He turned and left.

"How fast can we do this, Dalton?"

He reached for the case. "Pretty fast."

She closed her eyes and let him work, hating the feel of it, the touch of his hands. When he finished, she checked the results in the mirror. She was a dark-eyed, full-lipped stranger. "Men like this look?" she asked.

"Works for me." He dabbed some of the perfume on her neck.

"Dammit, Dalton!"

"He said to—"

"I think we're finished here."

The perfume felt cold, smelled of alcohol and lilies.

"We should go," she said.

People were talking in the club now, one of them shouting. It sounded like Fox.

They returned to the main room where they found everyone stuffing themselves. The stench of backed-up pipes was now overlaid with the salt-and-oil smell of condiments, meat, and cheese. The front door was still open, letting in blasts of rain. And there was Fox standing in front of it, silhouetted against the flashing storm, eating a hoagie with hands that were no longer bound with nylon zips.

"Hey!" She started toward him. "What the hell's going on?"

He turned.

It wasn't Fox.

"Sam? That you?"

It was Danny Love, dressed in Fox's shirt, jacket, and pants.

The real Fox was still tied to his bar stool, wearing a wife-beater and black boxers. The boxers had a pocket in front, a pouch for his man junk. She didn't want to notice that, but she did. It was actually less disturbing than his hand-tooled boots. They reminded her of another time, another life, things she didn't want to think about.

He was the only one not eating.

Danny stepped toward her. "Man!" he said. "You look . . . different."

"Yeah. You too."

It wasn't just Fox's clothes that had changed Danny. He was larger, taller, broader about the shoulders. Something about him had always reminded her of a ferret, but his features were rounder now, fuller. And his voice had changed too, deeper than before. "Kirill said I might as well wear Fox's stuff, so we stripped him down. His boots didn't fit. I let him keep those. And the hat? Screw that hat!"

"Clothes don't matter, son. Not where we're going." Fox glanced toward the three boys at the end of the bar. "When the dead rise, the judgment can't be far behind."

"He's been going on like that," Danny said. "He used to be a preacher."

"Don't care about used to be," Sam said. "He's my bitch now."

"Get behind me, Satan!"

"Don't force my hand, Fox." She raised her death palm. "Don't make me come over there."

Fox looked away, jaw pulsing.

She turned toward the boys at the end of the bar. Blood still stained their skin and clothes, but their features had changed. The little guy had lost his overbite. Some of Jason's fat had gone to muscle. And the tall one? He looked much the same, except his eyes. He had been helping the others work on a pile of uncooked pizzas, but now he stood a little apart, staring at her. She wasn't sure if he recognized her or just thought she looked hot. But his eyes, they seemed to be burning, not visibly, but with an internal heat she could feel from across the room. Her imagination? Whatever it was, she couldn't deal with it now. It was time to roll. "Everyone here needs a gun, Kirill. Guns and ammo—for Plan B. Just in case."

"No," he said. "No way."

"I'm not asking you, Kirill. Listen to me—"

"Not that bastard." Kirill glared at Fox. "No gun for *Fucks*."

"No. Not him. I mean the rest of us."

"Them?" He turned toward the resurrected boys at the end of the bar. "You want to give them my guns?"

She called to the boys. "Any of you ever fire a gun?"

"Yeah," the little one said. "Paintball."

"Laser tag," the tall one said.

Jason just stared.

"Maybe they don't get guns," Kirill said. "Maybe just me, Danny, and *Dolboeb*."

"I've never shot a gun," Dalton said.

"Maybe we just take one," Kirill said. "One for me. OK?" He grinned, and the expression was pure Kirill. "A strong gun. Very kickass."

"What gun?"

"MM1. Very kickass."

Had she heard him correctly?

"It came two weeks ago. Ilya sent it. Said he maybe had a buyer in Columbus. Told me to hold it for him."

"You're talking about a Hawk revolver?"

"Forty millimeter."

"A grenade launcher?"

"Twelve rounds. Rotating chamber. Semi-auto."

"You have ordnance?"

"Yeah. Ilya sent a case. Military grade. Very kickass. I asked Bird to store it, but he said he had too much of my shit already. So I kept it here."

"Upstairs?

"Yeah. To keep it safe."

She closed her eyes.

Thank you, Kasdeja.

"Go get it," she said.

Kirill started away.

She looked around at the others, wondering why Kasdeja had insisted on her raising an army of seven if Kirill had a gun powerful enough to rip through solid steel.

Testing me.

She looked at the three boys at the end of the bar. The tall one was looking at her again.

Always testing.

44

The stairs of the mansion's east tower led to a stone room with a conical ceiling. Bird leaned the Kalashnikov by the door and opened the four shuttered windows, each positioned at a compass point along the circular wall. Clouds covered the sky in all directions. Rain hadn't yet reached the hilltop estate, but to the south it fell in black horsetail plumes. Lightning flashed, and in the brightness he saw what looked like cruciform shadows flying toward him, moving ahead of the rain, losing altitude as they passed over the lower bends of the mile-long driveway. They shimmered, flickering with static fire, bending their bodies into S-shaped curves as they came down amid a stand of trees.

U'këë Ushaista!

He shouldered the Kalashnikov, disengaged the safety, watched the trees.

Wind gusted, blowing cold from the south. He leaned into it, scanned the grounds.

Where'd they go?

The south lawn waxed beneath a lightning flash, bright as day one moment, dark the next. He saw them in the brightness, 50 feet off and poised before a garden wall. Heads raised. Necks arched. There were perhaps six of them . . . maybe seven. He aimed at the closest, held his breath, considered the room he was standing in. Stone walls. Metal ceiling. Iron casements.

Should have brought ear plugs.

Too late for that. He squeezed the trigger.

Thwack-OOOM!

The report set his ears ringing as a tracer round cut a red line to the monster's head. The head shattered. The neck reared back. Bird fired again.

Thwack-OOOM!

He hit the monster again, cutting it in two. The pieces thrashed on the ground, taking out a line of shrubs before its body erupted into a cloud of sparking dust and chunks of clotted clay.

"Damn!"

The dust darkened as it settled. Was that all the serpents were, dust animated by static charges? Strange, and yet, wasn't that the essence of life—dust, current, and animating spirit. The big difference was that these creatures didn't decompose, they combusted.

He took aim again.

"Let's do some dusting."

Thwack-OOOM! Thwack-OOOM!

Another one down.

"Fish in a barrel!"

But the others were moving now, whipping their tails until their heads glowed. One opened its jaws.

Bird aimed at the open mouth, fired.

Thwack-OOOM!

The head erupted into a ball of blue-white sparks. The body went down, sputtering like a shorting cable.

"Three down."

But now the others were opening their jaws, turning their heads, taking aim.

"Shit!"

The serpents fired, spitting bolts of jagged heat that sent him diving for cover. The chamber rocked. He covered his ears against the thunderclap and trusted the tower's lightning rod to do the rest.

It did. This time.

He leaped up, shouldered the rifle, leaned out the window, and—

"Fuck!"

He leaped back, arms burning where he had tried bracing them against the casement. The iron was hot.

The serpents drew closer, tails twisting like corkscrews, recharging.

He raised the gun. Aiming wasn't as easy with nothing to brace against. The first shot went too far to the right, splintering a trunk near the garden wall. The next passed just to the side of a pair of opening jaws. He didn't get a third chance.

The monsters fired again.

He hit the floor, stayed there as another blast hit . . . then another. Too much of this, and they'd burn out the lightning rod's grounding cable. What then? How many direct strikes could the tower take? How much noise could Axle sleep through?

Can't just sit here. Have to return fire.

He gripped the gun, turned the selector to full auto, resigning himself to shooting into the blinding light. But then the barrage ended. He leaped up, ran to the window, then backed away as a blast of rain sheeted in. The casement steamed. The drops were heavy, leaden. They hammered the tin roof, formed rivers in the courtyard below. And the serpents? He didn't see them. He checked the other windows, making a circuit of the room. Nothing out there but rain. Had they taken off? Or had the rain turned them to mud and sludge?

He put down the gun, cranked the windows closed, and wondered if it was over. Would they come back once the rain passed, or was something more terrible coming?

He returned to the south window, ran a sleeve across the fogging glass, and went back to standing watch.

45

The storm filled Axle's dream, engulfing him in a whorl of wind and rain. He rode with it, through a region of thunder, then out again to find himself standing before a line of trailers on a gravel lot. Yeyestani's was one of them, dark and waiting.

He moved toward the porch steps. The screen-door shivered in the wind. No need to open it. He passed through, toward the sound of a television playing in the living room.

A boy sat in the cathode glow, perched on the edge of a couch, looking toward the closed door of Yeyestani's room. He called her name. No answer, just the murmur of the all-night radio. No music this time. No repeating song. Only voices on an AM call-in show. Sports and politics.

Axle paused as the boy got up, walked down the hall, and opened the bedroom door to find Yeyestani lying beneath a blood-stained blanket. Her hand, gaunt as a chicken claw, clutched something dark.

The boy trembled as he touched the old woman's face. "No," he whispered. Then louder. "No!" He touched the thing in her hand, wrenched it free.

Axle recognized it. He had seen it before. Three places. In life, memory, and dream.

In life he had seen it as he saw it now, but those impressions had all been overwritten in memory, transforming the thing into something it had never been. And now he was seeing it as he had glimpsed it elsewhere in the dream. Not as a knife, but as something delicate and beautiful—a stone carving shaped like an elongated bird.

I saw her making it!

He remembered Yeyestani standing in the kitchen, working the slate with a file and sandpaper. That memory was of something he had dreamed. But was it possible the dream had come from life, based on something he had seen and forgotten long ago? He couldn't be sure. He only knew that now, looking over the boy's shoulder, he clearly saw the contours of the slate, the carved likeness of a bird with a long, bladelike tail. And he knew what the boy was thinking. He remembered it as clearly as if he were thinking it now.

She killed herself!

The blood told part of the story, but the carving—so much like a knife with a spiral blade—told the rest. Yet there were details here that the boy hadn't considered, the dullness of the blade, the blood on Yeyestani's face. There was also blood on her hands, wrists, and arms. The adult Axle put it together, noting things that had been lost to the boy.

I see it now.

The blood had come from her mouth and nose, spilling from a hemorrhage somewhere in her head, chest, or stomach. He had no way of knowing from where exactly, or what had caused it. He only knew that the blood on her hands suggested she had tried stopping it. Had she sensed it was going to happen? Had she felt it coming on? Had she been warned?

He told me it was time.

He remembered her telling him of a dream, of Kwetis warning her that it would soon be time to give her blood back to the earth.

He said nothing of cutting.

Where did that memory come from? From life? Another dream?

Layers on layers.

And now here she was, dead, bloody, clutching an artifact of stone, lying cold and stiff beside a small bundle of money she had promised would be his one day, a meager life savings resting on a nightstand, ready to be passed to an undeserving heir. And the stone carving? Was it possible she had intended that as a gift too, a piece of heritage to go with the money?

Perhaps.

But the boy did not consider these things. He saw the blood on her arm and assumed she had cut herself, opened an artery, taken her life. And the thought horrified him, made him fearful of what people would say . . . about her . . . about him.

Akeo! The left behind.

The boy took the stone carving and dashed from the room. He entered the kitchen, threw it into the trash beneath the sink. Then he stepped back, leaned against the refrigerator.

Akeo! First his father left him. Then his mother. Now his great-grandmother.

But unlike his parents, Yeyestani had been old. Her time could have come at any moment, yet she had killed herself. Why? Was it him?

"No," the boy said. No longer shouting. Just mumbling. "They can't know. No one can know."

He didn't remember saying these things, but they seemed right and true. They were things he could have said as he stood in the kitchen, obsessing about a knife that wasn't a knife.

Axle stepped close, wished he could do something.

But the boy just stared, first looking past him, then walking through him as he returned to the trash, removed the carving, and broke it against the counter. It split in two, a slender piece that might have been a blade, a rounded section that resembled a handle. He picked them up and wrapped them in a towel. Then he ran for the door. It groaned open, banging shut as he descended the steps.

It was raining now, heavy drops breaking against the gravel, hammering the vinyl siding, soaking the boy's shirt and hair. He looked around, first toward the dumpster by the entrance to Cliff Mine Run, then toward the trees that grew thick between the court and the southern end of the mine, then back toward Yeyestani's trailer.

Axle remembered this too. Not doing it, but seeing it. This was the moment that Kwetis had brought him to in a previous dream, and now he was seeing it again on his own, watching as the boy dropped to the ground and crawled beneath the trailer.

Axle followed, moving with the ease of a spirit while the boy pulled himself between columns of concrete block, crawling deeper . . . deeper.

The storm flashed through the wicker skirting, painting the space with crosshatched shadows. The boy crawled on, one hand cradling the broken pieces of stone, the other clawing the dirt until he reached a vertical pipe that connected the trailer's plumbing to the communal lines beneath the ground. Then he dug, buried the evidence, and crawled away. The secret was his now, or so he thought.

Axle the dreamer remembered. These things seemed familiar, ringing with the clarity of unaltered memory. But something else was coming . . . a final shock that would cause the boy to forget that he had ever buried a stone carving beneath the trailer. Axle sensed what it was. He felt the looming terror of it, but this time he forced himself to watch as the boy stopped crawling.

This is it.

The boy tensed, tried rolling to his side. His shoulder snagged the floor above him. He reached for his chest and screamed.

46

S am watched Danny tie Fox's right hand to the wheel, securing it with a loose zip that gave him enough mobility to steer. Then she climbed onto the island beside him.

Kirill rode shotgun.

Danny and Dalton took the middle seats.

Jason and his friends filled in the rear.

Surprisingly, for as big as it seemed on the outside, the Hummer had barely enough room for all of them.

The windows fogged the moment the doors slammed shut.

Sam started the engine for Fox, turned on the fan, switched it to high. Then she tugged the transmission into drive. "Come on, Fox. Let's go."

He slid his zip-tied hand against the wheel, checking its range of motion. "This isn't safe, you know."

"Nor is this." She set her left fist against his shoulder, letting him feel the weight of the hidden palm. "Drive!"

He did, advancing through the rain until he reached a line of concrete blocks that marked the end of the lot. Then he stopped.

"No," she said. "Keep going."

"Shouldn't we take a look first? There was a lot of water down there the last time we checked. With all this rain—"

"We'll make it," she said. "Keep going."

He toed the gas, easing over a concrete block and onto the unpaved ground. The overpass towered above them, gray concrete curving into the sheeting rain. They passed beneath it, toward a rocky slope.

Fox slowed.

"Keep going," Sam said.

The interstate's exit ramp came into view, a vague shadow in the distance, two lanes of blacktop ending above a torrent of black water. Another section of road lay beyond the runoff. Police and EMT vehicles gathered on its edge. Behind them, a stretch of level pavement waited, curving north. All Fox had to do was get to it, but that meant crossing the runoff.

Sam shifted to low, then pressed her fist to Fox's shoulder, partly for support, mainly to remind him it was there. "Steady, Fox. Easy on the brake."

They nosed down, started sliding.

"Easy!" She gripped Kirill's backrest.

The Hummer's rear wheels slid to the right.

"Ease up on the brake, Fox. Trust the gear!"

They straightened out, picking up speed, heading for the water.

"A little gas, Fox. Keep moving!"

They jerked forward, bearing down as the currents hit the wheels.

"Too deep," Fox said.

"More gas. Come on. Drive!"

Waves broke against the fender, drummed beneath the floor.

"Drive!"

The engine revved.

Fog spread against the windshield. Sam cleared it with her fist. "Keep going!"

They were climbing now, water receding, wheels rising clear as they moved toward the flashing lights of a cruiser.

Someone came toward them, a cop in a poncho, palms out, waving for them to stop.

Sam shifted out of low. "Keep going. Steer around him. Gun it."

"The road's blocked."

"Go straight!" Kirill said. "Down the other side!"

Fox hit the gas.

The cop leaped away.

The Hummer crossed the pavement, lurched onto a shallow decline. There was water here too, inches deep. They splashed through and onto a rise that carried them up onto a weedy plain. A line of poplars stood in the distance, thrashing in the wind.

"Toward those trees," Kirill said. "There's a road."

Sam didn't see it. "Where?"

"A quarter mile. Maybe less. We can get there."

"That cop?" Sam checked the rearview. "Can anyone see what that cop's doing?"

Jason's crew sat in the rear seats. The window behind them was completely fogged.

"Wipe that off, Jason!"

"What?"

"The window," she said. "Wipe it off. See if anyone's coming after us."

He turned, ran a bloody sleeve across the glass, replacing the mist with a bruise-colored smear.

WHAM!

The front end rose up, came down again with an explosive thud. She lost balance, flew from the island, slammed the dash.

Kirill caught her, pushed her back.

She tensed until he let her go.

"We hit something," Fox said.

"No shit!"

The Hummer lurched, running rough now, lilting to the side.

"Front tire," Fox said. "Something's wrong—"

"Just keep going!"

They entered the trees, rain-swept trunks running in a hazy line beyond the windows. She looked back at the rear window. The tall guy was wiping it now, cleaning the blood to reveal nothing but distant flashers on the blockaded road. No one was after them. That made sense. Cops wouldn't be concerned about people leaving Windslow. But if Fox had stopped, if that cop had seen the mortar launcher, he certainly would have demanded a closer look. They had dodged that problem, but the Hummer was running rougher by the second, front wheel screaming, metal on metal.

"Feels like a bearing," Fox said. "Maybe the whole axle."

"Where's that road, Kirill?"

"Close." Kirill wiped the glass. "There! Over there!"

"You call that a road?" she said.

"Yeah! A utility road!"

It was a ribbon of muck.

"Steady," Sam said. "Easy on the gas, Fox. Don't get us stuck."

Dalton leaned forward from one of the middle seats, hovering like a dog that wanted to pee.

"Something on your mind, Dalton?"

"Yeah."

"You going to make me guess?"

"It's about something you said before. What you said the clay man told you."

"Why do you keep—"

"He said it had to be seven."

"What are we talking about, Dalton?"

"An army of seven. You said that's what he said you needed. An army of seven."

"I've got seven, Dalton."

"But he said *resurrected*, right? The army had to be *resurrected*."

"And?"

"And Fox isn't."

"Not that you know of," Fox said.

Sam pressed her fist to Fox's neck. "Just drive."

"I just thought I'd mention it." Dalton braced on the seat as the Hummer reached the utility road. "Just in case."

"In case I'd forgotten?"

"Yeah."

"Don't sweat the small stuff, Dalton."

"Sounds like Moses to me," Fox said.

"Just drive."

"You know that story? Moses and the rock?"

"Do you?" Sam asked.

"He probably does," Danny said. "He used to be a preacher."

"Moses was one of my specialties," Fox said. "I used to tell the story of how God promised Moses water if he struck a rock once. Once! But Moses struck it twice, figured that was close enough."

"Just drive."

"And the Lord said, *'Because ye believed me not, ye shall not bring this congregation home!'*"

"Screw you, Fox."

"I'm just making a point."

"You have no idea how much you're pissing me off." She opened her hand, held it close to his head. "And I'm about this close to having you join your friends." She waved the hand. "This close!"

They reached an intact section of Windslow Road, the Hummer's front end settling hard, lilting left as they steered onto the pavement. She closed her fist and set it on the dash, bracing as he eased into the northbound lane.

"Not running any better here," Dalton said.

Fox said nothing, maintaining speed as the grinding worsened.

"How far to Bird's place, Kirill?"

"Three miles."

"Shit."

"Then there's a long driveway. I don't think—"

Headlights cleared the bend up ahead, coming on fast. Sam wiped the glass, saw what was coming, recognized it for what it was—a sign, a gift!

"Cut it off, Fox!"

"What?"

"The van. Cut in front!" She grabbed the wheel, steering over the center line.

The headlights were a few hundred feet away, still coming on fast.

"Stop, Fox! Right here!" She grabbed the emergency brake, yanked it. The Hummer stopped.

The approaching vehicle stalled, skidding to rest with barely a couple yards to spare.

Sam read the markings on its cargo door.

Pittsburgh News 6

"OK," Sam said. "This'll work."

Dalton pushed his face over Kirill's backrest. "What're we doing?"

"Commandeering a van."

itting behind the wheel of the van, Sharo watched the Hummer's doors fly open. Three blood-smeared men leaped out, raced toward her. She tried restarting the engine, but one of the men came on fast, springing forward on long legs, reaching the door before she could snap the lock.

He grabbed her.

She fought back, but others rushed through the passenger side, overpowering her, forcing her onto the pavement where a man with a giant revolver threw her to the shoulder.

More people hurried by. A woman with fiery hair, a half-naked guy in a wife-beater, a young man in jacket and slacks. That last one looked familiar. She'd seen him around, though he looked bigger now, as if he'd put on weight. And the guy with the giant revolver? She recognized his suit if not his face.

Kirill Vorarov?

He climbed into the van's driver's seat. "Three miles!" he said. "I'll drive."

The red-haired woman opened the cargo doors. The half-naked guy was hustled in. The others followed. All except one, a stocky man with a shaved head. He wore a T-shirt and sweat pants, getting soaked as he stood by the open door, staring at her.

She met his gaze, held it.

"Hey!" The red-haired woman called from the cargo hold. "Dalton! Let's go!"

Dalton?

It was him, the man who had rescued her from snake-bite death in the clearing above the mine. He didn't look the same, but this had been a day for changes.

Dalton!

He climbed into the van, looked back at her through the open door. He had helped her once. Would he help her again?

"Dalton!"

The red-headed woman grabbed the cargo door, slid it closed.

The engine revved, reversing along the rain-slicked road.

"Dalton! Wait!"

The van spun around. Tires squealed, racing away.

She ran after it, pushing her new body to the limit. But it wasn't enough. The van took a bend, vanishing into the storm with Benjie still sleeping in the rear compartment, knocked out from exhaustion and oxycodone.

She sprinted back to the Hummer, knowing even before she checked that its keys were gone.

Kirill's words came back to her.

Three miles! I'll drive.

Three miles to where?

48

H ey *Dolboeb*. You know that monster woman?"

"Yeah," Dalton said. He rode in the back, sitting on the floor, leaning against a closed door in a foam-core wall. "She used to be a cop."

"Sounded like she wanted to tell you something."

"I wouldn't know." Dalton turned away, bracing against a side panel as the van took a turn.

Sam rode across from him, staring at Fox, who sat in the cargo hold's only chair. She remembered him now, from the days when her mother had been searching for a guide, someone to help make sense of the voices in her head, the waking dreams that haunted her eyes. She would hear a preacher on the radio, and the next thing Sam knew they'd be travelling the winding highways and country roads of West Virginia, Kentucky, Ohio—

"Do we know each other?" Fox said.

She realized she was staring at him.

"I've met many people in my day," he said. "Are you one of them?"

She looked away.

Jason stood beside the editing console, pondering the blank screens and row of controls.

"Don't touch anything," she said.

He scowled at her, brow knotted, lips pressed into an angry line. It was the same face that had come for her behind the strip club, only it was darker now, stronger, more formidable.

"Hey, Jason," the blond kid said. "Sit down!" The blond kid rode beside Sam, sitting on the floor, long legs bent against his chest. An ugly stain blackened his shirt, dried blood from the shot she had inadvertently lobbed between his shoulders.

She noted the strong lines of his profile. He had been good looking in life. Now he was even more so, blue eyes almost glowing, skin smooth as marble.

Jason remained as before, staring at the console. Spattered gore still clung to his shoulder, a starburst of bone and brains. But his head was intact, on the outside at least. It was hard to say what was happening on the inside.

"Jason! Come on, man. Do as she says."

"Fuck you, Vinny."

"Do it, man."

Jason pushed back from the console, glared at Vinny, then sat on the floor beside the other collateral-damage boy, the one they called *R.D.* "Wasn't going to touch it anyway," Jason said. "Didn't even want to touch it." He turned to R.D. "The fuck you staring at?"

R.D. shrugged, said nothing.

"He listens to you," Sam said.

"Sometimes." Vinny met her gaze, held it. His eyes had that same look she'd noticed in the strip club, but warmer now, as if he were responding to a similar look from her. The moment lingered, neither one of them speaking, just looking until she turned toward the front of the van where Danny Love rode shotgun beside Kirill. "Hey, Danny!"

"What?"

"Get back here." She stood, moved toward the cab. "I'm taking your seat."

"We're almost there," Kirill said.

"Move it, Danny! Now!"

Danny got up.

She slid into his place, buckled in.

"Problem?" Kirill said.

"How much farther?"

Kirill hit the high beams, illuminating the rain-swept distance. Wipers raced, clearing the rain as fast as it fell, but through it she saw a patch of red, the reflective glare of a no-trespassing sign on the beams of a wooden bridge.

"Right there."

She hunkered forward, hands against the dash. Across the bridge, a narrow road curved among blowing trees, vanishing onto darkness. "Where's the house?"

"End of the drive." The bridge deck droned as he drove across. "Not quite a mile."

Almost there.

49

Something flashed on the lower bends of the drive.

Headlights?

Bird ran a hand along the fogging glass, then resigned himself to opening the window and peering out into the sheeting rain.

The lights advanced, vanished into a low bend among the trees . . . reappeared . . . disappeared . . . reappeared again.

In spite of the no-trespassing sign mounted on the bridge at the edge of the estate, some people still mistook the drive for a public road, not fully realizing their mistake until they reached the stone courtyard. Was that happening now, or was someone coming to see him?

The lights vanished once more, down into a shallow dip, then up again. It was a van, side panels painted with bold letters.

Pittsburgh News 6

It stopped in the courtyard.

The driver's door opened. A woman stepped out, small and cringing against the rain. She looked like a reporter, but there was something off about her. No umbrella or shoes, no crew.

He left his post and descended the tower stairs.

By the time he reached the second-floor hall, she was at the door, slapping the shutters. "Hello! Anyone home?"

He entered the vestibule, looked at her through the steel grill.

"Please!" She stepped back, hugging herself, shivering. "Can you help me?"

50

The face peering at Sam through the grate was the same one that had confronted her twice before—once in the convenience store in Windslow, then again as she lay dying at the base of the dynamited dam. The only thing different now was the slow, deliberate way his eyes stared at her, sized her up, took their time until finally the shutters unlatched and the man stepped out. He looked at the van, then back at her. "You by yourself?"

"Yes."

He looked her over again, then met her gaze. "Reporter?"

"Yeah, I—"

"Where's your crew?"

"There's no one. Just me."

He glanced at the courtyard, scanning it with the wary eyes of a man who sensed something was coming. So far, he didn't seem to think it was her.

"Please, mister." The rain fell over the portico, sheeting behind her, spattering her feet. She shivered, and it wasn't an act. She was beginning to feel cold and weak all over again. What did that mean? Did she need to eat?

He stepped out, one hand holding the steel shutter, the other wrapped around an assault rifle. She sized it up instantly, an AK-47 with a 30-round magazine. That complicated things.

"Mister?"

"Give me a second. I'm thinking."

He wore his sleeves rolled up, exposing lower arms that Kirill had once told her were tattooed with flames. And yet this man's skin was clean, unblemished—too perfect to be entirely human. Like her, he had been remade.

What now?

She couldn't touch him here, not with him blocking the door and holding a gun. He was already on edge. The pain of her touch would alert him, and she couldn't risk being shot. Not now that she was so close, and especially not now that her powers seemed to be fading again. Better to wait until they were inside, until he trusted her enough to put down the weapon.

He stepped back toward the door, but he didn't open it to invite her in. Instead, he closed the steel shutters and grabbed her arm. "Show me!"

He led her back into the rain and through the courtyard, his hand strong and warm against her skin as he pulled her to the van.

"What're you doing?" she said.

He grabbed the cargo door, unlatched it.

"I told you, there's no one—"

He pushed it open.

She stepped back.

He looked inside.

"I told you," she said. "It's just me!"

The cargo bay was clear, but he wasn't convinced. He looked toward the back. "That closet?" He gestured with the gun. "What's in there?"

"Nothing. Just . . . just cables and gear."

He climbed into the cargo bay, opened the closet, looked inside. It was just as she said. Some cables and gear. Mostly empty. "So where's your crew?"

She climbed into the van, getting out of the rain.

"Your crew," he said. "Where are they?"

"I told you. I don't—"

"No camera operator?"

"He's back in Windslow."

"You left your operator in Windslow?"

"Look, mister. We had trouble. Got separated. Jesus—" She let her voice hitch, reaching deep into her past to channel a tone of helpless confusion. "I came here for help!"

He closed the closet, turned to face her. "Sorry." He reached for her again, gentler this time, pulling her close, just as Kasdeja had when lifting her from the flood. She had liked that. In a strange way . . . a different way . . . she liked this too.

"I'm jumpy," he said. "It's not your fault."

She balled her fists, put her arms around him, eased her face to his shoulder. His smell was darker than Kasdeja's, primal, more immediate.

Did she like it? She wasn't sure. Maybe.

Rain hammered the van.

Maybe more than maybe.

He looked out at the thrashing trees, eyes still wary, studying the shadows. "I should get you inside."

"No." She made a token effort to push away. "This was a mistake." She stepped toward the cab. The keys were still in the ignition. "Sorry, mister. I think I'd better—"

"You can call me *Bird*."

"What?"

"Bird. As in *Free Bird*." There was something rote about the way he said it, as if it was a line he often used to introduce himself, perhaps when picking up women. "People call me *Bird*. How about you? You have a name?"

She hesitated. Had he ever heard Kirill talk about her? Better to play it safe. "Elle." It gave her chills to say it. It was the name her father had called her.

"All right, Elle. Let's try this again. We're both wet, cold, scared. We need to fix that. Agreed?"

"Yeah."

"So let's get you inside."

51

Wrists bound with the last of the nylon zips, Fox sat in the corner of a toolshed beside the Frieburg driveway. The others were in there too, most of them gathered around the kid they had found in the back of the van.

"You're not here now!" the kid said. "Go away! You're dead!" The kid sat on a 40-pound bag of mulch, knees drawn to his chest, hands covering his face. "Dead and gone!"

"Someone needs to shut him up," Fox said.

"You keep out of this," one of the others said. "He's my brother."

"Then you shut him up," Fox said. "He's making too much noise."

"Who's going to hear him?"

"I hear him."

"And I hear all of you!" This came from Kirill, standing by the shed's open door, looking out at the long driveway. "Next man who argues gets a kick in the head."

"But you're not here! You're dead! Dead and gone!"

Kirill looked around. "But not him. No kick in the head for the little *dolboeb*."

"What?" Dalton said.

"Not you. You're *Dolboeb*. He is just the little *dolboeb*."

"His name's Benjie!" the brother said.

"Yeah. OK. That's how you say it."

They had discovered Benjie in the rear compartment shortly after starting up the drive. His waking cries had given him away, and his discovery had caused quite a stir among the formerly plastic-wrapped boys, none of whom could understand how the kid had ended up in the closet of a news van. And if Benjie had an explanation, he wasn't sharing. He just ranted on and on, insisting that the boys weren't really there, that they were all *Gone! Dead and gone!*

It was on account of that ranting that Sam had stopped the van beside the toolshed, telling everyone but Danny to hide out and await word that she'd gotten inside the mansion. And now Danny was coming back, running through the rain, stopping at the shed's door. "She's inside!"

Kirill hefted his monster gun. "Let's go!"

"Hold up!" Dalton said. "What about these two?" He gestured toward Fox and Benjie.

"Benjie stays here," the brother said. "He'll be all right if we close the doors."

"You're all gone! Dead and gone!"

"And what about Fox?"

"I'll stay with Benjie," Fox said.

"No." Danny took some coiled rope from a hook on the wall. "You're going back in the van." He tied a slip knot, slung the loop over Fox's head, and pulled him out into the rain.

The others followed.

Benjie's brother tried shutting the door, but Kirill had broken the latch to get them inside. Now the door just swung open again, banging in the wind. The brother gave up and started along the drive.

Benjie remained behind, screaming in the darkness.

52

Axle watched the boy stop crawling and grab his chest.

Lightning flashed. The storm raged harder, changing in pitch, the thud of rain on vinyl siding giving way to the clang of iron shutters. He was waking up, being driven from his spirit quest by the same terrors that had made him forget what he had done beneath Yeyestani's trailer.

He willed himself to stay in the dream.

Keep watching!

The boy grabbed his shirt, pulling the fabric as something moved beneath it. The shirt seemed suddenly alive, pulsing as he tugged at the buttons. The shirt opened. Dark things spilled out. Three of them. Five. More.

The boy screamed.

Axle watched, seeing the details with spirit vision, noting the sunken nest that the boy had lain upon while burying the pieces of stone. The heat of his body had awakened them. They had crawled out, into his shirt, over the warmth of his skin.

The boy screamed and fled through the crawlspace, emerging into the howling rain. He ripped off his shirt. There were more of them, small black bodies with rounded heads. They were garter snakes, non-venomous, but the terror was in what they represented, in the unrealized portent of things to come . . . visions as yet unrealized.

The boy ran into the house, ripped off his clothes, and stood beneath a scalding shower until the water turned cold and leaden.

Axle watched it all, hovering close, wondering how knowing these things could possibly give him a second chance to save the world. What good did it do for the spirit to realize things that the mind refused to know? And even if the adult Axle remembered the details of this spirit dream, how could that change things that had already happened, mistakes that had already been made?

The boy remained in the shower a little longer, the cold seeping into his bones. Axle watched his face and wondered if this was when he had first imagined walking to the mine with Yeyestani. Or had that fantasy come later, as he lay dying in the pressboard shack? In any event, the boy turned off the water and stepped from the stall. His skin was gray, lips pale. He dried off, dressed, and then returned to the living room.

A can of Sprite stood on the coffee table. The boy picked it up, shook it. Liquid sloshed in the bottom. One sip left. He drank it before turning toward the sound of talk-radio voices that wafted from Yeyestani's bedroom. Did he want to go back in there? Did he have a choice? He followed the sound. She lay on her bed, curled on a mattress stained purple with her blood. Beside her, on a nightstand, lay a two-inch brick of shrink-wrapped bills, the old woman's life savings withdrawn from the Windslow branch of PNC Bank and left for him to start his body shop in the Bottoms.

53

T he foyer was dark, the only illumination coming from candlelight beyond an open archway.

Sam smelled food. "Were you eating?"

He locked the steel shutters, then the door. "Yeah. Hungry?" He stepped from the foyer. "Come on." He led her through a cavernous hall, walls rising two stories toward a glass-and-iron skylight, curved stairs ascending to a line of bedrooms. Only one door was closed. The demon master was in that room. She sensed it. Knew it. But Bird still had the gun. When he put it down, she'd make her move.

They entered a dining room, stood before an array of platters and bowls. *So much food!*

"It's just leftovers," he said.

"Looks good."

"What can I get you?"

She stepped to the table. The food would not only quell her chills, it would strengthen her touch, provide the reserve she needed to kill both servant and master.

He put down the gun, leaning it against the dining-room arch. "Let me help you." He reached for a plate.

"No." She picked up a curl of thinly sliced roast, pushed it into her mouth, turned away from him as the power hit. The taste was salty, bloody . . . primal. Heat spread through her chest and neck. Her heart raced.

"Guess you are hungry." He came up behind her.

She swallowed, wiped her mouth on the back of her hand, reached for some more.

His hand landed beside hers. "You eat like me," he said.

They each took a slice.

She turned toward him, watched his face as he ate, saw the bliss in his eyes. He had amazing eyes, like Kasdeja's, but darker.

She ate with him, sharing the rush.

Where's this going?

She wiped the juice from her chin, took some more, then took a napkin from the table to clean her fingers.

He did the same, watching her the way the blond kid had in the club . . . in the van.

"Feeling better?" He drew closer.

She smelled him again, then tasted him. Salty and warm. She hadn't seen the kiss coming, didn't have time to think about it. It was just there. Part of her wanted it. Another part recoiled. "No!" She balled her fists, pushing away.

He held on tighter.

She looked past him, toward the closed door at the end of the second-floor hall.

Bird's expression changed, questioning. Did he suspect something? Had she given herself away?

"Hey." She touched his face, gently at first, fingertips only. "I'm still soaked. Do you think—" She lowered her palm, pressed it to his cheek.

His skin crackled. "Ow!" He recoiled.

She leaped away, tried racing for the gun.

He grabbed her.

She pulled free and dove for the only weapon in reach, the candelabrum. She swung it full force against his head. The candles went flying.

He went down.

She grabbed the table. It was heavy, solid wood. She lifted it easily. Platters of food slid, falling to the floor as she upended everything and sent it crashing down on top of him. A china closet stood against one wall. Eight feet tall, oak and brass. She sprang, landed atop it, then leveraged herself against the wall until the whole thing toppled. She rode it down, leaping free as it landed across the table, slamming down between the lion-claw legs.

Bird roared, voice muffled beneath the weight. He was trapped now, leaving her free to find the master.

She dashed away, over the scattered candles, some still burning. The lace tablecloth was there too. She slipped on it, fell, rolled, and got back up without losing momentum. An instant later she was on the stairs, charging up, guided by Kasdeja's invisible hand.

She knew exactly where to go.

Axle found himself in the center of a large, uncluttered room, four-poster bed on one side, chest of drawers on the other. Kwetis faced him, standing with his back to a shuttered window. On the bed, rumpled sheets held the sweaty imprint of a dreamer who was no longer there.

I'm awake!

The dream was behind him, but its memory remained. And with it, possibilities rose. What if the guilt he had carried for nine years had been completely unfounded? The question swirled, filling him with a sense of relief that could be his if the dream was true.

But was it?

There was only one way to know. If he could not physically revisit the past, he could still return to Coals Hollow, crawl beneath the trailer, and dig for an artifact of memory that might prove the dream. If he found it, and if it was in the same condition he had dreamed it, dull and incapable of cutting, he would know that Yeyestani's death could not have been prevented, that he had not sat idly by while she took her life in that lonely corner of their single-wide home.

That much would be clear. But a question remained. How would that realization change what had already happened?

He needed time to sort that out, but already the waking world was intruding, more immediate concerns making themselves known as voices rose from downstairs.

"Your adversary," Kwetis said. "She's in the house."

Axle faced the closed door as the sound of fighting rose from below.

"Bird let her in," Kwetis said. "She'll deal with him. Then she'll come for you."

The house echoed with crashing china, shattering glass, building toward a concussive clap that shook the floor and walls.

"Bird?"

"No time to worry about him."

Another crash, louder than the first.

"Did you bring it with you?" Kwetis asked.

It was the same question he had been asked in the dream. This time, he understood. "You're talking about the memory."

"Did you bring it?"

Someone was climbing the stairs, coming on fast.

"I have to go to Coals Hollow."

"No time for that," Kwetis said. "First the present. Then the past."

The footsteps reached the hall.

Was there another way out?

Axle crossed to the shuttered window, threw it open. A line of trees thrashed in the wind, rain striking his face as he looked down along the wall.

"Running isn't an option," Kwetis said. "You need to face her."

Axle stepped back, passed through the shadow of a wing, grabbed a bedpost. "Can you help me?"

"If you let me. You're still skyborn, still the spirit master. And I still have the power of the earth and air."

Thunder roared.

"Join with me, Axle. We might have a chance." Kwetis stood before the window, wind whipping through him, the line of thrashing trees visible beyond the shadow of his wolfish head. Lightning flashed, distant at first, then cutting the night like a jagged blade, a serration of heat and light that expanded into a blast of spewing debris. It had struck one the trees, blowing it to mist . . . and now the mist was in the room, swirling, speaking with a voice of charged light: "We'll fight this one together."

The bedroom door flew open.

am stopped when she saw what waited inside. Flashing light and churning dust, spinning to form an image from deep in her past, primal and
frightening. She grabbed the doorframe, held on as the years of her adult
life vanished and she was a child once again, staring in terror.

It was a man with dark hair, darker eyes. His face was young and strong,
attractive in ways that went straight to her heart, filled it with fire. As a
young woman, on the cusp of adolescence, she had begun noticing boys,
wondering about them even as her mother had made a point of warning
her to keep a distance.

"Out of the heart come evil thoughts. Adulteries and fornications!"

And now here she was, staring at a man enveloped in a cloud. He was
strong, painfully handsome. And he was naked. But there was more.

The cloud coalesced, assuming the form of a creature with broad wings,
feral face, glowing eyes.

Lucifer!

She knew it was him. Believed it. She stumbled backward. It was neither
the image of the man nor that of the King of Evil that took her breath. It
was the two of them together, the realization that her mother had been right
. . . that evil and desire were connected . . . that the very demons she had
spent a lifetime fearing were one in the same.

Lucifer!

He had appeared to her before.

In her other life she had driven toward him in a speeding car, staying
her course as his wings shimmered like a heat mirage. She had plowed into
him, and he had vanished. But this time was different. This time the man
gave substance to the mirage, the two became one, and the shape of all her
fears leaped from the darkness and through the open door. And then, with
a crack of powerful wings, Lucifer grabbed her wrist and carried her out
over the balustrade.

Far below, the upended table and toppled china closet shifted and heaved. A hand emerged. Bird was pulling himself free, straining against hundreds of pounds of wood, brass, and broken china. His head appeared. He looked up, eyes flashing in the light of a spreading fire. The candles had ignited the tablecloth, burning close to Bird's face as he pulled himself free. He was there for a moment, then was gone as the Devil banked against a paneled wall, circling like a caged bat.

The skylight flashed.

The Devil changed course, wrenching her arm as he climbed through the atrium, veered along the mezzanine, and circled again—faster this time.

Bird came back into view, running through the hall, heading for the assault rifle.

He would shoot her if he got the chance.

"Kasdeja! Help me!"

Bird reached the gun, swinging it to his shoulder as the Devil accelerated upward, this time hurling past the mezzanine to throw himself against the skylight. Glass shattered, raining past her as he broke through into the flashing wind. Rain misted in the heat of his wings, vaporizing before it touched him, enveloping him in an aura of shimmering fog. He flew parallel to the roof, riding a cross-cutting wind that seemed to emanate from the charged particles of his wings, skimming a catwalk that ran along the roof's center—so close that Sam's feet almost collided with the rail.

She struggled, twisting around to see that they were headed for a utility ladder, metal rungs ascending to the conical roof of the east-wing tower. The Devil climbed slowly . . . too slowly. If she hit those rungs, she'd lose her legs, break them off at the knees.

"Kasdeja!"

An updraft caught them, sudden and strong. The Devil climbed. She missed the ladder by inches, but another obstacle waited atop the roof—an ancient television antenna shivering in the wind, tines threatening to impale her as she hurtled toward it. She kicked, wrenching her arm in the Devil's grip. The antenna came at her, then angled away as the Devil banked over the courtyard. The van was there, right where she'd left it. And her resurrected army was there too, returned from hiding, staring in wonder as she and the monster soared out above the trees.

And then came something that had to be a sign, an omen that told her Kasdeja was watching, still protecting her. It started as a glow among the clouds, a quickening flash that became a three-pronged bolt of lightning. One prong leaped to her left, coursing so close that she felt its heat. Another passed to her right, farther off but brighter. A third sliced the air directly behind the Devil, striking him between the wings and turning all that had been dark to blinding brilliance. The bolt poured over him, surged through his wings, around his body, then down his arm and onto her hand. No pain. No heat. Just a sense of power as the lightning passed through her, leaped from her toes, and continued its path to the ground.

The bolt hit a gnarled sycamore. The tree exploded, and she—renewed by the sign—raised her legs to kick the Devil's flanks.

He must have sensed what she was doing. He pulled hard at her wrist, tried swinging her out into the air. But it was too late. Her kicking feet rose higher, passed through the charged mist of his demon form, and closed over the naked flanks of the man beneath. Then, embracing him in a scissor hold, she reached up with her free hand—her left hand—and hurled it toward his chest. Again, the devil flesh yielded like so much fog. The hand passed through, slapping flat against his skin within.

Wings clenched, folded around her.

They dropped together, the charged wind swirling around her as the Devil wrenched her hand away, squeezed until she was sure he would shatter the bones. Then he opened his wings, broke their fall, carried her back into the storm. He had her by both wrists now, but it didn't matter. She had done it.

"Kasdeja!"

The Devil carried her out above the trees.

"I did it! We—"

The Devil barrel rolled, swinging her in front of him, a dance in the air. She spread her fingers.

Pull me closer! Let me rake your eyes!

His eyes brightened, speaking with light. "Pray for me!" He slapped her hands together, palm to palm.

A jolt went through her, coursing out one hand, into the other.

Kasdeja's warning came back to her.

No folded hands for you, Samuelle. Good and evil must be kept apart.

But now those hands were together, the currents cycling, good into evil . . . evil into good.

And she couldn't pull them apart!

The Devil's eyes flashed once more, brighter, louder. "Pray for all of us!"

Then he snapped his wings, changed course, and flung her into the trees.

itting in the van, Fox saw the woman fall from the sky and vanish beyond the courtyard. He didn't see what had dropped her. Roped to the
floor-bolted chair, he could see only what lay framed by the open cargo
door and rain-smeared windshield.

Beyond the door, Kirill stood with his resurrected army. He looked even
bigger than before, forehead bulging with horn-like ridges, jacket splitting
at the shoulders as he aimed his monster revolver at the steel doors of Bird's
fortress. A puff of moisture left the barrel. There was no report, no flame,
nothing like you'd get from a proper gun. Instead, the delayed blast came
from the target, the steel shutters igniting with a flash of white heat as the
mortar hit.

Kirill shot again, then again, creating a smoking entrance into the house.

The tall kid started toward it.

The others followed, passing out of sight beyond the edge of the cargo
door.

Kirill held back a moment, lowered his monster gun, then advanced like
an upright bull.

Fox kicked against the floor, swiveling the chair to watch the progress
through the windshield. The tall kid was still in the lead, running toward
the blasted shutters. The metal glowed, molten red and smoking in the rain.
Fox wondered if the tall kid was going to get through without burning
himself. But the kid never got the chance to try. As he neared the steps, a
pencil-thin ray leaped down from the tower, struck him in the head.

ThaaaaCCCK!

The kid somersaulted, trailing red mist as a second ray hit the smaller
kid running behind him.

ThaaaaCCCK!

The others scattered, leaping away as more shots rained down, rapid fire
now, full auto. It looked like tracer rounds, bright red and machine straight.

It fell everywhere, shattering the pavement stones before catching Benjie's brother, cutting him to ribbons near a line of hedges.

The others dove for cover, onto the stone steps to huddle beneath the portico arch. Just three of them now—Danny, Dalton, and Kirill.

The tracer fire stopped.

Kirill rocked his head as if working out a kink, then lumbered back onto the steps. He raised his gun. The barrel puffed. The top of the tower exploded in a blast of stone, glass, and sizzling light.

Debris landed atop the van, bounced off to crash against the courtyard. Some of it sounded heavy enough to breach the roof and smash Fox like a hog-tied bug. He would have covered his head if he could. Would have taken cover beneath the editing bay if he hadn't been bound to the chair with knots that got tighter when he pulled. Nowhere to run. Nothing to do but stay in his seat and watch the show.

Up on the porch, Danny Love slipped through the hole in the smoking shutters.

Dalton started to follow, ducked down, then drew back.

Kirill pushed him. "Go!"

Dalton stumbled, shirt snagging on the hot iron.

"Inside!" Kirill pushed him again, all the way through this time. Then he just stood there, staring at the hole, waiting for something. Nothing happened. "Hey!" He drove his fist against the glowing iron, struck it once, then shook his hand as if burned. "Hey, *Dolboeb.* Open this thing!"

Fox could only imagine what might happen if Kirill started discharging that mortar launcher in the house. He didn't really want to be around for that.

The van's key was still in the ignition. Fox could drive away if it weren't for the ropes. But Danny had tied him good. Three knots, one at his wrists, a second around his booted ankles, and a third securing the whole shebang to the base of the chair. He tried giving his hands another pull, slower this time, as if he might coax his wrist free without tightening the knot. But he stopped when he realized he was being watched.

Something crouched at the edge of the courtyard. He glimpsed it through the shadows, then got a better look as it leaped onto the stones, bounded nearer, and climbed through the cargo door. It was the monster woman they'd left stranded on Windslow Road, the one who had been driving with a manchild stashed in her cargo hold. She glanced around, looking to see if Fox was alone in the van.

"He's not here," Fox said.

She looked angry enough to kill.

"He's down—"

"I know where he is. Screaming in a tool shed!" She looked toward the cab.

"The keys are there," Fox said.

She moved toward him.

"A terrible thing," he said. "What they did—stealing your van, leaving your boy in the middle of—"

"Not my boy!"

"No?" He was out of his element here, lacking the proper terminology to identify young men who were locked up in closets and driven around like spare tires. But this was a time for finding common ground, not quibbling over differences. "Whatever the case, I'm not your enemy," he said. "I'm as much a victim—"

"I want you gone!"

"Fine. No argument there."

She turned his chair to get at the knots. She freed his ankles, then his hands, pulling everything loose until there was nothing holding him but the nylon zip around his wrists. Was she going to help him with that too?

"Get out!" she said.

Apparently not.

"Now!"

He hobbled down from the van, hands still crossed against his back. He hurried through the courtyard and pushed in among the shrubs. The wind was less intense there, and as he looked back at the house, he got his first clear view of the top of the tower. Part of the conical roof had been blasted away. Smoke swirled like a mini cyclone. Whoever had been up there was certainly dead . . . as wasted as the three dead-again bodies bleeding on the courtyard stones.

Fox noted these things as the van started up, turned around, and left the scene.

Then, slowly at first, one of the bodies started moving. It was the tall kid, blond, good looking. He drew his arm across the bloody stones, raised his head, and looked toward the blasted shutters.

Fox scuttled into the woods, hobbling with hands still lashed across his back, putting distance between himself and the rising dead.

Clearly, the final hour was at hand.

57

Kwetis returned to the mansion, riding the spirit wind low over the broken skylight. He did not try flying back through it. The broken mullions and glass panes were angled outward, jutting like giant teeth in the buffeting currents. He might pass through them easily enough in spirit form, but now—fused to the flesh of a wounded man, he needed a safer entrance.

And he needed to reach it soon.

The human part of him was dying.

The spirit wind failed as he soared low over the catwalk, reached the end of the roof, cleared the eaves. The open shutters of the guest room raced toward him. Curtains blew through the casement. He dropped fast, wings crumbling now, falling rather than flying. He reached for the sill, missed it, caught himself on a mortared seam five feet below the window. His wound burned hotter as he clung to the stones, caught his breath, then climbed.

Rain pelted him. His wings grew heavy. His wolf-like head and feathered shoulders deliquesced and poured away. By the time he grabbed the windowsill, his nightflyer form was running down his skin and onto the stones, the residue of spirt powers he no longer controlled.

He pulled himself up between the blowing curtains, then stopped when pain flared in his shoulder. He dangled, legs hanging in the wind, head inside and staring at the darkened room.

Kwetis was already inside, his spirit form pressed like a shadow against a paneled wall.

"Help me!" Axle said.

"I have."

"I'm going to fall."

"That's one way to end it."

Axle screamed. No words. Just rage.

"That's the spirit," Kwetis said. "Now turn it into action. Get in here."

"I didn't ask for this."

"Don't be so sure about that. Now climb."

He gripped the sill, pulling with his good arm, bringing himself forward until his chest was all the way in. He pushed, tumbled, landed in a spreading puddle on the hardwood floor. Then he tried standing, made it as far as one knee.

"Did you bring it with you?" Kwetis asked.

"Yes," he said. "Still have it." But it was only a memory. He needed to see it, make sure it was real. "Coals Hollow," he said. "Yeyestani's trailer. I need to go there." He pulled himself up on the bed, tried walking, managed two steps before his legs gave out. He caught himself on a bureau, his reflection staring back at him from a beveled mirror.

"I dreamed this?" He steadied himself, standing taller, hands still gripping the bureau. "But it wasn't me in the mirror. It was Bird. Is that important?"

"You tell me."

His reflection stared back, naked and shivering, the hand-sized wound smoldering on his chest. "How long do I have?"

"Hard to say." Kwetis faded as he spoke. "You were skyborn. That will buy you time."

Axle opened one of the bureau drawers. Clothes lay inside. He took a pair of jeans, held them to his waist. The legs were too long, but they would do. He pulled them on, rolled the cuffs, then rummaged for a belt as new sounds rose from downstairs.

"More adversaries," Kwetis said. "Not a death hand among them, but they can kill you all the same."

Axle found a belt, pulled it through the loops, drew it tight. He was feeling stronger now, getting a second wind. But how long would it last? "What about Bird?" he asked. "Is he all right?"

Kwetis didn't answer.

The dream spirit was gone.

Voices rose from downstairs. People talking, moving in the darkness. He opened the bedroom door, peered across the mezzanine rail, down toward the shadows below.

58

Smoke filled the mansion's main hall. Some of it rising from a burning cloth, the rest wafting in from the blasted iron shutters. All of it was dispersing, drawn by the draft from the shattered skylight.

Dalton scanned a line of rooms beyond a second-floor balustrade as Danny Love came up beside him. "See anything?"

"No."

Kirill pushed past them, raised his monster gun, fired into the ceiling. The house shook. Plaster fell. Fire spread across the beams, illuminating the hall, mezzanine, and a dining room of upended furniture and spilled food.

"No monster." Kirill lowered his gun.

"But it flew back here." Dalton stepped toward the stairs, looking up along the line of open rooms, one closed door. "And there were two, right? That's what Sam said. Master and servant."

Kirill crossed to the edge of the trashed dining room. "She killed them."

"We don't know that."

"She killed the demon. Touched it right on its tit." Kirill put a hand to his chest, illustrating. "Probably dead by now."

Dalton wasn't convinced. "You two need to look around."

"What about you?" Danny said.

"I'll go outside, look for Sam."

Kirill picked a piece of meat off the floor, stuffed it in his mouth. "This is good beef." He took another.

Outside, an engine rumbled. Headlights came on, shining through the blasted shutters, panning across the walls.

Dalton hurried toward the foyer.

Someone was driving away, taillights spilling red across the courtyard. Sam? It had to be Sam. It was the only explanation.

She's finished here. She killed the servant . . . killed the master . . . now she's leaving.

That had to be it. Who else could be driving? Not Fox. Danny had tied him good, slipknots over nylon ties. And the others? The three guys who had been cut down by tracer fire from the tower? Dalton scanned the courtyard, verifying that the bodies were still there. They were. But one of them was up, kneeling in the rain, staring at the house. It was the tall one. What was his name? Vinny?

"Jesus!" Dalton steadied himself on the foyer wall. The kid looked like shit, slipping on stones as he rose to his feet, staggering like a drunk. He had a big hole in the side of his head, bubbling in the rain, percolating from within, healing. And now the small guy was getting up too, lifting a half-gone face from the stones. Like Sam, they evidently had the power to heal.

Dalton pushed into the rain.

Vinny seemed to recognize him. He whined, shrill and breathy, reaching out. "Daal!" He grabbed Dalton's shoulder, fell against him.

"Need to get you inside."

"Daal." His broken head made a popping sound, healing as the rain washed blood from his hair and shoulder.

The other kid cried out. No words, just sounds spilling from a broken jaw. He was in worse shape than Vinny, but not nearly as bad as the kid who had been cut down by automatic fire. That last kid remained facedown in a spreading pool of black rain, apparently too far gone for resurrection.

Dalton led Vinny and R.D. out of the rain and into the trashed dining room where Kirill and Danny Love were already building their strength by chowing down. Danny sat cross legged on a toppled china closet, a tureen of macaroni salad between his knees. He ate with his hands, smearing his face and dripping mayonnaise on Fox's shirt. His hands seemed bigger than before, with the suggestion of claws curling from his fingers. And his face looked fuller, jaw swelling as he chewed.

He's still changing!

Kirill gnawed a meaty bone, gripping it by the shank. He turned as Dalton helped the resurrected boys into the room. He didn't stop eating. Didn't hold up the bone, wave it and say: "This is good shit, *Dolboeb*." He just glared like a feeding lion, warning Dalton and the boys away. *Find your own. This is mine!* As with Danny Love, Kirill's gradual bulking up had accelerated. He now had shoulders like an ape, head like a horned lion.

Dalton left Vinny and R.D. in a corner with half a pie and a bowl of pasta. Then he returned to the hall.

The rafters still smoldered, glowing in the updraft, illuminating the second floor. Balustrade rails threw shadows across open doors. And one of those shadows seemed to be moving, creeping low along the mezzanine floor. A trick of the light? Or was someone up there?

He walked toward the stairs, started up, then stopped when something thumped in the foyer. He looked back, gripped the rail, and almost heaved as a mass of tortured flesh entered the hall.

The third kid, the one who had been ripped to ribbons by automatic fire, was coming to dinner.

59

ars ringing, eyes burning from grit and the garlic stink of spent ordnance, Bird woke on the tower stairs. A steady draft blew from the second floor, escaping through a steaming hole in the conical roof. He remembered firing wildly out the window, emptying the magazine before Kirill emerged from beneath the portico and took aim with his monster gun. Bird had run for the stairs then, and that was all he remembered . . . until now.

He sat back, steadying himself through a rush of dizzying pain. His face was wet, smeared with blood, burning from where the woman had touched his cheek. The touch had taken his powers, made him mortal again.

And now something was coming toward him, slipping into the arch at the base of the tower stairs.

He raised the empty gun, bluffing. "Hold it, you son of a—"

"Bird?"

"Axle?"

"Yeah."

Bird lowered the gun. "Jesus, Axle. What—"

Axle hunkered down, looked back the way he'd come. "There's a guy on the stairs. I think he saw me. I think—"

"Hey!" A voice roared from below. "Hey, goddamnit! Get out here!"

Bird held his breath, waited.

"Now, dammit!"

Axle hunkered down, peering along the stairs as footsteps moved through the first-floor hall. "He's not talking to us," Axle said. "He's calling to the adversaries."

"How many?" Bird said.

"Two. No, there's more. And there is something else. Can't tell what it is. Can't . . . Jesus! It's screwed up, whatever it is." He remained by the arch a moment longer, not saying anything, just looking while more sounds filled the hall. Then he drew back, met Bird's gaze.

Bird sized him up, noting how Axle looked smaller than before. No longer skyborn. Just a man in a pair of over-sized jeans. A glowing wound festered beneath his right shoulder. He looked broken, defeated—possibly dying.

Bird sat on one of the steps, set the Kalashnikov across his knees. "That woman, Axle. The adversary. Did she touch you?"

"Yeah."

"You warm?" Bird said.

"Burning up."

Bird coughed, spit on the stones. "She got me too."

"So we're mortal again."

"Dying." Bird wiped his mouth. "We're both dying."

"But I got her," Axle said. "Threw her into the woods."

"I saw," Bird said. "You were Kwetis."

"Yeah."

"Any chance you can do that again?"

"What? Turn into Kwetis? Carry the rest of our adversaries through the skylight?" He cocked his head toward the commotion near the bottom of the stairs. "I don't think so. Even if I still had my skyborn powers, one of those guys has some kind of big-ass gun. Don't think I want to mess with something like that."

"Mortar launcher," Bird said. "The guy's Kirill. At least, I think that's who it is."

"Your friend?"

"Not anymore, and you and me are pretty much screwed unless you did what you needed to do."

Axle moved to the other side of the arch, still trying to see.

"So did you?" Bird said. "Did you find what you were—"

"I think so."

"And?"

Axle pulled back from the arch. "I need to go to Coals Hollow. I think maybe—" His eyes widened. "What the hell?" He moved closer, staring at the thing around Bird's neck. "Where'd you get that?"

"This birdstone?"

"Looks like a knife handle."

Bird slipped it off. Part of the birdstone had broken away, probably when he'd fallen on the stairs. Only the elongated body and upturned head of the bird remained. It looked a bit like a knife handle, but only when one dismissed the finer details, etched lines suggesting wings, feathers, and beak. "Okwe elders used them as legacy gifts." He handed it to Axle. "I didn't get mine from an elder. Had to buy my own."

Axle turned it over in his hand. "Was it sharp?"

"You mean the tail? The part that's missing?"

"Could it cut?"

"You mean like a knife?"

"It wasn't, was it?" Axle said. "Not like a knife at all."

"Not exactly. Shaped like one, maybe. But not—"

Axle handed it back to Bird. "I need to get back there."

"Coals Hollow?"

"I don't know how long I have, but I need to get there."

"You think it'll set things right?"

"For me, it will."

"But what about the bigger picture?"

"Not sure there is one of those." Axle looked back toward the bottom of the tower stairs.

The light from the fire in the hall seemed dimmer than before. Perhaps it was going out. Or maybe it was Bird's eyes, the final vestiges of his spirit senses failing as he sat in the stairwell listening to Axle talk about things he needed to do.

The voices that had been shouting at the bottom of the stairs seemed farther away now. Bird wondered if they were in the dining room, eating, getting stronger before launching their attack.

"Maybe you should make a run for it." Bird raised the Kalashnikov. "I can maybe hold them off if you get to the door, buy you a few extra seconds."

"Bet you can do better than that. You're a good shot. I know that from experience."

"Yeah. I'm good enough," Bird said. "Problem is, I'm out of ammo. Best I can do is bluff, shout, and get in the way."

Axle crept back to the arch.

"You going for it?" Bird asked. "Making a run?"

"Only if the way is clear. A few extra seconds won't help if they catch me on the stairs."

Bird crept beside him.

Together, they peered down through the fire-lit hall.

The thing that Dalton saw slithering in from the foyer looked less like a man than a piece of large roadkill. A bear, perhaps. One that had been hit hard enough to break its back, fracture its hips, open its belly. It didn't have much face left either. Just an eye, part of a nose. No jaw.

Its clothes were shredded but still intact enough to hold some of it together as it crawled over the threshold and onto the parquet floor of the main hall.

"Hey!" Dalton called toward the dining room arch. "Hey, goddamnit! Get out here!"

Danny Love peered out. At least, the clothes suggested it was Danny Love. The face had changed, more grotesque than before.

"Now, dammit!"

Danny Love lumbered out, followed by an equally disfigured Kirill.

They hauled the thing that had been Jason into the dining room, pulling it by the arms and leaving a dark trail on the polished wood. Then they helped it eat, liquids mostly. They started with juice, pouring into the hole that they assumed was a throat. It choked, coughed some of it back up before they got the hang of it. Then they tried some room-temperature soup, getting noodles everywhere before trying some two-percent milk that Danny Love found in the fridge. And all the while the thing's body bubbled and oozed, realigning into a functional shape that didn't look much of anything like the human it had once been.

The others were only marginally better, with each developing features that seemed to channel his inner monster. It was enough to keep Dalton from eating. So he stood by, watching from the dining room arch, keeping an eye on the mezzanine. He was pretty sure he'd seen movement earlier, but he wasn't about to go up there alone. Actually, he wasn't sure he wanted to go up there at all.

"Hey, *Dolboeb!* You still think the demons are up there?" Kirill spoke in a low drone, words reverberating in the cavities of an oversize head. "Master and servant?"

"I don't know. Don't know what I think anymore."

I see devils, what do you see?

"But you saw something."

"Yeah. On the mezzanine, heading for that stone arch. It might lead to the tower."

Kirill wiped his hands on what remained of his Armani jacket. Seams popped with the movement of his shoulders, then split wide as he reached for the monster gun. "Enough eating." He belched. "We're ready." He started for the door and roared at the others to follow.

Dalton held back, let them pass, then tried heading for the foyer and out into the night. That was his intention, anyway. But his body had other plans.

He climbed the stairs.

61

Crouching behind Axle in the tower stairwell, Bird looked down the mansion's main staircase to see a band of monsters coming toward them. "Shit!" Bird drew back. "What now?"

Axle kept looking, hair blowing in the updraft.

"Any ideas, Axle?"

"Yeah." He turned, hurried past Bird. "This way." He started up the stairs.

"It's a dead end, Axle!"

Axle kept climbing.

Bird returned to the arch for another look. The massing shadows were now halfway up the stairs. No way out. He grabbed his empty gun and followed Axle, catching up with him at the top of the tower. A quarter of the chamber was open to the sky, wall and ceiling blasted away. Rain sheeted in, hammering the stones.

Axle leaned into the wind, looking up at the break in the ceiling. "Lift me up," he said.

"What?"

"I need to get to the roof."

"You going to fly?"

The adversaries kept coming, voices louder, closer.

"Trust me, Bird. Get me up there."

Bird put down the empty gun, made a stirrup with his hands. "Hope you know what you're doing."

Axle stepped up, grabbed the broken ceiling, pulled himself through.

A moment later, the adversaries entered the chamber.

Bird didn't reach for the gun; instead, he backed up, making sure they kept their backs to the north window where Axle was already descending the ladder, scuttling down to the catwalk that ran along the center of the roof. Of course! Axle had known the walkway was there. He'd flown over it as Kwetis, and now he was moving back along it, past the shattered skylight, heading toward a second utility ladder that led down to the patio roof. From there it would be another eight-foot descent to the ground. Beyond that, Bird had no idea what Axle had in mind. He only hoped he would make it . . . do whatever it was he had to do.

The adversaries kept advancing, out of the shadows and into the sheeting light of the storm. The thing that had been Kirill was in the lead, still carrying the giant revolver. Surely he wouldn't fire it here. Discharged at close range, a round from the launcher would just bounce around the chamber until it went off, releasing an explosion that might set off all the rounds in the revolving cylinder. There'd be nothing left then. No monster boys. No tower. No Bird. They'd all be toast. Kirill had to know that . . . or at least he must have known it when he was human. It was hard to tell exactly what the monster version knew, what it was thinking.

"The other one!" Kirill's voice boomed, reverberating from the stone walls as he jabbed the 40mm barrel at Bird's chest. "The demon master? Where is he?"

Demon master? If anyone looked the part, it was Kirill, with a curved horn above each eye and skin lined with necrotic veins. The guy to his left looked even uglier, like a weasel on steroids and Botox. He also looked familiar. Danny Love? Jesus!

But the others were worse. A tall kid with stiletto fingers, a smaller one who looked like ten miles of bad road, and a third who resembled a leaking garbage bag. What a freak show!

But there was one exception, a broad-shouldered man with bronze skin and frightened eyes. He stood apart from the others, one foot in the wind-swept room, the other inside the arch that led to the stairs. He wore a T-shirt, sweat pants, and an uneasy expression that suggested he'd just as soon run for the hills. Bird had no idea who he was . . . or who he had been.

"Hey, Bird!" Kirill said. "Where's your master?"

Bird's hair whipped in the wind. But the wind didn't cool him. The rain seemed to sizzle on his skin. "Hot in here, eh, Kirill?"

"No. Not hot. Cold as hell. Where is he?"

"I don't know who you're talking about." Bird fingered the wound on his jaw. His hand glowed, brightening as he brought it to his face, dimming as he pulled it away.

"Hey!" Danny Love said. "He's glowing! Like Boone and Prutko."

Bird raised his hand again. The glow returned, reflecting from his face.

"Boone and Prutko?" Kirill said. "What about them?"

Danny never got the chance to answer.

62

A utility ladder ran along the north wall, slicked with rain, bolted to the stones. Axle climbed down, reached the patio roof, and dropped to a flight of concrete steps that descended to an in-ground pool. He glimpsed its surface through the rain, then saw it again in daylight clarity as the mansion's east tower exploded, a starburst of brilliant white. Debris rose with it, chunks of stone and metal that arced against the clouds, lost altitude, flew toward him.

He dove into the pool, swam to the bottom as debris rained down. The water hissed. He surfaced at the far end to find the deck strewn with metal and stone. The metal glowed, sizzling on the pavement, misting in the rain.

A low wall stood behind a line of deck chairs. He climbed it, paused at the top. The other side was dark. He couldn't see the ground, and when he dropped, the fall was twice the distance of the climb up. He landed hard, tumbled along sloping grass until the ground leveled out. His pain was worse now—chest throbbing, head pounding, right arm tingling with terrible heat. He got up, fell to his knees, tried again. This time he found his balance and pushed on.

The terrain changed, manicured lawn giving way to stones and jaggers as he neared the shoulder of Windslow Road. The wind was stronger here, blowing in a wide spiral toward a column of black mist and flashing lightning. The column widened above the trees, spreading into a racing wheel that covered the sky. Roadside debris flew toward it—branches and leaves tumbling in the air. Sometimes the pieces struck him. He seldom saw them coming. They attacked out of nowhere. He covered his head, hands folded across his crown, elbows extended like blinders to protect his eyes. It didn't help. The pieces kept coming, pummeling harder until something struck like a fist at the back of his head.

The pavement rushed up, and the next thing he knew he was on his knees, mouth filling with blood, wounded chest reflecting against the wet asphalt.

"Giving up?"

The voice seemed to come from his left. But there was nothing there, only darkness, sheeting rain, swirling debris.

"Over here!"

The voice came from beyond the trees, from the direction of Coals Hollow.

The trailer park was calling to him.

63

Sam woke to find the east tower burning beyond the trees. Fox sat beside her, face bright with reflected fire. She stirred, tried getting up, made it to one knee, then dropped back to the ground. Her hands were pressed together, cemented by crackling pain, as if current were passing from one palm to the other, cycling through her in a searing loop. She rolled onto her back. "Help me!"

"Are you praying, sister?" Fox's hair hugged his head like a helmet. His T-shirt and boxers were soaked to the skin. He hunched over her, backlit by the burning tower. She couldn't see his face, only his outline, dark against the aura of flame. But he seemed to be amused. She heard it in his voice. "It's the last resort of the unbeliever," he said. "When all else fails, turn to God. I know that from experience."

She rolled to her side, drew up her legs to kneel in the coursing rain.

"That's right, sister. I can't do it, but you can. Kneel and pray."

She reared back, shoulders clenched, body bent into a sopping S. She tried standing. No good. Kneeling was as far as she could go. And the pain was getting worse, a deep aching heat permeating her bones. And where was Kasdeja? Why wasn't he helping?

"I'd pray with you if I could, sister. I'm just a little tied up at the moment, if you see what I mean."

"Stay away." If she could free her hands, she would strangle him. That would be the first thing.

"Prayer might actually help, you know. I never knew it until today. But this has been a day of visions . . . of revelations. A day of seeing things I never believed."

"Never believed?"

"You heard me."

"You were a preacher," she said. She wondered at the coincidence, their paths crossing then and now. Once at a fire-hall revival, now here.

"I've never been anything more than a mercenary," he said. "Never really believed in anything . . . until today. Today I saw the signs. Too late to make a difference, but I saw them just the same."

A spasm shot through her. She cramped, bent forward. "*Ahhhhhhhhgh!*"

"Your hands," he said. "What's happening to your hands?"

They were glowing now, pink light outlining the shadows of her bones, the pain becoming a vast and powerful agony. Perhaps if she had eaten more, built up her strength as Kasdeja had advised, maybe then she could have pulled them apart. Or maybe if she had raised an army of seven rather than six, or charged the Devil instead of letting him charge at her . . . maybe then things would have turned out better. But none of that mattered. It was over, and her soul was burning. Rain struck her face. But it didn't cool.

"I saw you preach when I was a kid."

"That a fact?"

"You preached the flood."

"Really?" He looked up at the rain. "That can't be coincidence."

But she had her doubts. They burned within her, taking shape as the fiery glow spread to her wrists. Kasdeja wasn't coming. She had given him what he wanted, and now it was over. "They play with us," she said. The words tasted like arcing current. "We're nothing to them. They're out for themselves."

"Who?"

"The angels. They're just like us."

"We can't judge them."

"But they are. Just like us. Like me. Like you."

"You don't know me, sister."

"But I do! I know you. *I know your works!*" Her breath was so hot that it seemed to glow, spilling from her mouth like forked flame. When she spoke again, it was with her mother's voice, fire from the past: "*I know your works . . . and you—*" She coughed, doubled over. Her skin glowed, fanning in rays through her water-heavy clothes.

Fox got up. He evidently knew the quote, knew where this encounter was going. He tried hurrying away, wrists crossed against his back.

She called after him, voice igniting as her heat expanded: "*I know your works, and you . . . you are dead!*"

Heat exploded through her skin, filling the forest with a moment of cosmic clarity. A vision in which nothing was revealed . . . and *no thing* was the answer.

64

Axle followed a flooded easement down to the hardscrabble neighborhood of his youth.

Coals Hollow.

The air seemed clearer here. No flying debris. Nothing but sheeting rain, as if all the loose pieces of surrounding landscape had been gathered up and swept away. The trees trembled, but for now they remained rooted, standing their ground as he splashed through a flood of runoff and emerged into the eastern end of the trailer court.

Mobile homes lined the lot, frames groaning in the wind. He walked past them, coming to a trembling single-wide that looked smaller than he remembered. There were new curtains in the windows, an upended tricycle beneath the porch, painted rocks in a flooded garden.

The voice that had called to him had come from here, but he stood alone, nothing but the howling storm, shifting trees, creaking trailers. The ground was moving too, gravel shifting in the wind, grinding beneath his bare feet.

When the voice spoke again, it seemed to come from everywhere at once: "Looking for something?"

Axle turned in place. "Where are you?"

"Where are *you*?" it replied, voice blending with the sound of shifting gravel. "Where are you now, *Akeo*?"

"Yeyestani?"

"A piece of her." The gravel was moving faster now, rolling in a wide clockwise arc that rose like a whirlwind of stone, spinning into the semblance of a face. Hollow eyes, pitted cheeks, mouth like an open trench. "Where are you, Akeo? Where is your body when you dream?"

"But I'm not dreaming."

"It's all dream, Akeo. Remember what I told you? Long ago? Memory is spirit, and spirit is dream—past and future, one moment."

Wind tugged the wicker skirting that covered the crawlspace beneath Yeyestani's old trailer, part of it giving away, curling back, bending.

"You think it's still there, Akeo?"

"The birdstone?"

"The knife."

"It's not a knife," he said.

"You need to prove that."

"I saw it."

"But only in your dream."

"But dream is memory," he said.

"Prove it!"

The face rose higher, resting now on gravel mounds that moved like rolling shoulders.

"What are you?" Axle said.

Open wounds lined the face—wide, deep, and dark. Yet something about them suggested they were as old as the stones, ancient wounds that had never healed.

"What are you?" He shouted it this time.

Its expression changed. It had no lips, yet it seemed to smile as it returned the question: "What are *you*?"

The wind blew harder, coursing along the gravel, hammering the trailers. Down the street, a mailbox flew from its post, tumbled past, banged twice against the stones, then flew into the air.

"What are you?" it asked again, louder, shouting with a roar like thunder. "*Why* are you?" It rose higher, looking down over a pair of gravel berms, piled atop the other like a pair of crossed arms. "*Why* are you here, Akeo?"

"To set things right, give the earth another chance."

"And what if it all happens again? Another failure. On and on. An endless cycle. What then?"

"But we have a plan, right? That's why I'm here . . . so we can start over."

"No. We never start over. Not completely. The deepest wounds always remain. And the next time, our adversaries will have the upper hand. They'll strike first . . . and fast."

"How fast?"

"For you? Hard to say. Months maybe. Maybe years. But for us it will be an instant."

"But we have a plan, right? A better plan. Same path, different fork?"

"We'll salvage what we can."

"And me? How much will I remember?"

"Not much. Maybe a few things, the semblance of dreams."

The wind changed, shifting violently. Down the street, a trailer broke free from its foundation, rose up like a sinking ship, and shattered in the wind. The debris raced toward them—gutters, shingles, wooden beams, aluminum panels spinning like blades. The giant head leaned left, gravel falling from its brow, covering the face in a slide of stones as it came between Axle and the shattering trailer. The pieces struck hard, crashing into the creature's back. The head trembled but held, protecting Axle as more trailers shattered. The head came toward him. It was featureless now, spreading into a protective wall. Then it collapsed to reveal a nearly empty courtyard, all trailers swept away except the one beside him, the one covering the key to his past and future. The wicker skirting broke, sailed away.

Rain swirled, making shapes in the wind. For a moment Axle saw the ghost of a boy dropping to his hands beside the trailer, crawling beneath it.

All around him, gravel rumbled, speaking with the voice of settling stones. "Follow the memory, Akeo."

He pushed through the howling wind, got down on his knees and pulled himself through the break in the skirting. Then he continued on. There were no snakes this time. The harmless garters that had frightened him nine years earlier were gone. Only their papery skins remained, curled and lifeless. The old terrors had moved on.

He reached the vertical pipe and started digging. The earth was soft, full of eyeless things that must have sensed his presence, boneless lives with no understanding of the world beyond dirt and darkness, creatures for whom a man's digging hand was at once destructive and unknowable. If worms had the power of reason, what would they know? What names would they give to the force of a digging man? What stories would they tell, and would any of those tales come close to envisioning the truth?

The earth glowed as he dug, reflecting the light that blazed from his skin, burning with heat that hissed and sputtered against the dampness.

The pieces of polished stone that he had buried long ago were still there, half an arm's length down, visible in the brightness of his wound. He reached in, felt the dull contours of the piece he had taken for a blade. He was sure of it now. It wasn't a knife.

Kwetis said nothing of cutting!

It was merely a length of carved stone, the stylized likeness of a bird that she had made shortly before her death. Perhaps she had intended to give it to him. A legacy gift to go with his modest inheritance. He still wasn't sure.

Someday you'll need to know the things I show you tonight.

He carried the birdstone back into the storm. His whole body glowed, turning the rain to jewels as it fell around him, undimmed by bolts of flashing lightning. His pain was brighter too, searing his chest.

He rose to his knees.

The air screamed, reverberating with shifting metal, wood, and vinyl as his childhood home rose up, shattered, and blew away.

A window box flew past him. Then a screen, tumbling so fast it seemed to change shape in the air. And now the gravel was moving again, stones rolling in wide arcs. And he was at the center, holding his ground while the funnel cloud hurtled toward him from Windslow Mine, plowing a course through the trees, screaming with a voice like a thousand freight trains.

He raised his arms. The wind was all around him now, cooling his burning flesh as it drew his glowing aura into a pair of shimmering wings.

The ground fell away, opening into a whirling sinkhole. But he didn't fall. Instead, he hovered, suspended in the contending winds until one grabbed hold and hurled him into the sky, through a region of spinning darkness that swirled with a million possibilities, a billion potential dreams, a whirlwind of infinite futures—all rising from this moment of loss and discovery.

65

Axle passed through darkness, then upward into a column of rushing air that flung him high above a wind-sheared cloud. He slowed as he climbed, finally reaching a point where he seemed to stand above a moonlit desert—silver dunes, dark canyons, feathery plains. The cloud covered the earth, horizon to horizon, turning beneath him in majestic silence. And then, slowly, he began to fall, descending feet-first as the cloud darkened . . . then hardened to become a stretch of two-lane pavement.

He wore a leather jacket, jeans, and boots. Mist broke around his heels as he came to rest on solid asphalt. Beside him, his vintage Mustang sat parked across a double-yellow line.

I've done this before.

The impression was fleeting. There for a moment, then gone, dissipating as quickly as the mist at his feet.

Roadside weeds rustled, stirred by his partners in crime—Reddy and Tejay, the boyfriend-girlfriend team set on robbing a trust-fund brat named Bird.

Tejay claimed Bird carried a lot of cash on Sunday nights, transporting it in a briefcase to Kirill Vorarov's strip club. The heist wasn't Axle's idea. He was just the driver, providing his services for a flat fee that would cover repairs on his car shop and maybe keep him in business through a nasty stretch of hard times.

One night's work. Do it and walk away.

The guy in charge, a young hustler named Spinelli, had just called Axle from two miles up the road, letting him know that Bird was on his way. Now Axle was waiting, listening to the shifting of roadside leaves, a sound that seemed to have nothing to do with Reddy and Tejay getting into position beyond the shoulder. The sound he heard was different, a windless shifting of branches that his great-grandmother had told him was the whisper of the earthborn guardian. She had called it *teyunies*—an Okwe word, a piece of mythology that she always seemed to rework and revise in the hopes of giving him a sense of purpose.

You will be a great leader! A caretaker of the land!

A chill went through him.

He opened the Mustang's door, climbed back in, and reversed away from the center lane.

"Sombitch!" Reddy leaped from the weeds, swinging his shotgun. "Axle!"

A hum rose in the distance, Bird's SUV approaching from the north.

Axle lowered his window. "I can't do it!"

"What?"

Axle shifted to low. "Get in if you want. Either way, I'm done."

Tejay emerged. "What's going on?"

"Sombitch is leaving!"

Axle let out the clutch, started pulling away.

"Goddamnit!" Reddy leaped after him, grabbed the door.

Axle hit the brakes.

The door swung wide. Reddy moved with it, diving toward the pavement. He hit hard, shotgun skidding.

Tejay looked in through the open door. "You can't quit now, Axle."

"Watch me."

"We have a deal."

"Sue me!"

She climbed in.

Reddy retrieved his shotgun, dove in after her.

Up ahead, approaching headlights fanned the roadside trees, coming through the bend.

"Sombitch, Axle. Give me one good reason—"

Axle gunned it, burning rubber into the bend, racing past the lights of Bird's SUV, following a new path—one he had to follow.

66

A few miles before crossing the border into Pennsylvania, Sam Calder pulled to the shoulder and removed her Jeep's roof panels and doors. Then she stowed them in the back and drove on with the night blowing around her. She felt strange, as if something were burning inside her, not a fever, but the memory of one.

Maybe she was getting old.

She steered onto the Windslow exit, beneath the overpass, and toward a Readerboard at the side of Boundary Street.

XXX

LOCAL GIRLS NITELY

XXX

What a hell hole!

She hated coming here, but working for Kirill meant checking in at least once a month. Fortunately, Kirill never made her go inside.

Danny Love stood in the doorway. She glanced at him, then did a double take as she swung around to stop a few yards from the entrance. He looked much as he always did: pencil-thin moustache, swept-back hair, open-collar shirt, pleated slacks—a weasel in silk and polyester. But for some reason she sensed he had changed from the last time she had seen him.

What's with me tonight?

Danny approached her Jeep, pulled an envelope from his pocket.

"Good crowd tonight?" she said.

"Yeah. Coming in?"

"Yeah, right. Does Kirill have anything for me?"

"Just the usual." He passed her the envelope. "Things are cool."

"Works for me." She put in the clutch. "See you next—"

The club door opened. Kirill stepped out, followed by a man with shoulder-length hair and the face of an angel. He had his sleeves rolled up, exposing forearms covered with tattooed flames. He looked like a picture of a fire angel from one of her mother's books, a picture that had captivated her as a child. He was talking to Kirill, laughing, his mouth wide and strong.

"Who's that?" she asked.

"You never met him?"

"No." She would have remembered.

"People call him *Bird*. He's working on the Mountain Downs project."

Bird was 20 feet away, out of earshot, but he suddenly turned to look at Sam as if sensing she was there. He said something to Kirill, and now Kirill turned too.

"Got to go, Danny." She let out the clutch and steered a wide arc toward the parking lot's exit.

She caught Bird's glance once more in the rearview.

Why?

She considered going back.

What am I so afraid of?

But it was safer this way, keeping a distance, avoiding friendships, avoiding men.

When she checked the rearview again, he was gone. Only the glow of the strip club remained, coating the top of the hill like a halo in the night.

Officer Sharo Jenkins nearly rammed the white pickup as she rounded a bend on Cliff Mine Run. She'd been dreaming, caught in a burst of micro-sleep, driving on reflex.

She hit the brakes.

The truck's driver had missed the turn, and now his front end lay smashed against a guardrail, rear bumper angled out into the uphill lane.

Three men stood in the cargo bed, faces ablaze in Sharo's lights.

She hit her flashers, reversed to the shoulder, and called Becky at dispatch with the plate number.

"Need backup?" Becky asked.

"Yeah. Good idea." She climbed out, closed the door, and snapped on her personal radio.

One of the men tried climbing down from the truck bed.

"Stay put!" She panned her flashlight over each of them: a raggedy kid with an overbite, a blond hunk with an athletic build, a couch potato with a starter beard. The potato boy looked particularly wasted, sitting down on the lid of a cooler as she hit him with the light. "Anyone hurt?" she asked.

"No," the athlete said. "We're OK."

"My truck!" the raggedy kid said. "My truck's freaking hurt!"

"The truck is yours?"

"Yeah." He slapped the cab's rear window. "The retard drove it off the road!"

"Hey, Ditwitter!" The big kid rose from the cooler. "Don't call him *retard*."

"Fuck you, Jason! You call him *retard*!"

"He's my freaking brother, not yours."

"Gentlemen. We all right here?" She panned the light over each of them. "Let's relax, OK." It was times like these when she was mindful of her size. Even the raggedy Ditwitter outclassed her in weight, and yet for a moment—when he and Jason had started yelling—she'd felt an uncharacteristic impulse to leap into the truck and step between them, as if she were somehow bigger than all of them combined. "Let's just sit back down, OK? Just sit and chill. I need to talk to your driver."

"The registration's in the glove box," Ditwitter said. "Insurance too. You'll need to tell him that."

She stepped toward the cab, pausing as a second cruiser came flashing up the road. It pulled to the front of the truck, backed in close. Officer Zabek climbed out. She felt relieved to see him, not just for the backup, but because she'd somehow been worried about him . . . as if she wasn't sure where he was, how he was doing.

Get it together, Sharo! Focus!

She pointed to the back of the truck. "The three in back, Robert. They're all yours."

Zabek walked past her.

She knocked on the side window. The driver cranked it down, turned toward her. She put the light on him, and for a moment she thought he looked familiar.

"Sss-sss-sorry." He rubbed his head, not drunk, just dazed.

"Driver's license," she said. "And registration and insurance. Your friend says they're in the box."

He stared at her, seemed about to say something more, then he turned away and got the papers.

She put her light on his license, read the name: *Benjamin William Herrington*. "All right, Benjie. Keep it in park. I'll be right back." She snapped off her personal radio and returned to the cruiser. That's when she realized what she had done. *Benjie*. She had called him *Benjie*—not *Ben* or *Benny*. And it had felt right. For a moment, standing beside the truck, it was as if she knew him.

Dalton Davies woke to find himself lying beneath the broken roof of an abandoned farmhouse. The night beyond the rafters was clear, stars strewn across a blue-black sky. No wind, and yet something moved, swooping low over the house to land on the exposed beams. It was the guardian, the winged man who tolerated Dalton's presence in the derelict house.

Tonight, for some reason, the guardian had returned early.

"Dalton!" the guardian called down through the rafters. "Get up. Now!" He dropped to a crossbeam, then landed beside the bed. "Something's happened, Dalton. Everything's changed."

Dalton sat up, stretched his painted arms, tried remembering what he'd been dreaming. "Changed?"

"Where were you just now, Dalton?"

"Me? Right here. Sleeping."

"And in your sleep, where were you?"

A piece of it came back to him. "Someplace . . . burning. A flaming tower . . . with a pack of monsters." It didn't make sense, but there it was. "Why?"

The guardian turned away, heading toward his nest in the back of the house. "Get ready. This is going to be interesting."

"What is?"

"Same journey, different path." He passed through the door of his back room, a trace of moonlight filtering through the plastic-covered windows, illuminating the dark curve of his wings.

I see angels . . . what do you see?

EPILOGUE

Most nights, Alex worked late.

Business was booming, and sometimes it seemed the days didn't end, but instead cycled together with barely a few hours of downtime in between. Sometimes he told himself it was all good. He was successful, living his dream. Other times, he felt there had to be more to life, that there were surely adventures waiting to happen if only he could step away, walk out the office door, become the master of something bigger. His great-grandmother had told him he would be a great leader. Well, maybe he was. But he wondered if running an auto-service center was really the destiny she'd had in mind.

Much had changed since he'd walked out on a fast-money scheme that might have kept him in Pennsylvania . . . or landed him in jail. He'd made three enemies that night, but he had found peace with himself. Looking back, he realized that he had reached a kind of crossroads. He had no way of knowing where the path he hadn't taken would have led. He only knew that the one he took had carried him back to his shop in Windslow Bottoms with a renewed commitment to find a legal means of keeping the business alive. Months later he sold the place for a profit, and now here he was. Modestly successful. Charting his own destiny.

His office looked out over six service bays staffed by two shifts of mechanics and detailers, all presided over by a couple of overworked assistant managers who were just as harried as he was. Right now, one of those guys was coming through the office door, looking both stressed and amused. "There's a man outside." He cocked his thumb toward the window, gesturing toward the lot. "Wants to talk about your Mustang."

"The fastback?"

"Yeah. Says he wants to make an offer."

"It's not for sale."

"Told him that. Want me to get rid of him?"

Alex looked toward the lot. The Mustang was parked by the street, out of sight around the building's wall. "I'll talk to him." Alex got up. "I need a break anyway."

He stepped from the office and out into the ratchet and clang of the shop. It was a good place, so much of it a part of his youthful dreams. But the night beyond the bays was the stuff of memory, the cool wind ripe with the scent of trees and pending rains. In many ways, eastern Ohio was much like western Pennsylvania. Perhaps a little flatter. He missed the hills. But the smell and feel of the summer nights still reminded him of his youth, when his great-grandmother had taken him on long walks and told him stories that he had always suspected were revised to suit her needs.

The man came into view as Alex rounded the shop wall. He wore a cream-colored suit, wide lapels, western boots. He had a full head of hair, combed back in a silver pompadour. In all, he looked a bit like an aging country-singer.

"Help you?"

The man turned. "Alex?"

"That's me."

"Name's Fox." He offered his hand.

"You a car enthusiast?"

"No. Actually, I'm a minister."

"What denomination?"

Fox smiled. "I'm freelance, son." He reached beneath a wide lapel. "And as much as I have been admiring your car, I'm actually here on a spiritual matter." He produced a large handkerchief, unfolded it to reveal two pieces of carved stone. "I've been told to give you this."

It was Yeyestani's birdstone, broken and cradled in the handkerchief.

"A Windslow contractor found it while putting in an expansion lot for Mountain Downs." Fox folded the handkerchief, rewrapped the pieces, handed them to Alex.

Alex took them. Even through the handkerchief, he felt the chill, the pressing weight. "This contractor, does he know me?"

"Let's say he knows *of* you. I can tell you about him . . . if you care to listen." He looked toward the trees at the edge of the lot. "Nice night for a ride." He smelled the air. "What say we take a drive, son? I have stories to tell. Some of them might interest you."

The air was still, but with a sense of things stirring beyond the parking-lot lights.

"Curious, son?"

Alex turned, headed back to his office, and got the keys.

SHORT STORIES BY LAWRENCE C. CONNOLLY

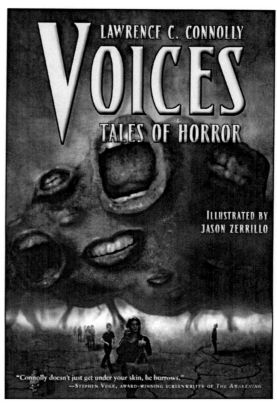

CPSIA information can be obtained at www.ICGtesting.com
Printed in the USA
BVOW03s2102281014

372732BV00006B/11/P

9 781934 571057